SHADOW
STATE

SHADOW STATE

A NOVEL

FRANK SENNETT

CROOKED
LANE

NEW YORK

Copyright © 2023 by Frank Sennett

Published in the United States by Crooked Lane Books, an imprint of The Quick Brown Fox & Company LLC.

Crooked Lane Books and its logo are trademarks of The Quick Brown Fox & Company LLC.

Library of Congress Catalog-in-Publication data available upon request.

ISBN (hardcover): 978-1-63910-240-2
ISBN (ebook): 978-1-63910-241-9

Cover design by Nebojša Zorić

Printed in the United States.

www.crookedlanebooks.com

Crooked Lane Books
34 West 27th St., 10th Floor
New York, NY 10001

First Edition: February 2023

10 9 8 7 6 5 4 3 2 1

For Mary Doheny, who got me writing again.

And for my Pop. Sorry I didn't finish this in time for you to read it. Oh shucks, oh darn.

I

I

CHAPTER

1

F ROM HIS POSITION in the parking lot seventy-five yards
from Washington, DC's Friendship Academy, Rafael
Hendrix tracked his target's brisk progress down the main
entrance hall.

The window wall provided a full view of the young
woman through his scope, from her choppy black bob to
a blue peacoat too bulky for her small frame to the smart
white linen pants that clashed with a pair of neon-green
running shoes engineered for flight.

Her face, in profile, was a study in determination, thin
lips pursed, eyes locked on the corridor ahead.

Hendrix was ready to put the woman down before
she reached the interior hallway leading to the classroom
hosting the First Lady, and the one next door where his
eleven-year-old daughter, Becca, was enjoying a free reading period with her classmates.

"Situation is fluid," the op commander said. "We have
not confirmed she is acting alone. Do not take the shot.
Repeat: Do not take the shot. Acknowledge."

Hendrix said nothing.

Time slowed as he tugged his collar to wipe away the sweat trickling down his neck. The hot asphalt smell of the parking lot and the *pew-pew* calls of pissed-off starlings on the tree branch above him faded as his concentration sharpened. These were the trade's most intimate moments, when the world was stripped down to sniper and target.

He calmed his breathing, made sure his gun rest was solid, rechecked the sight. She was ten paces from the corner and ten more to where President Wyetta Johnson's wife and forty-five of DC's most privileged children remained oblivious to the grave danger this woman represented.

"No shot. Acknowledge. Goddammit, Hendrix. No shot. No shot. There are—"

He ripped away the earpiece, put the crosshairs on the woman, then moved them slightly to the right, leading her. She was two paces from disappearing.

He took the shot.

It was clean, just above her right ear. Instantaneous death.

As the woman's nervous system collapsed, her right hand released the triggering device. Less than a second later, her body and the wall of windows vaporized.

The classrooms around the corner remained intact.

Until the second bomber, the one emerging from the girls' bathroom adjacent to Becca's classroom, heard the blast, flung herself through the door, and detonated her suicide vest, engulfing twenty-three fifth graders and their teacher in a column of flame.

Hendrix couldn't see the carnage from the parking lot. But in the dream logic of his nightmare, he reached the classroom just as Becca turned to him, screaming, from inside the inferno. He couldn't rescue his daughter, but he was sure she saw him, and blamed him.

He awoke, heart pounding so hard he could feel it in his ears and the veins of his neck.

Hendrix sat up, peeled off his sweat-soaked T-shirt, and mopped his face. He swung his legs over the side of the bed and rested for a few minutes in the desert quiet, head lowered, waiting for his nervous system to reset.

He stood, stretched, then filled a tall glass with cloudy water from the kitchen tap and drank it down in three swift gulps. The wall clock read three AM, as it did after the nightmare pretty much any night he didn't drink himself into a stupor.

That meant he'd endured a straight month of nightmares since he'd cut out the tequila that had been softening him physically and mentally. He was done falling asleep on the toilet and passing out in his folding chair on the back patio.

He was damned if he was going to turn into a public embarrassment, old ladies whispering as he stumbled through the market with a bag of limes. If he wanted to check out, he'd do it with a single shot from his nine.

So he'd quit. It wasn't that hard, changing the habit of a year and change. He'd never been much of a drinker in DC, on active duty in Afghanistan, or even on his high school football team in western Pennsylvania, where booze was a birthright.

But this bout of post-traumatic stress disorder was worse than the one he'd suffered after Hell Man. That's what U.S. forces had dubbed the Helmand River Valley where they'd targeted Afghan insurgents from Camp Dwyer, a permanent Marine base with no permanent buildings, just a series of trailers and tents they moved around to keep the enemy guessing.

Helmand, which accounted for more than 40 percent of the world's opium production, was the most dangerous province in Afghanistan. That was one hairy final tour. After some initial reluctance, Hendrix had embraced the therapy he'd been offered when he got back stateside. He'd made it through in one piece physically, but emotionally he was an unstable mix of paranoia, depression, and night sweats.

At Walter Reed, he worked with a woman who'd helped identify and create therapies for PTSD. Hendrix credited her with saving his life. He was twenty-six when he mustered out and she was past retirement age, but they had clicked. His trust in her continued to grow as she helped him carve out a hard-fought recovery, and ultimately gave him the clean bill of mental health he'd needed to join the Secret Service.

Hendrix had lost touch with her in the intervening decade. After the bombing, he discovered she was living in a memory-care facility in Bethesda. He visited, but her face remained as blank as a whitewashed wall when he said hello. She'd lost the ability to speak but let out an occasional unsettling moan from somewhere deep inside.

Instead of finding a new therapist, Hendrix had given up on therapy. He had no relatives to turn to. He was an only child and his parents had been killed during a kayaking trip, capsizing in rapids while Hendrix was on his second of three active-duty tours.

By taking that shot at Friendship Academy, he had saved the First Lady from near-certain death. The bombers, Russian separatists from Donetsk, weren't there for a hostage negotiation. That much had been confirmed in the investigation. The terrorists were making a definitive political statement against U.S. military support for Ukraine during Putin's war. That was why Hendrix wasn't in prison now.

Because he had not been thinking only about the First Lady in that moment, itself a tremendous dereliction of duty.

As any parent would be, he was also desperate to save his daughter in the classroom next door.

But the First Lady was spared, as were the teacher and the children in the classroom she was visiting. The wall connecting the two rooms was breached, but the blast did not harm anyone on that side of the wall.

Hendrix learned all of that later. As soon as he'd heard the second blast, he dropped his rifle and ran straight into the smoking rubble, pushing what was left of his daughter's classroom door off its hinges.

Hoping for a miracle.

Finding fiery hell.

There was nothing recognizable left of the room or its occupants. And there would be nothing recognizable about Hendrix's life after that moment. The op commander found him sitting cross-legged on a chunk of ceiling that had fallen into the gore. He had been taken, in shock, straight to Walter Reed.

* * *

When Hendrix returned to his prewar Colonial home in Silver Spring two days later—he remembered how bizarrely normal it had seemed when he walked up the driveway—his wife, Judy, was packed and ready to leave with their three-year-old son, David. If he'd arrived a few hours later, he would not have had the chance to say goodbye.

That evening, Hendrix discovered Judy had left only his closet and their daughter's room intact. He ventured into Becca's pink and purple lair long enough to retrieve her prized snow globe from their Montreal vacation a

couple of years back, and the framed photo of the two of
them in a receiving line of princesses on a Disney cruise
the family had taken when she was five.

That had been nearly halfway through Becca's life,
Hendrix realized as he suppressed a choking sob. The
beautiful, funny eleven-year-old who'd embodied raw
potential in a ponytail, flying across the soccer field as a
striker on Saturday mornings or eating up extra readings
on the science subjects that fascinated her, that girl, in the
shoulder season of childhood, was gone in a blink, as was
the woman she would never have the chance to become.

Hendrix put the house on the market and hired a service to box up Becca's things and deliver them to a storage
center on the outskirts of town. He couldn't bear to look
at them but wasn't ready to throw them out. Besides, Judy
and David might want to go through them someday. He
set up the storage on autopay and put it out of his mind.

Hendrix had kept to himself and tried to avoid the
blanket media coverage, especially the obituaries of
the children, but he knew the blast had shattered many
families beyond his. The President, whose family he had
managed to save, did not reach out lest she be accused of
interfering with a federal investigation. The day he realized he wouldn't be hearing from his best friend was the
day he felt truly forsaken.

When prosecutors decided they had nothing to charge
him with after three months, he was told there were no
leads on identifying the bombers or their network other
than the group taking credit via a post to a dead-end social
media account originating in Russia. The school families
had come up clean, as expected, with no connections to
the crime.

The next day, a card came in the mail from the President. Hendrix couldn't bring himself to open it. He'd just

sent his own letter to the White House resigning his post as head of the President's Secret Service detail, a formality. There didn't seem to be anything more to say.

*   *   *

With his daughter murdered, the investigative trail cold, his career cut short, the President ghosting him, and Judy taking David to live near her parents in Michigan, Hendrix had wanted only to disappear.

So he did, driving west from DC until he'd seen the for-sale sign on this 900-square-foot shack in the Chihuahuan Desert scrublands outside of Fort Stockton. The West Texas town had grown from a military fort established in 1858 near Comanche Springs, which pumped out 30 million gallons of fresh water every day until farm irrigation sucked it dry a hundred years later. These days, the town was best known for hosting Paisano Pete, the world's second-largest roadrunner statue.

It was the perfect place to fade away. If only his memories hadn't come along for the ride.

Breaking into the old Caswell County Jail had been disappointingly easy.

He'd watched the Yanceyville main square go from quiet to deserted on a pleasant North Carolina afternoon punctuated by a breeze that kept the late summer humidity at bay.

After taking in a muted sunset from the pine grove in the arboretum tucked behind the brick jailhouse and Civil War–era courthouse, he'd walked back through the town's memorial garden, pausing to read a few of the inscriptions to the departed that lined the brick path. Plenty of room for more, he noted as the streetlights sputtered on and he came to the back of the empty jailhouse.

Still alone on the square, he stepped behind a bush large enough to hide most of his body, eased the shim into the gap between the upper and lower windows, and pushed the crescent latch open on the second try. Thirty seconds later, he was inside and easing the bottom window closed.

He slipped the penlight out of his right front pocket, clicked it on, and played the slender shaft of light across the floor until it illuminated the stairs leading to the second floor, where the hanging chamber awaited behind a large iron door.

The unlocked cell was set up just as it had been when it was built in 1906, complete with a noose hanging over the open metal trap door. No one was ever hanged here, however. North Carolina had banned the deadly drop a year after the jail opened. So the cell had been a museum piece for more than a century. The noose was a sturdy recent addition. He hoped no one would mind too much that he'd borrowed it.

Back downstairs, he wiped off the window and sill, opened the back-door deadbolt, and exited into the darkness. The noose was tucked into a cloth shopping bag, but no one was around to hide it from.

The old courthouse next door now served as the county history museum. It was as easy to break into as the jail. Navigating again by penlight, he entered the storage room off the main floor hallway and made himself as comfortable as possible on the stepstool he found there.

He closed his eyes and tried to sense any ghostly presence in the room but felt nothing. Unique among U.S. political assassinations, the murder of John W. Stephens by the Ku Klux Klan had concluded with the Republican state senator's body lying undiscovered by the authorities overnight because the storage room had been locked and the only key taken.

When someone climbed a tree next to the courthouse at first light and saw the corpse through the window, a lawman had forced the door open.

He wondered why they'd waited for visual confirmation. What if Stephens had only been wounded and incapacitated? He could possibly have been saved. But supporters of Black rights were none too popular down South among white officials in the 1870s.

Much the same could be said today, he mused, leaning forward and opening the shopping bag between his knees. With the light shining down from his mouth, he reached past the noose and the short, horn-handled knife for a cheese sandwich and a bottle of water.

Again in darkness, he ate over the still-open bag. This was the hardest part, he thought as he finished the first half of the sandwich. Tom Petty had been right about that. But morning would come soon enough, and he had plenty of thinking to do about the logistics of the next job.

Sipping the water and waiting for his eyes to adjust, he wondered who would show up to open the museum. Probably a retiree happy for a few hours of volunteer work to fill her otherwise empty day.

Good news: That was one problem he was well equipped to solve.

2

H ENDRIX PULLED ON running shorts and a fresh T-shirt, this one sporting the panther mascot of Fort Stockton High, where he had enjoyed watching the varsity football squad take on the likes of Lubbock, Big Spring, and Canyon on fall Friday nights. It wasn't much of a social calendar, but it was something. Other than the games and occasional supply runs to town, Hendrix kept to himself out among the creosote bushes, his nearest neighbor half a mile up the dirt road that ran past his rusty gate.

He sat on his front step and tightened his shoelaces. The dry desert air was cool, and stars blanketed the cloudless sky. He stood for a moment marking the constellations. Other than those stars and the security light high on a pole at the edge of his neighbor's property, Hendrix was enveloped by darkness.

He slipped on the headband light, eased open the gate, though he didn't know who the squeaking metal could possibly bother, and turned left on the dirt road leading out into an expanse of gray scrubland that made him feel like he was running on the moon.

This was the next step in his reclamation project, running ten miles every time the nightmare got the best of him. He'd covered 300 miles in the course of the month. He'd bought good shoes and concocted a stretching routine based on what he'd learned from his high school coaches and Special Forces training. He was glad his body was proving to be up to the challenge at the hang-fire age of forty-one.

He didn't have a fitness bracelet to track the distance, so he'd driven five miles from his shack and nailed an aluminum pie plate to the nearest wooden fence post. It reflected the light from his headlamp beautifully in these predawn hours.

By this point, closing in on eighteen months of exile, he'd made a decent mental map of the chuckholes and other obstacles on the hard clay road with its light gravel overlay. But the lamp kept curious critters at a safe distance. The last thing he needed was to trip over a skunk or porcupine.

His routine did not include earbuds. He tried to keep his mind blank as he focused on his breathing, pace, and surroundings. It was the reset he needed to have a productive day of gardening, reading, maintenance, and chores. Simple was the solution.

He reached the pie plate in just under an hour. It was four fifteen and there was a hint of pink on the horizon. By eight AM it would be a scorcher, but he'd be showered and fed long before then.

He eased his back up against the thick, weathered fence post and gave himself a good scratch as he ticked off more constellations.

His father had encouraged his childhood interest in astronomy. Those peaceful hours at the telescope had made the choice to become a sniper feel natural to him, ironically enough, after he scored forty out of forty on his Army marksmanship test.

His natural aptitude for range estimation and target stalking accelerated his ascent into the top ranks of Ranger snipers. Drones were useful, but as the human advance recon element tasked with telling the rest of the unit what they were walking into—and eliminating as many threats as possible when the shit started flying—Hendrix and his sniper colleagues were revered.

This status didn't translate to many extra comforts—he never had to stand long in a chow line, and he drew appreciative nods wherever he walked on base—but he was proud to play such a critical protective role. Hendrix felt he had been born to do it.

When he wasn't training the scope of his Mk 11 on rugged Afghan hillsides to lock in on potential hostiles, he'd taken up stargazing again in camp. It gave him a sense of peace as he accepted his insignificance in the world and reflected on how minor his concerns were in the face of a never-ending universe.

Under the benign and ancient gaze of the constellations, he felt an almost religious absolution for taking so many enemy combatants' lives. If every living thing had come from stardust, perhaps returning them to that elemental state was part of the natural order.

It was the elaborate dissociative coping mechanism of a young man. It fell apart when he returned to civilian life, but the philosophy had helped him perform with peak efficiency in-country. Self-doubt was deadly over there.

Stargazing was also how he had helped Wyetta Johnson, his bunkmate and best friend through his last two Afghan tours, kick heroin in the week before her medical discharge came through.

Hendrix and Johnson had been on a routine Blackhawk run through the Helmand River Valley when their copter had taken an RPG from what they'd thought were a group of shepherds leading their goats to water. The pilot had been killed instantly and the helicopter touched down hard but upright on the river, which saved Hendrix and Johnson's lives.

Johnson was knocked out by the impact. Before Hendrix could cut her loose from her safety harness, her left leg had been burned to the bone from ankle to mid-thigh.

"That's some nasty-ass barbecue," she said when he'd roused her.

He carried Johnson on his back to safety across the shallow river, keeping the downed copter between them and the insurgents, who in any case looked to have headed back into the hills.

After pushing Johnson up onto the opposite bank, Hendrix found a spot where high spring waters had eroded a divot into the dirt just behind a stand of dense bushes, like a giant rabbit burrow. He dressed her wound using the torn sleeves of his uniform and told her not to move or cry out while he was gone.

"Bite down on your knife handle whenever you feel a wave of pain," he said.

"Hendrix, there's no wave," she said. "It's just pain."

And then she'd passed out.

He'd managed to cover the three clicks to camp undetected. Three Blackhawks and a caravan of Humvees had been deployed on the rescue and recovery mission, and base comms radioed Johnson's location to them when Hendrix made it inside the wire.

"We got her," came the reply after too many tense minutes had passed.

The base surgeon made the call to amputate as soon as Johnson was wheeled into the operating tent. For the next three days, nothing they gave her could touch the pain.

She screamed until she was hoarse, and then they'd knock her out to give her a few hours of rest.

A medic Hendrix was friendly with told him in mess about a Pashtun heroin hookup outside the closest village. Hendrix slipped beyond the wire that night and brought back enough pure product to put down that herd of goats and every last shepherd.

The medic showed Hendrix how to kill Johnson's pain without killing her. For the next ten days, he kept her flying and stayed by her side. Word of her medical discharge came a week before she would be airlifted to Bagram and then on to Germany and the States.

"I can't go back an addict," she whispered. "Get me clean. That's an order."

Johnson loved to remind Hendrix she outranked him by one grade as a first lieutenant, the one instance in which a silver bar was more valuable than a gold one. So much more valuable that second lieutenants were routinely referred to as "butterbars," a condescending reference to their yellow bar insignia.

"Hendrix, do you know the only difference between a Private First Class and a Second Lieutenant?" Johnson asked during their first meeting. She delivered the answer with a smirk he came to know well: "A Private First Class has already been promoted." Message received: He was as junior as officers got.

So Hendrix and the medic followed Johnson's order to wean her off the opiates. Hendrix distracted her at night, when her withdrawal was at its worst, by mapping out every constellation visible through the small telescope his parents had sent him for his birthday just before their fatal kayak trip.

During the days, when she wasn't sleeping, he held her hand and they talked.

"You remember the day we became friends, don't you?" Johnson said in a hoarse whisper one afternoon when she was particularly lucid.

"You can't let it go," Hendrix said.

She laughed until she coughed. After drinking some water, she said, "You were such a cocky son of a bitch, Hendrix, big shit sniper on campus. All that wavy, fair hair slicked back with nasty grease, muscles bulging out the torn sleeves of your T-shirt. You looked like a rough-trade dreamboat."

"That's offensive," Hendrix said.

"Oh, I know, you're a he-him who only has eyes for the she-hers. And when that London war correspondent parachuted into our lives, you were locked and loaded."

He smiled and shook his head. "Definitely not the way I remember it."

"We should have put a drool bib on you," Johnson said. "Don't even try to deny it. As soon as Constance walked into the mess in her form-fitting khakis, you had your sights dialed in."

"All right," Hendrix said. "I think you're having withdrawal delirium."

Johnson shook her head. "You were so gallant hopping up and giving her your seat. Remember what she said?"

Hendrix exercised his right to remain silent.

"'You fancy a ginger, do you?'" Johnson said in a tortured posh London accent. "'My name is Constance, but you can call me Con.'"

Hendrix sighed.

"She had you in her clear-coat manicured clutches, Hendrix. For once, you were at a loss for words. Kind of like you are now."

"Just get it over with," he said.

"When you came back to quarters that night and found Con had beat you there, that must have felt like the answer to your prayers. Until I walked over and stroked those red locks. Guess I fancied a ginger too. Even better, she fancied me."

"You're so proud of yourself," Hendrix said. "But in the end, you were just a one-night stand."

"Two," Johnson said. "But who's counting?"

"You always keep score," Hendrix said.

"I am competitive," she said. "Which is why it's so lucky I always win. By the way, where did you bunk during my two nights of bliss?"

"What do you care?" he asked.

"One of the nurses has been giving me the eye," Johnson said. "You might just have to go back there tonight."

They were the most confident soldiers on base and, in their way, the most macho, two talented twenty-somethings cutting a wide swath. That had been what bonded them: They were both out to squeeze the most possible juice out of life. It didn't hurt that Johnson was the funniest person Hendrix had ever met. Her withering commentary on the comings and goings in mess made the shitty food almost palatable. He wouldn't have predicted she'd become President back then, but if someone had told him she'd end up in the White House, he would have had no trouble believing it.

Hendrix still had the telescope that had helped Johnson through her worst nights. It was one of the few personal effects that mattered to him, beyond cherished photos of Becca and David. He was otherwise unmoored in the vast expanse of the universe, alone as the most distant star.

As he prepared to start the second half of his run, Hendrix heard a yelping cry in the distance.

Time to explore the world beyond the pie plate, Hendrix thought as he started jogging toward the sound.

He found the source of the yelps less than a mile up the road. It looked like a feral dog, its left hind leg caught in a small animal trap. Thankfully, the metal was smooth, not serrated, but the trap had snapped shut with enough force to break the dog's leg.

When the animal saw the approaching human and his headlamp, it bared its teeth and growled.

"Hang tight, my friend," Hendrix said. "I'll be back before dawn."

He picked up the pace on the run back and covered the distance in under an hour. He grabbed his thickest pair of gardening gloves from the shed, took his .22 rifle and an old blanket from the front closet, and picked up a plastic bowl and two bottles of water from the kitchen. Three minutes later, his pickup was bouncing down the road toward the pie plate. Hendrix hadn't been looking for a dog-rescue mission, but it felt good to have meaningful work.

By the time his headlights picked up the animal's eyes, the desert sunrise was ready to spring, spreading a deep red slash across the horizon.

Hendrix took the water, dish, and blanket to the dog, who was whimpering and licking at its broken leg.

He poured half a bottle of water into the dish and nudged it toward the dog's head with his foot. The dog eyed him warily, but then started lapping up the water with big sloppy sloshes of its tongue.

"Easy there, partner," Hendrix said.

He was distracted enough by the dog's eager gulping that he didn't notice the truck coming toward him with its lights off until it was about a hundred yards away. Hendrix stepped into the road and held up a hand.

The truck stopped about twenty feet from him. Whoever was in the passenger seat turned on the spotting light mounted to the top of the cab and turned it so that it nearly blinded Hendrix.

He started walking slowly backward toward the open driver's side door of his truck, where the rifle rested across the seat.

"You can stop right there, buddy," the driver said as he climbed out of his rig, casually pointing a handgun in Hendrix's direction.

"No problem," Hendrix said. "I'm your neighbor from back up the road."

"We don't have no neighbors," the man said. "Nearest house is six miles that way," he added, pointing the gun over Hendrix's shoulder.

"That's me," Hendrix said. "I run out this way every morning before dawn. This time, I heard an animal in distress. That's why I came back with my truck."

The passenger hooted in disgust through his open window.

"Animal in distress?" he said. "That's the damn coyote been killing our chickens. We've been trying to catch him for three weeks."

Hendrix nodded. "Makes sense," he said. "But if you take a look, you'll see that's not a coyote."

The driver put his gun back in his belt and called over his shoulder: "Shine a light on that thieving son of a bitch."

Hendrix was glad to be done with the glare as the man in the truck trained the spotlight on the wounded animal.

"I reckon you're right, mister," the driver said as he got close enough to give the animal a full inspection.

"I thought it might be a wild dog," Hendrix said.

The man chuckled. "You're not from around here."

"No," Hendrix admitted.

"What is it, Pop?" the passenger asked from the truck.

"Not even the young people who grew up here know what this is," the man said to Hendrix, adding, "Haul your ass out here, Donny, you need to see this."

The son, a filled-out version of his wiry father, toted a .410 shotgun.

"Should I shoot it?" he asked.

"No," Hendrix said.

"Not yet, anyway," the older man said. "Donny, this is something you'll never see again around here if you live to a hundred. This is a Mexican gray wolf."

The kid let out a low whistle, but Hendrix could tell he had no idea why encountering this creature was significant. Hendrix was also unsure.

"You ever seen one of these?" the man asked Hendrix.

"No, sir," he said.

"There's maybe a hundred of these critters still living in this desert north of the border," he said, "and those are only said to roam Arizona and New Mexico. This guy's an awful long way from home."

You and me both, pal, Hendrix thought.

"Sounds like an endangered species," he said.

"Always the way," the older man said. "The nanny state says we should let him eat every one of our chickens and then invite him inside for dessert."

"Just like everything else that comes up from Mexico," the younger man said, looking to his father for approval.

Once again, the man ignored his son and kept his eyes on Hendrix.

"You're not fixing to report me to Fish and Wildlife, are you?" he asked. The man's hand rested on the gun handle sticking out of his waistband.

Hendrix shook his head. "No, sir. You weren't looking to trap an endangered wolf hundreds of miles out of his range."

The man held Hendrix's even gaze, then nodded.

"All right, we'll take it from here, neighbor," he said.

"Let's let him loose and shoot him on the run," the younger man said.

"This is serious business, son," his father replied. "It's not sport. We'll put him out of his misery and give him a proper burial."

"The injury doesn't look that bad," Hendrix offered.

"Like I said, we'll take it from here," the man responded without looking back.

Hendrix took a last look at the wolf and returned to his truck. He slid the rifle over to the passenger side and climbed in. He kept both hands in sight as he turned around on the narrow road and started driving home.

The sun was coming up fast over the horizon, plenty of light now. Hendrix slowed, then stopped about two hundred yards from the would-be wolf killers.

Hendrix rolled down the driver's side window, opened the door, then climbed down from the cab toting the rifle. He walked around the door to face the men through the open window.

In one smooth motion, Hendrix raised the rifle, steadied it on the window well, chambered a round with the bolt, put his eye to the scope, and squeezed the trigger.

When the spotlight exploded behind the men, they jumped for cover. Hendrix worked the bolt again and took out the driver's side headlight.

When the other headlight remained intact after thirty seconds, the men scrambled for the truck.

Fast learners, he thought as the older man turned the vehicle around by driving it into the ditch, narrowly missing the fence on the other side of the road. After the dust died down, Hendrix backed up his rig to retrieve the wolf. He wrapped it in the blanket and placed it into the bed of the pickup after prying open the trap.

"It's your lucky day," Hendrix said as he closed the tailgate. "You met a creature out here crazier than you."

As he stood before the creamy white World War II memorial in Bayfront Park, placid Biscayne Bay stretching out on both sides, he gave thanks for Chicago Mayor Anton Cermak. If not for Cermak, he would have had to cross Miami off his list as another in the history of near-miss presidential assassination attempts featuring loathsome malcontents like Richard Lawrence, John Schrank, Oscar Collazo, Griselio Torresola, Richard Pavlick, Arthur Bremer, Squeaky Fromme, Sara Jane Moore, and John Hinkley Jr.

All in all, it was harder to kill a President—or even a presidential candidate—than one might suppose given the outsize infamy of the successful plots against Lincoln, Garfield, McKinley, and the Kennedy brothers.

He'd found Pathé newsreel footage from the February 15, 1933, event on YouTube. The headline: "America's President Elect, on the Eve of Taking Office, Has Marvellous Escape from Gunman's Bullets." Didn't work out so well for Cermak, though.

FDR, fresh off a post-election vacation in Bermuda, was on his way to DC, where he would start the first of his four terms in March. After leaving Vincent Astor's yacht, he took an open-air touring car to greet a crowd of 4,000 gathered at Bayfront Park to send him off. Roosevelt hoisted himself onto a seat back and delivered brief, non-political remarks—he had just gone fishing but wasn't going to tell the crowd a "fish story"; he liked Miami and planned to come back soon—with Cermak by his side.

But one of the well-wishers actually wasn't. As soon as Roosevelt finished his roadside chat, an anarchist mope named Giuseppe Zangara emptied an $8 pawn-shop revolver in FDR's direction. He wounded five people, including Cermak, who died a few weeks later, but missed the President-elect thanks to an onlooker who jostled Zangara's gun hand after the first shot popped off. The unemployed bricklayer got the electric chair five weeks later, and America got the New Deal.

Cermak got a round plaque in the ground that was overshadowed a few years later by this Art Moderne war memorial. You had to be looking for the plaque to find it, and few people did. But it was there, grass neatly trimmed around it. Cermak famously told FDR he was glad he'd taken the bullet instead of the President, which may be the most accurate self-assessment a politician has ever made.

Cermak's sacrifice then meant a nice winter break now from chilly DC. This was the outing he'd been looking forward to ever since he'd mapped out the full itinerary. Room with a sweeping bay view at the InterContinental, a fantastic Cuban lunch on Calle Ocho, and then a pleasant reconnaissance walk around the park perimeter with the sun warming his bare forearms before he ended up here.

He adjusted the .32 revolver in the right front pocket of his khakis. This one had cost more than $8, but it was on the inexpensive side. Reliable, nothing fancy. It was the right caliber, which was the important thing. The trick for tonight was to set the scene well enough to generate local media interest beyond a headshaking five-second recap of the latest urban shooting. The coverage would be there waiting when he needed it to be found.

The memorial was off Flagler Avenue, which was convenient, except the flagstoned portion of Flagler that cut through the park before dead-ending at the bay was closed to regular vehicle traffic. There were no barricades, and service vehicles used it daily, but in the early evening, none of the convertibles *cruising up Biscayne Boulevard would be hanging a right and presenting him with the perfect target.*

There also wasn't much cover. The memorial was flanked by tall, skinny palm trees, and that was it. Open grass all around. He'd have to stand behind the memorial itself, which wasn't ideal for two reasons: it would leave his back exposed to anyone taking an evening stroll or skate along the lakefront path, and it meant his view of the target would be limited until a few seconds before go time.

He turned around and took in the scene. There were a few pedestrians on the sidewalk next to Biscayne Boulevard more than a block away. The advantage of the open park layout was that it provided several options for escape. He could jog north or south on the waterfront path. He could head west on Flagler to Biscayne and blend in with the urban bustle, or he could grab a passing cab and exit the area immediately. He preferred that option.

He unfolded the newspaper he'd tucked under his right arm and removed the bottle of lighter fluid wrapped inside it. After taking one more look around, he walked to the open garbage barrel positioned under a shade tree ten yards southwest of the war memorial and looked inside. There was enough cardboard and paper trash to keep a fire going for at least five minutes, maybe longer once he added the newspaper.

He did that now, and then started squirting lighter fluid into the barrel, soaking the trash before tossing in the empty bottle. He pulled a matchbook from the InterContinental bar out of the pocket of his white guayabera, lit the pack, and tossed it in as he stepped back to avoid the whoosh of flame that shot three feet over the top of the barrel.

He walked back to the memorial and slipped behind it. As the orange flames licked the barrel wall, he scanned the perimeter for motion. Less than a minute later, he saw the electric maintenance cart bumping down the waterfront trail from the north. When the vehicle whirred onto Flagler en route to the fire, he saw that it held a two-man crew.

Which one of you is FDR? *he thought, pulling down the brim of his ball cap with his left hand as he hefted the revolver in his right.*

And which one is Cermak?

3

B Y THE TIME Hendrix pulled up alongside his front gate, the sun was casting the harshest possible light on his decision to rescue the wolf. Even wearing his wrap-around shades, he could feel its judgment piercing him.

He stuck his left arm out the open truck window and extended his middle finger. If the Mexican gray could howl at the moon, what was the harm in a man flipping off the sun?

Hendrix enjoyed a rare chuckle as he pulled out his phone to look up the hours of the Fort Stockton veterinary hospital. It was closed for another forty-five minutes, but he hoped there might be a doctor making early rounds of the kennels.

When he arrived ten minutes later, he discovered he wasn't the only one with that idea. Two trucks sat idling in front of the hospital, both containing one anxious driver and one sick or injured dog.

He glanced in the rearview and saw the wolf curled up on the blanket in the shade of the canopy, head resting on its front paws. Perhaps sensing it was being watched, the animal raised its eyes dolefully.

"Take a number," Hendrix said as the wolf flopped its chin back onto an outstretched paw. Its broken back leg lay at an unnerving angle on the blanket's edge, twitching every few seconds.

"It's not supposed to bend that way, I know," Hendrix said. "We'll get you fixed up, though, bud, I promise."

The wolf had a distinctive face, fur frilled under the chin like a raggedy beard, cream-colored cheeks melding to brown, and even a little burnt orange on its long nose, forehead, and around the eyes. It was smaller than Hendrix thought a wolf would be, but given the sparse prey available in the high desert, that made sense.

"You might not make a bad pet," he said. "But I don't think you'd like that."

When the hospital receptionist unlocked the doors a few minutes before opening time, Hendrix followed the other two men inside to register his patient. They were both carrying their dogs, but he'd left the wolf in the running truck after cracking the window between the cab and the bed to give it some air conditioning.

"If you see a carjacker, bite him," Hendrix had said before closing the door.

He told the receptionist he'd rescued an injured wolf and asked her to please step out and wave at him when it was their turn to be admitted.

"You're one of the smart ones," she said as she handed him the paperwork on a clipboard. "You should see the dangerous animals people think they can just plop down into my waiting room. Wild-eyed coyotes, venomous snakes, rabid raccoons—it's a wonder I haven't ended up in the emergency room myself. I'll let you know when the doctor's ready for you, and I'll have you drive around back for unloading."

Hendrix thanked the woman and walked back out into what was becoming a blast furnace of a day.

He closed his eyes and grimaced as soon as the resulting image entered his conscious mind, stopping in the middle of the sidewalk as the door swung shut behind him.

An old woman holding an even older-looking cat almost bumped into him. When Hendrix noticed her, he apologized for blocking her path and turned back to hold the door open.

"I'm just glad you're all right," she said. "You looked like you'd seen a ghost."

Back in the truck, Hendrix opened the other water bottle he'd brought on the rescue mission and drank it as the wolf watched him and whimpered.

"We'll get you all the water you can handle in a few minutes," he said.

Hendrix took off his sunglasses and pushed the palms of both hands against his eyes. Almost home, he thought. He saw the liquor store down the block opening up. No, he decided, what I really need is a nap.

*   *   *

Half an hour later, the receptionist came outside, waved, and pointed toward the intersection his truck was facing.

"The doctor will see you now," he said, but the wolf didn't look like it believed him.

*   *   *

The vet wore a blue rubber smock and safety glasses along with what looked like a pair of falconer's gauntlets.

"You're a brave man to pick him up with a blanket and gardening gloves," she said after he explained how he'd freed the wolf from the trap, leaving out the encounter with the ranchers.

"So he's a him," Hendrix said.

"Yep," she said.

"I thought so, but I wasn't curious enough to confirm it."

She laughed. "You'd already had enough excitement for one morning."

"It was enough to last me the rest of the year."

"These guys usually roam in small packs, and they mate for life," she said. "I don't see a wolf roaming this far on his own, especially an older one like him."

"Maybe his wife kicked him out," Hendrix offered.

She nodded. "Or she died, more likely. And he's not going to find a replacement way out here."

"Occupational hazard for lone wolves," he said.

The doctor looked like she was going to continue the banter, but apparently thought better of it. "Well," she said, "we'll take him from here."

The phrase sounded friendlier coming from her than when the rancher had said it an hour ago.

Hendrix and the vet watched as her assistant, also decked out in full protective gear, wheeled the wolf into the hospital via a rolling kennel contraption that looked like a school AV cart. He gave Hendrix the ultimate hangdog look on his way inside.

You don't know how good you've got it, he thought. He turned back to the vet.

"Thank you, doctor . . ."

"Melody Sanchez," she said, "but everyone here calls me Doctor Mel."

She didn't look like a Mel, not even with all the bulky gear. Warm eyes and a killer smile were always a winning combo.

"I'm Rafe," he said, extending his hand and then withdrawing it when he realized she was still wearing the thick leather gloves.

"Uh huh," she said, "Rafael Hendrix. I recognized you. Listen, I'm very sorry for your loss."

He nodded and felt his mouth go dry.

The doctor pulled off the gloves and offered a hand for a proper shake. He gripped it briefly and mumbled, "Thanks again."

"No, thank you," she said. "You did a nice thing today. Most folks would shoot a trapped wild animal like that. But you went out of your way to save a unique specimen of an endangered species. Fish, Wildlife, and Parks will have a field day studying him and tracing his route, either over from New Mexico or up from the south. Maybe the numbers are getting high enough that the Mexican grays are reclaiming more of their old territory. And I'm lucky enough to get to treat him before handing him over to the feds."

"Speaking of that, my address is on the paperwork," Hendrix said. "You can send me the bill."

"Not necessary," she said. "He's not your pet. You're the one helping us."

He nodded. She was around thirty-five, he guessed, probably too young for him. But the encounter had lifted his spirits.

"Good to meet you, Rafael," she said. "Or you said Rafe, right?"

"Yes."

"I got so used to hearing Rafael on the news, but I guess the reporters always use full names," she said. "Rafe suits you better. I like it."

"I'm sure I'll see you around," he said. "Maybe at the next football game."

"It's such a small town, once you meet someone, you bump into them everywhere." She nodded toward his shoes. "Plus you're a fellow predawn runner. Not many of us around here."

He couldn't help smiling.

"I usually hit the high school track around five AM if you're ever in the mood for a change of scenery," she said. "It'd be a lot easier on your joints than that gravel road."

Hendrix felt his breath catch, in a good way for once. "That's not a bad idea," he said as he climbed into the truck. "Besides, I think my old route's pretty well shot."

*　*　*

After a lunch of crackers and a cheese stick over the kitchen sink, washed down with plenty of water, Hendrix checked the load on his nine-millimeter and placed it on his bedside table before turning on the ceiling fan and crashing hard. He didn't think the assholes up the road would try anything during the heat of the day, but having his weapon ready helped him rest a little easier.

Or a lot easier, as it turned out. Hendrix was surprised to wake up in pitch blackness. He checked his phone. It was nearly midnight. He'd been out for more than ten hours, with no nightmares he could recall. It was the longest uninterrupted sleep he'd gotten since the bombing. He felt groggier than normal, but otherwise good.

The shack was quiet. When he stepped out of the bedroom, he saw the front door was still locked. He stood beside the living room window and cracked the blinds. Seeing nothing moving in the shadows, Hendrix turned on the porch light.

The truck was where he'd parked it, but there was something off. Hendrix killed the light, retrieved the pistol from his bedroom, slipped on his shoes, and opened the front door.

After his eyes adjusted to the dark, Hendrix crouched low and sprinted to the gate.

All four tires were slashed.

* * *

Hendrix opened the shed in the side yard and wheeled out the wide-tired bike abandoned by the previous owner. He hadn't ridden it much in the past year, but he had oiled the chain and pumped up the tires in case the urge struck. Or some peckerwoods vandalized his truck.

He slipped on the headlamp and slid a roll of duct tape onto the right handlebar until it came to rest on the front fender. Then he tucked the nine into his waistband and pedaled into the darkness.

* * *

By the time he reached the pie plate, he'd worked up a good rhythm and a decent sweat. He switched off the headlamp and proceeded more slowly. He hoped the ranch house was close.

It was. The shot-up truck was parked in the dirt driveway facing the road. There were pole lights on all four corners of the perimeter, but no other visible security.

The weather-beaten house was flanked by a large detached garage and the chicken coop that had proven so tempting to his friend the wolf.

Hendrix grabbed the duct tape before stashing the bike in a ditch. He made his way to one of the few trees on the property. And then he waited.

After two hours, he was fairly certain the inhabitants of the house were asleep. If they had a watchdog, it wasn't a good one. Probably why the wolf had picked this particular henhouse.

There was no basement, which would make getting inside a bit trickier. The house did have a front porch, but it was fully enclosed, which meant getting through two front doors. There were bedrooms on the second floor, but there could be one off the kitchen or living room as well. Too risky.

Hendrix settled on a side window leading into the living room. The garage was twenty yards away, giving him the best available cover. He pulled out his small Buck knife to open the half-moon lock, but when he gave the frame a push, he found the window was unlocked.

He eased the window up halfway. No alarm sounded. He waited fifteen minutes. Nothing stirred. No curious pets jumped up to take in the breeze.

Hendrix placed both hands on the frame and hoisted himself up and over in one reasonably smooth motion before lowering himself onto the living room floor. He was out of practice, but his infiltration training was holding up.

A recon of the main floor confirmed all the bedrooms were upstairs. He hoped not to encounter wives or children. He hadn't seen wedding rings on either man, and neither of them seemed like much of a catch, but junior had to have come from somewhere. He hoped his mom had run off with the UPS driver.

Staying against the wall, Hendrix inched up the stairs to keep the floorboard creaking to a minimum, stopping for five minutes any time his footsteps made a sound.

On the landing, he saw three doors. The middle one was open and led to a bathroom. To his left lay the master bedroom, which looked out over the front porch. To his right was the second bedroom. The door to the master was closed, but the one leading to the smaller bedroom was open a crack. He'd start with that one.

After checking the bathroom, Hendrix sliced off a six-inch strip of duct tape with his knife and nudged the door to the smaller bedroom open enough to get a full view of the bed against the far wall.

There was Junior, splayed on his back, enjoying the blissful sleep of the ignorant. A glistening strand of drool trailed off one side of his sickly smile. Hendrix took three quick steps across the floor and sealed the length of tape over the young man's mouth.

That caused him to stir. Hendrix stood over him and watched as he awoke. When his eyes opened and he saw the intruder, he froze before tensing up to scream. Which was when Hendrix brought his gun butt down hard on the shithead's temple.

Sweet dreams, he thought as he rolled the now-limp body onto its stomach and proceeded to secure the kid's arms behind his back and wrap his ankles tightly with tape. He ran several loops around his head and over the mouth to keep him quiet if he came to earlier than anticipated, making sure he could breathe through his nose.

He returned to the landing, opened the unlocked door of the master, and woke the older man by shoving the barrel of the gun into his mouth.

"Make a move and your son's going to have a hell of a time cleaning this room," Hendrix said.

The older man's eyes were watery with fear. He nodded.

"Do you know who I am?"

The man nodded again.

"I mean besides being the guy who shot the lights out of your truck, do you know my name and where I come from?"

The man swallowed and blinked his eyes, then nodded once more.

"Good," Hendrix said. "Then when I tell you this all ends right here and now, and that if you cause me any more trouble I will kill both of you without any hesitation, you'll know that's a promise I'm well equipped to keep."

He eased the gun barrel out of the man's mouth.

"I understand," he said. "Your tires, that was my son. He's a hothead."

"He's an idiot."

That seemed to wound the old man. "Sir, his mom died in childbirth and I haven't been much of a father to him, but he's all I have, and I can tell you, he's got good in him."

Hendrix nodded. "Then help him get back on the right path. I know what it feels like to lose a child to violence. You do not want to be sitting out here alone in this farmhouse for the next ten years knowing your son was killed because of events you set in motion."

A loud *thunk* came from the other bedroom.

"Go tend to that boy," Hendrix said. "I gave him a goose egg and trussed him up good. But he'll have a long life ahead of him if you both play this right."

"Understood, mister," the man said. "No one should die over a mangy old chicken-killing wolf."

Hendrix slipped the nine back into his waistband and helped the man out of bed.

"I should've known it was you the minute you took out that spotlight from two hundred yards," he said. "You're a damn fine shot."

You had to hand it to the anarchists of the late nineteenth and early twentieth centuries: They were a small political force, but they had an outsized impact—thanks to their proclivity for assassinating any official they held responsible for their poor lot in life.

They enjoyed an impressively brutal run. In 1894, an anarchist stabbed the French president to death, in 1897 another one killed the Spanish prime minister, another killed Empress Elisabeth of Austria in 1898, and yet another murdered King Umberto I of Italy in 1900.

An anarchist attempt to assassinate the Prince of Wales was thwarted in 1900, as was an attempt on King Leopold II of Belgium in 1902, but more plots succeeded than failed during that period, in large part because the anarchists had the zeal to walk right up to their targets and shoot or even stab them to death on the spot.

The new century brought more of the same old strife. Less than seven months after Queen Victoria died, taking the Victorian Age to the grave, anarchist Leon Czolgosz shot William F. McKinley twice in the gut on September 6, 1901, causing the President to shuffle off this mortal coil from Buffalo shortly after his visit to the Pan-American Exposition.

McKinley probably would have survived if he'd had better medical care—he succumbed to gangrene a full week after he was shot while offering to shake Czolgosz's hand. His death spurred Congress to task the Secret Service with protecting the President, ushering in the modern era of the White House bubble.

The Temple of Music where McKinley fell was long gone, replaced by a residential neighborhood, its existence recalled only by a marker the county historical society had placed on a grass median in Fordham Drive.

The exact spot of the assassination was lost to time, with speculation centering on homes at 30 and 34 Fordham.

He stood on the sidewalk between the houses, covering his revolver with a white dish rag just as Czolgosz had done, and watched as a young man in a bright green T-shirt and khaki shorts approached.

"Do you have a few minutes to talk about endangered bird habitat?" the kid asked, a well-practiced grin stretched across his face.

When he got close enough to extend his hand for a shake, he saw the gun barrel poking out from beneath the towel. The grin evaporated. These charity muggers—or chuggers, as city residents referred to the clipboard-toting pests—made it hard to escape their donation pitches by delivering them at point-blank range.

Well, two could play that game.

CHAPTER

4

Aᶠᵗᵉʳ ʜᴇ ᴘᴇᴅᴀʟᴇᴅ home, Hendrix was too keyed up to
go to bed but too tired to go for a run. So he brewed a
pot of coffee and did something he never thought he'd do
again: opened the Facebook app on his phone. He'd joined
to see the photos his wife posted of the kids and to keep
up with a few high school and Special Forces friends. After
the bombing, social media was the last thing on his mind.

He typed Melody Sanchez into the search box. Thanks
to geolocation, the doctor was midway down the first of
many pages featuring women of that name. He clicked on
her profile and was glad to discover her page was open so he
could peruse her posts and photos going back several years.

She was a born-and-raised Fort Stocktonite, or whatever the locals called themselves. She'd attended veterinary
school in Austin but returned home after graduation to
open the animal hospital. She apparently had two sisters in
town, as well as her mother, but there were no references
to her father.

Mel enjoyed visiting national parks, especially Joshua
Tree, Big Bend, and the Grand Canyon, but she'd also

documented one trip each to Yosemite, Grand Teton, Yellowstone, and Glacier. She never seemed to vacation alone, but her companions on each trip were varied. Sometimes she'd gone with her mom and sisters, other times with friends. She didn't appear to be in a relationship, but she might just keep that part of her life offline, shielded from stalkers like Hendrix.

She liked horseback riding, monster truck rallies—that made him smile—and, of course, running. Mel also shared brief reviews of movies she'd seen and books she'd read, often pulling out provocative or inspiring quotations. She seemed well-rounded and delightful, with most of her selfies and group shots displaying the crinkly-eyed smile he'd noticed at the hospital.

Hendrix poured a second mug of coffee and headed outside into the first light of day. He picked up the newspaper from the yard and sat on the front porch to enjoy the last of the overnight cool while he caught up on the county's marriages, births, deaths, and upcoming civic events. There was a rock show at the senior center—the kind featuring polished stones, not guitars and drums. He thought he'd check it out after he got a tow into town for a new set of truck tires.

After that, maybe he could stop in at the hospital and check on that wolf. No, he thought, best not to be over-eager. But he would head over to the high school tomorrow morning to get a good run in on that joint-preserving track. Having seen his best friend lose part of a leg, Hendrix never took his for granted.

Six months after Johnson was transported stateside, Hendrix had taken his own chance to get out of Hell Man and ended up in DC. He visited her at Walter Reed every day after his therapy sessions, which she'd talked him into pursuing. When she completed her PT, they'd kept in touch. But then she moved home to Chicago, became a community organizer, and entered politics, while Hendrix was busy getting married, starting a family, and making his way up the Secret Service ranks.

The Secret Service training had helped take his mind in new directions. The ten-week criminal investigator course was unlike anything he'd encountered in Ranger School, which focused primarily on punishing physical exertion and developing mental toughness.

Analyzing combat situations was part of his Special Forces training at Fort Benning, too, but Hendrix had never stretched his brain quite as much as he did during the CI course at the Federal Law Enforcement Training Center, 235 miles and a world away from the Rangers on the Georgia coast. The 1,600-acre facility at Glynco was the closest he'd come to a college campus environment with dorms, classroom buildings, and quads. Of course, this campus also had eighteen firearms ranges, an explosives range, and an evasive driving course with a cadre of instructors who would tell their charges outlandish urban car chase stories after a few tequila shots at the strip clubs of nearby Brunswick.

"Bogotá, 1985," one of the instructors, a hard-bitten man named Stevens, said to Hendrix and four other trainees squeezed in around a too-small table at the back of a club called The Fox Hole one night. "We were working with the DEA to disrupt a cartel money-laundering operation. We didn't realize we were blown until a hit squad of three sports cars and six motorcycles started gunning for us just as we were arriving at a downtown bank to arrest the launderers.

"There were civilians everywhere," Stevens continued. "The cartel gunslingers were popping them left and right as we took evasive maneuvers. It was like a fucking Bond movie, driving through pedestrian plazas, up on sidewalks, through market stalls, the works. The only thing we didn't see was two guys walking across the street with a giant pane of glass."

That drew laughter, which Stevens acknowledged by narrowing his eyes.

"We were in two vehicles, a DEA and a Secret Service agent in each one. We got away from the central city and lost all but one of the tails, four desperadoes in a Shelby GT. Our vehicles split up, and the Shelby stuck with us." Stevens paused to snare a shot from a trainee who was too enthralled with the story to mind his drink.

"I would have killed for that car," Stevens continued, wiping his mouth with a shirt sleeve. "Anyway, the crazy DEA agent driving the armored Cadillac SUV in which I was literally riding shotgun, he says fuck it and pulls the parking brake to 180 us into a heads-up showdown. I'm still not sure how he managed to keep that beast from tipping over.

"The Shelby's about two blocks away at this point," Stevens said, pointing toward the back wall, which caused one of the trainees to whip his head around to confirm the cartel wasn't invading the strip club. "DEA floors it and says, 'Exit on two.' Then he throws open his door and yells 'Two!' as he rolls into the ditch. I get the idea and do the same on my side just before the SUV plows head-on into the Shelby."

"Holy shit," one of the trainees managed. Two others shot him a look to convey that he should shut the fuck up and let Stevens finish.

"We were far enough out in the countryside that the DEA agent and I landed in grass," Stevens said. "I was pretty banged up, but because I rolled out later than my partner, I was the first to reach the Shelby. Total carnage.

Three dead cartel goons. And then the driver, he was in bad shape, but the airbag saved his life, or maybe slowed down his death. He saw me, screamed something in Spanish, and tried to clear his weapon. So I shot him in the head with my twelve-gauge Remington."

Silence around the table as a Vince Neil song blared over the sound system.

"The airbag looked like a fucking Jackson Pollack painting," Stevens concluded. "DEA finally hobbles up, assesses the scene, and says, 'I didn't know you were into modern art.'"

The other four trainees howled at the punchline, loosing the kind of relieved, choking laughter you get when a story's so tense you forget to breathe while you're listening.

Hendrix, the only combat veteran in the group, quietly took in the scene. He watched the light go out of Stevens's eyes as he signaled for another round. This was his therapy, but it apparently didn't do much to keep his demons at bay. Hendrix vowed not to become a danger junkie in the Service.

After the CI course, in which Hendrix had been part of a small task force investigating an ongoing case—doing everything from drafting and executing search warrants and interviewing witnesses to setting up surveillance operations (his strong suit), making arrests, and even testifying in a mock courtroom—he had returned to DC for an additional eighteen weeks of instruction at the Secret Service Training Academy.

As a new agent, he looked forward to investigating financial crimes and cyberattacks, but other than one boring case of food-stamp fraud that had him working undercover in Dubuque, Hendrix was pegged for protective duty because of his military training and physical prowess. He set up sniper positions during all-hands operations to protect the presidential family, but he was usually one of the guys with the earpiece and glasses scanning the crowd for odd behavior during events attended by lower-level protectees.

That's how he'd met Judy. He was walking through the shopping district of Georgetown with the security detail of a visiting head of state Hendrix was convinced no one in the U.S. had heard of when an athletic, self-assured young woman popped out of an art gallery, shouldered past him, and said, "Welcome to America, Your Excellency."

It turned out His Excellency had excellent taste in art and an unlimited budget. Judy's timely outreach persuaded the potentate to detour into her gallery. She seemed too young to be so successful, but Hendrix soon discovered she was one of those people who knew they were going to make it big and forced the world to agree. The foreign leader spent $3 million during his initial fifteen-minute visit and dropped tens of millions more on pieces Judy recommended to him in subsequent years.

Hendrix should have been an asterisk in any account of that meeting, but while Judy was making her big sale, she was sizing up the tall, strapping Secret Service agent trying to make sense of the avant-garde paintings on the walls. She liked what she saw enough to slip Hendrix her card as he held the door open for the foreign leader's departure.

They had their first date three days later, planned by her. Hendrix proposed to Judy three months later. Within two years, they had the house in Silver Spring and a baby Becca to go with it. All before they were thirty.

Looking back, Hendrix couldn't think of anything they had in common aside from the ambition to succeed in their chosen careers. He'd never been to college; she had degrees in business and art history. She craved culture, while Hendrix was happiest when he was active and outdoors. And yet Judy was a breathtaking force of nature. He enjoyed watching her build an art-selling empire out of the unassuming storefront gallery tucked off M Street. She'd chosen Hendrix for some reason, and he trusted her taste and judgment enough to roll with it despite their many differences. But in some sense, they started breaking up the day they got together.

Judy made such a killing with the gallery that she told Hendrix to stash most of his salary in a college fund for Becca and later David. When she exited his life after the bombing as abruptly as she'd entered it that day in Georgetown, he had $600,000 in the bank. Pocket change for his soon-to-be ex, but more than enough for Hendrix to spend a couple of years getting his life back on track.

*   *   *

After a day spent perusing agates with rock-hound retirees, spending $1,500 on a tow and a new set of tires—and resisting the urge to stop by the animal hospital—Hendrix turned in early so he'd be fresh the next morning. He showed up at the high school at 4:45 AM with a thermos of coffee for what he hoped would be a pleasant post-run chat with Dr. Mel. For the second night in a row, he hadn't been awakened by the nightmare, so he was feeling uncommonly relaxed and rested.

He got out of the truck and went through his stretching routine in the gravel parking lot. Then he walked over to the small set of bleachers to await her arrival.

By five fifteen, he started to feel foolish. At five thirty, he decided to at least give the track a try. He put in five half-hearted miles and called it a morning. He poured himself a cup and sat on the bleachers to watch the sunrise. The track had been easier on his joints, as advertised. It wasn't exactly like running on a cloud—the asphalt bed was exposed in several places where the rubberized surface had worn away—but it beat gravel by a long shot.

Maybe he'd give it another try one day, but comfort wasn't the point of these workouts and he felt awkward about showing up again. He'd opened himself up to the universe, as his ex-wife had always put it, but the universe hadn't noticed.

He shook the last drops out of the metal thermos cup, screwed it back onto the bottle, and stood.

"You're looking pretty good in those tight shorts, old man," Melody Sanchez called out from twenty yards behind him. "Might give some cheerleader the wrong idea."

Hendrix caught himself grinning and did his best to suppress it before he turned around.

"You snuck up on me," he said, walking toward her.

"I live right over there," she said, pointing to a small brick house across the street from the track.

He chuckled. "You've been watching me." So much for situational awareness. He'd been too busy moping to hear her approach.

"Like I said, I've been enjoying the view. You have any of that coffee left?"

He held the thermos up to his ear and shook it. "It's nearly full."

"Well," she said, "why don't you step into my kitchen and pour me a cup like a gentleman."

Hendrix fell in beside her as she started back to her house. She reached over and patted his ass.

"After that, it's probably time to hit the showers," she said.

*   *   *

Sitting on her well-shaded back patio an hour later in the sweats and T-shirt she'd let him borrow, Hendrix watched

Dr. Mel water her flower bed in a red silk robe short enough to show off the full length of the tan, athletic legs he'd so recently felt wrapped around him.

When she turned back to the table and caught him looking, she gave him a squirt from the hose.

"Enough of that, mister," she said. "Some of us have to get ready for work."

He let her see the grin this time.

"You can watch me get dressed if you'd like," she added.

He did like. It had been a minute since he'd sat on the edge of a bed and watched a woman go through her intricate morning routine. It brought back fond memories of the early years of his marriage, pre-kids, pre–White House.

"Don't get too comfortable," she said. "You can drive me to the hospital when I'm ready."

"Happy to," he replied.

After watching her discard three tops that all looked great to him, he said, "Mel, what is all this, exactly? I'm not complaining, but it's a pretty unexpected development."

"What is all this?" she replied, gesturing across her chest.

"I definitely know what that is," he said. "I'm a few years older than you, but my memory's pretty good."

"More like five or six years older. And yes, you did win the Fort Stockton lottery today."

"Feels like it," he admitted.

"It's like this, Rafe," she said. "I haven't been on a date since I came back from Austin and opened my practice. I hang out with my mom and my sisters and I work. That's pretty much it."

"And you lure unsuspecting men to the track."

"Not until this morning, no," she said. "But I'm tempted to make a habit of it."

"Why me?" he asked.

"For starters, you rescued that wolf, risking bodily harm," she said.

You don't know the half of it, he thought.

"That goes a long way toward winning a veterinarian's heart."

He nodded.

"You're considerate," she continued. "My receptionist told me all about how you didn't try to unleash a vicious wild animal in her waiting room."

"True," he said. "Speaking of animals, what kind of veterinarian has no pets at home?" He gestured toward the patio door. "Not even an iguana in there."

"When I was growing up, my pediatrician was a single woman, and something of an inspiration to me," she said. "My mom asked her once if she wanted to have children of her own and she said she had a firm policy to never take work home with her. Besides, she got to watch several generations of local kids grow up. It was enough for her. It's the same with me and animals—though I wouldn't mind having a horse. I enjoy riding."

Hendrix nodded. "Did you have pets growing up?"

"Oh, yes," she said, lighting up that smile again. "I actually did have an iguana, along with several dogs, a grumpy old cat, hamsters, guinea pigs, frogs, you name it. I've always been fascinated by animals. But I get more than enough interaction at the hospital."

"So I rescued a wolf and I'm considerate," he said. "That was enough to take me to bed?"

She laughed. "Not quite. You have other appealing qualities. I won't list them all because I don't want to give you a swelled head. But it helps that you're not a local. You've been halfway around the world, worked in the nation's capital. Hell, the President of the United States is your best friend. Meanwhile, every guy I went to high school with has either gone away or married and gone to seed. And you most definitely have not gone to seed."

"Right back at you," he said.

She laughed. "You want to know what my receptionist said? 'He's got great hair and a nice ass. If you don't fuck him, I will.'"

"She should have seen me when I wore it longer in my bad boy youth," he said, rubbing his head. "So you just wanted to beat the competition."

"Pretty much. It had been too long, almost to the point where I wasn't sure if I was going to have sex again. And I could tell you liked me."

"That's true."

"What was it that turned your head?" she asked.

He gestured across his chest.

She tossed a hand towel at him. "Yeah, with the smock I was wearing, pretty sexy."

"Your smile," he said. "It got me. You smile with your whole face. It's open and warm and intelligent and . . . fun."

The doc rewarded his description with the best smile he'd seen yet.

"For me, there's also that whole sad wolf thing you've got going on," she said. "It's like catnip to a cat doctor."

Hendrix felt his cheeks flush and his jaw muscles tighten. As he stood, she closed her eyes and let out a long breath.

"Shit, Rafe, shit," she said, stepping forward to take his hands. "I'm sorry, that was . . . I shouldn't have said that."

"I'm no one's rescue dog," he said, pulling away. "Before I left DC, I got enough looks like that to last several lifetimes. And the letters from women who saw me on TV and wanted to nurture me back to life . . . Not for me, Mel."

There was no trace of a smile in her eyes. "This is a lot," she said.

He nodded. "Yes. All of it."

"Listen, I'll drive myself to the hospital."

"That would be best, I think."

"I'm such an idiot," she muttered.

He was upset about being the object of her pity porn fantasy, but he felt a creeping regret for snapping at her.

"Hey," he said, "you are not an idiot. You're the best thing to happen to me in quite a while. I wish . . ."

He took her hands again and caught her gaze. He wondered if he looked as wounded as she did. It was a raw moment where there should have been afterglow. He'd never been good at any of this. Why should this time be different?

"Will you run with me tomorrow if I promise not to ogle your ass?" she asked as she reached around to give it a quick squeeze.

He nodded, relieved to feel the storm passing. "Fair warning, though," he said. "I'll be wearing my baggiest sweats."

* * *

It wasn't quite nine AM when Hendrix drove his rig past Historic Fort Stockton and the Road Runner Mobile Home Park to start the winding drive down U.S. 285 to Sanderson. It lay sixty miles south through a series of limestone hills and scrub plateaus, a slice of high desert badlands perfect for helping him sort through the morning's events.

Every April, dozens of Texas characters descended on this stretch of two-lane blacktop in everything from European super cars to battered Trans Ams for the Big Bend Open Road Race. But on this midweek morning in

September, Hendrix had the road to himself. He tapped it light as he took in the scenery.

Melody Sanchez. Dr. Mel. She was right. He had liked her right away, and he had also sensed in those moments at the clinic that the feeling was mutual. Why rush it, though? He knew he cleaned up okay and he'd stayed in fighting trim, but women didn't throw themselves at him. He hated that his tragic story might have been the catalyst. That was no basis for a healthy relationship.

She was lonely. So was he. They'd felt a spark and acted on it. It's not like Fort Stockton had a robust Tinder community for hookups. From that perspective, it made sense. Their lovemaking had been hungry, almost desperate, like they were trying to consume each other. It was electrifying but also unnerving.

He could smell traces of her, maybe a botanical shampoo scent or pleasant hand lotion, on the borrowed clothes. He killed the truck's air conditioning and touched his nose to his left shoulder. He could almost taste her lips and the sweat on her neck.

He snapped to attention and swerved to miss a javelina crossing the road. Like wild boar but somehow even uglier, javelinas roamed the valleys of the nearby Glass Mountains between Fort Stockton and Marathon, drawing hunters in all seasons except the scorching hot summers.

Feeling the heat building in the cab of his truck, Hendrix cranked the AC back up. Maybe he'd head west from Sanderson to Marathon and return to Fort Stockton on U.S. 385. It was similar country, but at a higher elevation. That would get him back home by around noon. If he'd just nailed that javelina when he'd had the chance, he could have grilled it up for lunch.

He'd have to ask Mel if she'd ever gone on a javelina hunt. He doubted it, given her profession, but he also hadn't expected to see on her Facebook profile that she liked monster truck rallies. In truth, he knew almost nothing about her.

Except that he liked her, and she liked him. And when had consenting adults needed more than that to go on?

He had to slow things down, though, that much he'd decided by the time he'd made the turn to Marathon. Get some runs in. Meet for coffee somewhere that wasn't a few feet from her bedroom. Take her out on real dates. See what it all added up to and take it from there. Maybe the universe wasn't ignoring him after all.

*   *   *

As he started up the third leg of the triangle, Marathon back to Stockton, Hendrix spotted a billboard: "The Monsters Are Coming. America's Wildest Monster Truck Show Returns to Midland, Texas."

The event was next Saturday at the Midland County Horseshoe Arena, about a hundred miles northeast of Fort Stockton. That sounded like a proper Texas first date.

He called the animal hospital and asked for Dr. Mel. The receptionist seemed pleased when he gave her his name.

After a few minutes, he thought the call might have dropped as he passed between cell towers. But just as he reached for the phone, her voice came over the truck's speakers.

"Did you forget something at my house?" she asked.

"Not that I know of," he replied.

Neither of them spoke for five seconds.

"You mentioned it's been years since you'd been on a proper date," Hendrix said finally.

"Did I?" she asked. "You make me sound like a real catch."

"I'd like to take you on one Saturday," he said, pushing on in hopes that she'd soften a bit.

"What kind of date, exactly?" she asked in what he judged to be a slightly interested tone.

"Classic. Dinner and a show," he said. "Up in Midland."

"That's a haul," she said.

"The way I understand it, a hundred miles is right next door to a Texan."

She sighed. "You got me there, Rafe."

"Besides, it'll give us a chance to get to know each other better on the drive," he said. "Can I pick you up at five thirty?"

Another pause.

He was about to speak again when she said, "It's a date."

Suddenly, the scrubland on this stretch of U.S. 385 didn't seem quite as monotonous as before. Hendrix turned on the radio and found an upbeat Tex-Mex station that soon had him tapping the steering wheel.

It wasn't even midday, but the skies had darkened as a vast cloud bank rolled over the prairie like God was putting up his convertible top. Hendrix noticed headlights about half a mile behind him, probably automatic ones that had sensed the lower light conditions.

He slowed five miles an hour and saw that the vehicle was a pickup, a sky-blue Ford he could have sworn he'd seen on his way out of Fort Stockton on the first leg of the trip.

The driver of the other pickup dropped back instead of maintaining speed and passing.

"What the hell are you up to?" Hendrix asked as he watched the truck resume its spot half a mile back.

Hendrix picked up speed, adding back the five miles per hour plus five more. Within a minute, the other pickup, after first fading further back, sped up enough to maintain its earlier distance.

It wasn't his neighbor's truck. This one was newer and both headlights were intact. But maybe the idiot son had a rig of his own parked in the garage the night Hendrix had dropped by their farmhouse. That was the most likely explanation.

Hendrix was in no mood for whatever trouble the driver of this truck might represent. He punched the accelerator and soon had his rig humming at 105 mph on the flat, mostly straight highway.

Five minutes later, he checked his rearview and didn't see the truck behind him. He spotted a pullout ahead and slowed so he could ease off the road without kicking up a dust cloud.

He grabbed his rifle, rolled down the window, jumped out of the vehicle, and faced back toward where the other truck would be coming into view. He trained the scope on the farthest spot that gave him good resolution and waited. At least he should be able to see what this tail looked like.

It didn't take long for the Ford to shimmer into focus through the high-noon heat. It was hauling ass, but Hendrix held the scope steady and got a good look inside the cab.

"Shit," he said.

The driver was wearing a *lucha libre* mask. Hendrix doubted he was being stalked by a Mexican wrestler, which meant someone was making a serious effort to keep him from making an ID.

The truck was less than twenty seconds away. Hendrix had a decision to make. He could take a potshot, shatter the windshield, and try to make a getaway. But that might lead to a crash and he couldn't risk killing the guy when he didn't know who he was or how hostile he might be.

So Hendrix climbed into his still-running rig, buckled up, and swerved back onto the road.

He punched the accelerator, but the other truck was closing fast. Seconds later, it was in the left lane coming up alongside his rear fender.

Hendrix leaned over to pop the glove box and grab his nine, which would have been sitting next to him if he hadn't been operationally rusty.

When he heard multiple rounds raking the canopy, Hendrix slammed the brakes and stayed low as his truck swerved to a halt on the right shoulder of the highway.

The automatic weapon fire shattered his back passenger windows. More rounds arced through his still-lowered driver's side window and over his body, which he flattened against the bench seat. Glass from the front passenger window showered his head.

Hendrix threw the shifter into park and grabbed the nine, waiting for the attacker to come back and finish the job. But the other truck kept going. After a thirty count, he raised his head over the dashboard and confirmed it was gone.

This was either a sloppy killer, which didn't jibe with the precautions the guy had taken not to be spotted, or someone was sending a message. He hoped he'd survive long enough to find out what it was.

*   *   *

Hendrix raised eyebrows at the body shop when he dropped off his truck, but they accepted his explanation that he'd escaped a roadside kidnapping attempt on an ill-advised drive into Juárez.

"You're lucky to be alive," the shop owner said. "My brother-in-law got kidnapped outside the *ciudad* a couple years back and we had to pay $5,000 to spring him."

"I doubt anyone would pay five bucks for me," Hendrix said as he handed over the keys. "You wouldn't happen to have a loaner I could use for a couple of days, would you?"

The owner, a beefy forty-something man with a tight Afro, pointed across the shop's small parking lot to a late-model silver Malibu parked under the sparse shade of a scrawny tree.

"I don't normally lend it out," he said. "But I served in Afghanistan the same time you were there. Kandahar."

"I appreciate it."

"You got a raw deal, Mr. Hendrix. I'm happy to help. Just stay out of Mexico, okay?"

"You got it."

"I'll have an estimate ready by the end of the day," the owner said.

"Not necessary," Hendrix said. "Just do whatever you think needs to be done."

The man nodded and offered his hand. Hendrix took it and was impressed by the easy firmness of his grip. He imagined he'd been a good man to pair with on patrol.

"Will Plummer, Mr. Hendrix," the man said.

"Please, call me Rafe. Glad to meet you."

"Should be ready by Friday," Plummer said.

"Perfect timing," Hendrix said, though he wondered if he should cancel his Saturday outing with Dr. Mel.

*   *   *

After picking up five boxes of .22 LR rounds and an upgraded scope, Hendrix spent the rest of the day setting up targets and shooting them with his no-frills rifle in the scrub near his shack. He knew he should upgrade to the more reliable .223 center-fire rounds, but he hadn't had any issues with the rimfire LRs, and he never thought he'd be using the gun for anything other than target practice and scaring off rattlesnakes.

Given that personal protection from human varmints now topped his list of use cases for the rifle, Hendrix had picked up the most powerful LR rounds available, sixty-grain Sniper Subsonic. The name was cheesy, but he was a trained sniper after all, so what the hell.

He could have opted for faster rounds, with muzzle velocity up to 1,435 feet per second, compared to the Subsonic's relatively modest 950 fps, but he'd traded speed for stopping power. If he saw the man in the *lucha libre* mask again, he'd want to take him out at 100 to 150 yards, if possible, to avoid another spray-down from the automatic rifle. At that distance, Hendrix would need as much heft as possible to put the man down and, more importantly, keep him down. What he really needed was a more powerful rifle, but that wasn't a path he was ready to go down.

It was a grim business, preparing to take another man's life, but Hendrix took satisfaction in the sighting-in process. He didn't use laser boresighters or other high-tech aids. He simply removed the bolt from his rifle, looked down the bore and started sighting in on targets placed fifty yards out. He continued sighting farther out in twenty-five-yard increments until he got to 150.

Hitting anything over 150 yards was tricky for a typical low-power .22 round. You had to account for a pretty big bullet drop at extended range. Hendrix was practiced enough to have taken out his neighbor's truck lights from beyond that distance, but making an accurate kill shot at 200 or 300 yards required luck and maybe prayer in addition to skill and preparation. He'd keep it to 150 to give himself the greatest chance of success if he had another crack at *el mysterioso*.

During a water break after he'd worked through the first three boxes of ammo, Hendrix thought back to one of his early missions with Wyetta Johnson in Afghanistan.

The platoon was on patrol in the outskirts of the nearest town when they started taking sniper fire from an abandoned building. They'd found cover in a small apartment building across the street, hustling the three families there to safety out the back door.

They were too close to the abandoned building to call in an airstrike, and they couldn't pinpoint the sniper's position. Meanwhile, in his first round of shots, the asshole had taken out one young corporal and badly wounded another. They needed to get back to the Hummers they'd abandoned in the street and get the kid back to base for urgent medical attention.

"Any ideas?" Johnson asked the platoon.

"I'll go up on the roof and take him out," Hendrix said.

"Such a stud," she said. "Who are they going to cast in the movie about you?"

"Depends on how pretty I am when we get out of here," he said.

"Get to it, then," she'd said.

But as Hendrix was settling into position behind the large fan unit that provided the roof's only cover, he was astonished to see the abandoned building destroyed in an explosion.

He ran back down in time to find Johnson putting away the AT-4 she'd used to take out the opposing sniper. "Sometimes an anti-tank missile is better than a finesse play," she said.

"You could have saved me the trip," Hendrix said as he shouldered his rifle and followed the platoon back to the vehicles.

"I like to keep you guessing," she said.

At mess that night, after they'd confirmed their injured comrade would pull through, Johnson confided that the blunt-force solution occurred to her when she realized the sniper had chosen to set up in an abandoned building.

"When you don't have civilians to worry about, a bazooka becomes an appealing option," she said.

Hendrix thought then that there would always be a time and a place for precision targeting. But now, with drones growing ever more sophisticated, he was no longer sure there needed to be a human element in that equation. Just one more reason to be glad he was out of the game.

After cleaning the rifle and stowing his equipment, Hendrix showered and changed into a fresh T-shirt and sweats. He was about to leave the bedroom en route to a steak and sunset on the back patio when it finally hit him: He wasn't glad to be out of the game, not really.

He'd gone out of his way to bring some kind of heat onto himself, and preparing to defend himself felt good, almost healing. He stopped at his bedside table, opened the drawer, and took out the card from the White House.

After finishing a rare ribeye and garlic potatoes, Hendrix pushed away his plate, picked up the envelope, and opened it. In the last light of sunset, he read the brief note inside:

"I was wrong not to reach out to thank you and give you my support. I will never again place political considerations above our friendship. My debt to you can never be repaid, but I will try. From here on out, I will always have your six just like you've had mine."

It was exactly what he'd expected her to say. But Hendrix hadn't wanted to see those words until he was ready to forgive her. He was glad he'd waited. Piece by piece, he was finally rebuilding his life.

* * *

At the end of the otherwise uneventful week—a drive past the neighbors' compound Saturday morning in his beautifully repaired truck hadn't revealed any rigs aside from the one he'd shot up during the wolf rescue—Hendrix decided to keep his date with Mel.

That afternoon, he made one last check of his shaved face in the truck's rearview and stashed the nine in the plastic storage bin at the bottom of the driver's side door. If there was another ambush, he'd be ready to return fire.

He was grateful to Will Plummer for the restoration work. He didn't want to explain the bullet holes to Melody Sanchez on the drive to Midland.

He momentarily lost the ability to explain anything when he pulled up to Dr. Mel's house and caught sight of her on the front porch swing. Her long brown hair, which he'd last seen in a ponytail, cascaded around her face in silky waves. Subtle makeup accentuated her fine cheekbones, which induced an extra flutter when she gave him a smile.

She wore a short, shimmery black dress and dark cowboy boots. A dark leather clutch completed the look. He shook his head and whistled as he mounted the steps.

"You sure you don't just want to stay here?" he asked as she got up and leaned in for a hug.

"That's what got us into trouble the first time," she said before playfully pushing him away.

"It's my first salon blowout," she added. "Do you like it?"

"You mean your hair?" Hendrix asked. "Yes, very much. Whatever that procedure is, I'm a fan."

"Procedure?" She laughed. "It's done with a blow dryer and a comb, no scalpel required."

Hendrix nodded, grinning.

"You don't look too bad yourself," Dr. Mel said. "I mean, not nearly as good as me, but you made an effort. You shaved."

"I did."

"New shirt, too. And you got your truck detailed."

"Kind of," he said.

"I'm impressed. Now where are you taking me?"

"I heard there's a good sushi restaurant in Midland," Hendrix said.

"Yum," she said. "Good choice. What about the show?"

"I got us great seats at the monster truck rally," he said.

"Uh, you want me to watch monster trucks dressed like this?"

He winced. "Good point. Would you like to change?"

"No, Rafael, I would not like to change. Do you know how many hours I spent to look like this? Not that you deserve it."

"I thought you liked monster trucks."

"Who the hell told you that?"

Shit, he thought, realizing he'd tripped himself up.

"I went through your Facebook page one night," he admitted.

Dr. Mel looked confused, but then laughed. "That bitch!" she exclaimed. "My older sister is always getting on my phone when we go out and posting silly shit on my Facebook. I'm going to kill her for this one."

"Sorry," Hendrix said. "I should have asked."

"Rather than creeping on my Facebook? Yeah, that would have been the smart play," she said. "But you know what? Fuck it. Let's give it a shot. If nothing else, we can make fun of every ridiculous moment."

"All right," he said.

"But you are totally buying me an expensive T-shirt. I'm not going to sit with a bunch of families and teenage boys all night with my tits hanging out."

"All the dads will be crushed," he said as he opened the passenger door for her.

"Believe me, Rafe," she said. "I know."

*   *   *

"We'll have quite a sunset on the way over tonight," Mel said as they headed northeast on U.S. 385 to Odessa on their way to Midland. "No clouds all the way to the horizon."

"That's one of the things I love most about living here," Hendrix said. "The landscape, the sunrises, the sunsets, they speak to me."

"That's one of the reasons I came back from Austin," she said. "What brought you to Fort Stockton? Are you from Texas?"

Hendrix shook his head. "Western Pennsylvania, outside Pittsburgh. My folks were real yinzers."

"What's that?" she asked. "Some kind of Jewish thing?"

Hendrix laughed. "No. Yinzer comes from how people say *y'all* where I come from. They say it as *yinz*. So they came to be called yinzers. My folks were of German descent, both third-generation Pennsylvania yinzers. My dad worked in the steel mill, the whole deal."

"Why didn't you go back?"

"Nothing for me there anymore," Hendrix said. "I enlisted right out of high school. My parents drowned in a boating accident while I was deployed in Afghanistan."

She reached over and gave his right leg a gentle squeeze. "I'm so sorry, Rafe."

"After I got my head straight, I started in the Secret Service, met my wife, and we had our two kids," he said. "Those are the years I try to hang onto."

"I'm glad you had them," she said. "You deserved better than how it turned out."

"No story has a happy ending if you follow it long enough," he said.

She turned to look at him. "I understand why you feel that way. But that's no way to look at life."

"I'm a realist."

"Whenever I think those thoughts, like what if I never meet the right person and die alone, I take solace in knowing there's something good waiting for me beyond this world."

"I'm not religious, unfortunately," he replied. "I'm glad you have that, though. I don't look down on it."

"I think we all have it, whether we believe it or not. But I'm sorry you can't take comfort in it."

"My mom took me to Sunday school when I was little," Hendrix said. "But then I realized my dad was watching the Steelers while we were learning Bible stories. Church didn't stand a chance after that."

"Are you still a football fan?"

"Mel, I don't even own a TV. I do enjoy the Fort Stockton high school games. They remind me of that period of my life, another time I was happy."

"Those games are all on Friday nights," she said. "Which leaves Sunday wide open for you to go to church with me."

"I appreciate the invitation," he said. "I doubt it will turn my head, but I'm happy to go with you to see that part of your life."

"We can meet there tomorrow morning at ten," she said. "You still have to go home and sleep in your own bed tonight."

"Lead me not into temptation," he said.

"Lead me to Negi Hamachi," she said as they hit the outskirts of Midland. "I'm starving."

*　*　*

After a surprisingly good dinner—they sat at the sushi bar and ordered the chef's choice selection, which he assembled

with care and precision as they watched and sampled—
they headed to the arena, where Hendrix bought Dr. Mel
an oversized T-shirt that read "Save a truck, ride a driver."

She pulled it on and did a half-turn for him.

"Truly awful," Hendrix said.

"Get used to it," she said. "It's my new favorite
nightgown."

As they made their way to the seats, it became clear
Mel's fashion choice fit right in with the heavy-metal tees,
Texas flag hats, and giant belt buckles favored by rally
attendees.

"It's very loud," she shouted to Hendrix once they were
situated in the third row.

"You can really taste the diesel exhaust," he replied.

They made it through one racing heat in which Soul
Reaper, a shiny black behemoth bedecked with giant chrome
skulls and two crossed scythes emerging from its diesel
stacks, defeated the Bunker Buster, a three-story, military-
themed rig topped with a giant shrieking eagle that shot
fireworks out of its talons. Soul Reaper sealed the victory by
slamming into Bunker Buster as it caught air on the track's
last dirt berm, tipping it on its side and breaking off one of
the eagle's talons as the skull wagon streaked to victory.

"Okay, I'm done," Mel hollered. "Tick that one off the
bucket list."

Relieved, Hendrix led the way back to the quiet parking lot. They were alone except for a dad walking about
twenty feet ahead of them. He was carrying his young son,
who had his arms wrapped around dad's neck and his head
nestled on his shoulder.

"Did you have fun, buddy?" the father asked.

The boy raised his head and nodded. As he turned to
cozy back up on dad's shoulder, he gave Hendrix and Dr.
Mel a tired, toothy smile.

The boy was about the age David had been the last time Hendrix had seen him, buckled into his car seat in the back of his wife's SUV as she drove them out of his life to start over in Michigan.

He remembered how Davey had pointed at his eye, then his heart, then at Hendrix as the vehicle pulled from the curb. Hendrix had returned the gesture, but his wife drove away so fast, he doubted his son saw it.

"Hey," Mel said, "you okay?"

Hendrix realized he'd stopped dead in the parking lot.

He squeezed her hand but couldn't get any words out. She put her free hand on his cheek and pulled him in for a hug. He closed his eyes and placed his forehead against hers.

"I don't have any business being with anyone," he said.

"I'll be the judge of that," she replied.

She drew her head back and held his gaze for a long moment. Then she closed her eyes and waited until he leaned in and kissed her.

"Let's get out of here," she said.

* * *

They didn't speak until they were back on the two-lane to Fort Stockton. The skies were still clear, and the stars stretched from horizon to horizon.

"Tell me about your son," she said.

"The last time I saw him, two years ago, he was three. I haven't spoken to him since."

"Not even on his birthday?"

Hendrix shook his head and kept his eyes on the road. "My wife, my ex-wife, she told me I should never reach out or try to see him. She's remarried, to a good man from what I've been able to find, her high school sweetheart, reconnected online. She wants David to know him as his father."

"You agreed to that?"

"Becca had just been killed in the bombing," he said. "My wife blamed me. Most of the world blamed me. I blamed myself. Judy and I had been drifting apart for a while, and now we were both devastated. I didn't have the heart to fight her on it."

"What about now?" Dr. Mel asked. She placed her hand back on his leg and left it there. It was a comfort.

"I think about him every day," Hendrix said. "He's five and I'm not there to teach him how to ride a bike—not that I was fully engaged when we were still together, but I know I'd treat the time with him as more precious now."

"You should talk to Judy about a new arrangement."

"I'm not sure Davey even remembers me," Hendrix said.

"He does," Mel said. "I know he does. You're his daddy."

"It would be too confusing for him," Hendrix said. "He's better off without me."

"Rafe, you're a good man. What little kid doesn't need more good grown-ups in his life?"

Hendrix let out a long breath. "It's not something I've talked about with anyone," he said. "I appreciate everything you're saying, but it's still raw."

"I know," she said. "I'll shut up now. But your needs are important, too. Not everything has to be a sacrifice."

He dropped his right hand off the steering wheel and placed it over her hand resting on his leg. Even though he knew he wouldn't break his promise to stay out of Davey's life, it was good to have someone in his corner again.

* * *

The next morning, he met Melody Sanchez, her mother, and her two sisters at the mission-style 1875 Catholic church downtown. The landmark adobe building was well preserved, and Hendrix felt transported back to old Fort Stockton when the traditional Mass commenced.

A simple mural of the crucifixion on the inside back wall showed Jesus alone on the cross against a backdrop of rolling white clouds. Hendrix was moved by how Jesus seemed to be at peace with his sacrifice. He had never seen one of history's most dramatic moments depicted with such a sense of calm.

Of course, Jesus knew he was on the right path. Hendrix was only guessing that his course of action, or inaction when it came to David, was the best one. It was agonizing. He wished he could know how the story turned out, and that he could go back and make a different choice if he didn't like the outcome.

After the service, Mel rode with Hendrix and gave him directions to her mother's house, where they were invited to brunch. It was a modest, well-kept home. Mel's father had died of a stroke ten years earlier, but the four women of the family were as close as he'd ever seen a family be, finishing each other's sentences, teasing, laughing, and welcoming in the men lucky enough to be there—her sisters' husbands and Hendrix.

"You're not very talkative," Mel's mother said to him at one point.

"Just taking it all in," he replied. The family feeling washing over him felt so warm and inviting, he was in awe.

"The way you girls coo over each other, he can't get a word in," one of the husbands, a gentle soul named Eduardo, said in his defense.

"Oh, Ed," his wife said. "You know you love it." He grinned.

"The food is excellent, Mrs. Sanchez," Hendrix said. "I can't remember eating a brunch this good. Thank you for having me."

"Well, my daughter can't stop talking about you, so I thought I'd better meet you and take your measure myself," she said.

"Mama!" Mel scolded.

"It's true, *mija*," she said. "You're smitten."

"She's a special woman," Hendrix said as she gave his hand a squeeze under the table. "I don't know about smitten, but I hope she lets me take her to the football game on Friday, anyway."

"It's one day at a time for you, Rafe," Mel said. "And Friday's out, I'm afraid."

"Why's that?" asked her older sister, the one who'd posted the note about monster trucks on Mel's Facebook. "Another suitor in the wings?"

"No, but I like the idea of keeping Rafe on his toes," she said. "I'm heading to Dallas this weekend for a veterinary conference."

"Since when?" her mother asked. "Why didn't I know about this?"

"I just found out myself," Mel said. "There was an email waiting for me when I got home from our date last night. A new pharmaceutical rep invited me to attend, on her company's dime. All I have to do is have lunch with her on Saturday. It looks like there are a couple of good breakout sessions, and it just sounds like fun."

"Do you get a lot of offers like that?" Hendrix asked.

"First conference invite for me," Dr. Mel said. "Various reps have taken me out for a meal or a drink when they've come through town over the years, but they mostly give out free samples in hopes you'll see good results and start prescribing their drugs."

"Good news," Hendrix said.

"I might get a little shopping in," she said, "or even a facial at the hotel spa."

"Ooh, take me," her younger sister said.

"If she does," her husband said, "you and me are going to have to hit the bars and have a wild night of our own, Rafe."

"Sorry, this trip's solo," Mel said. "It'll mostly be conference sessions Friday and Saturday, and then back by Sunday evening. But if anyone wants me to pick something up for them at the Highland Park Village mall, let me know."

"You better not go there without me," her younger sister said.

"Relax, I couldn't even afford to park there," Mel said. "But I think I will get that facial."

"You deserve it," her mother said.

"Thank you, Mama. Now I forgive you for 'smitten.'" She gave Hendrix a wink. "But he is pretty good company, that much I'll admit."

*   *   *

Hendrix dropped Mel off at home after brunch. He was about to pull away, but instead hopped out of the truck and jogged up to the porch to catch her before she went inside.

"Uh-uh," she said with a smile.

"I know," he said, placing his hands on her shoulders. "I just wanted to say a proper goodbye."

She looked up at him. "You really are a tall fucker, Rafe," she said.

"Only six one, not so tall," he said.

"When you're stretching to get to five five, it's all a matter of perspective," Mel said.

He leaned down to meet her. "You know what I call that?" he asked. "Perfect kissing height."

*   *   *

They were sticking to their take-it-slow plan, which still made sense to him, but Hendrix was more disappointed than he thought he'd be at the prospect of attending the football game alone.

When he got back to his shack after running errands, he texted her: "Have dinner with me Thursday. I'll give you a proper preconference sendoff."

He misread her reply— "xo"—as "no," and clicked the screen off in irritation. When he saw what she'd actually typed a few minutes later, he closed his eyes and gave thanks.

"xo," he wrote back. "Bring a big appetite."

*   *   *

On Thursday morning, Hendrix picked up a bag of fragrant mesquite chips at the local garden center in preparation for some slow and low grilling. Then he marinated two prime, thin-cut ribeyes in a mix of soy sauce, olive oil, lemon juice, Worcestershire sauce, basil, garlic, and a generous slug of hot sauce.

He tossed together a colorful salad with ingredients from the farmers' market and then combined sliced strawberries, muddled mint leaves, sugar, and red wine into a light dessert he popped into the fridge.

Once he'd set the small patio table for dinner and slid the steaks onto the grill, Hendrix rewarded himself with an iced-down Modelo Negra. There was enough wine left over from what he'd used for the dessert to tide them over through dinner, but he needed to conserve it until then.

He found a good Cuban jazz album on YouTube and streamed it through the Bluetooth speaker he kept in his cactus planter on the patio.

"Impressive," Mel said when she peeked around the corner.

"You found me," he said as she crossed the patio for a hello kiss.

"I just followed that incredible smell," she said. "My God, Rafe, don't tell me you can cook, too."

"I grill," he replied. "A few things. I don't have many tricks up my sleeve."

It was enough. Dinner was a hit and they became so engrossed in conversation they only realized they were sitting in the dark an hour after the sun had set.

"Before I turn on the light, do you want to do some stargazing?" Hendrix asked.

"Rafe, that is the cheesiest pickup line I've ever heard."

"Hold that thought," he said as he left the patio to take in the dishes and retrieve his telescope from the breakfast bar.

"You're serious?" she said when he returned. "That makes it a little better, I guess."

"Fun fact: West Texas has some of the darkest skies in the continental United States," he said as he set the telescope up on the patio table. "Not as dark as Afghanistan, but I like the company better over here."

"You haven't been to Big Bend National Park yet, have you?" she asked.

"No."

"We can go camping next weekend, if you want. The night sky there is spectacular."

"So you do like national parks," he said.

Mel laughed. "Yes, those Facebook entries are real. Carlsbad Caverns is next on my list. Maybe another road trip?"

Hendrix shuddered. "I'm not a big fan of bats."

"Really? When I was going to school in Austin, I loved to watch the Mexican free-tailed bats swoop out from under the Congress Avenue Bridge at sunset. Imagine a cloud of bats rising to meet the moon, Rafe."

"I'd rather not, thanks."

"Now that I think of it, bats are the one animal where my profession and yours overlap," she said.

"If I let you tell me how, do you promise never to talk about bats again?" he asked.

She rolled her eyes. "Have you heard about the bat bombs?"

"You mean like Batman keeps on his utility belt?"

"No, Rafe, it's much crazier than that. I learned about this in a history class at UT and it's one of the few non-veterinary things that's stuck with me over the years."

"Bat bombs."

"Yep. There was a dentist—I think he was from your home state—who came up with the idea during World War II to strap firebombs to bats and drop them over Japanese cities. He figured they'd roost in the eaves of all those wooden buildings and then when the timers went off, everything would burn down."

"A Pennsylvania dentist came up with this?" Hendrix asked. "I think you're bat-shitting me."

"Scout's honor," Mel said. "He became intrigued by bats during a visit to Carlsbad Caverns."

"Naturally," Hendrix said. "And how did he convince the military to test his scheme?"

"He was friends with Eleanor Roosevelt!"

"Naturally." Hendrix couldn't help smiling.

"So Eleanor told FDR, and he ordered the Army to test it in the early forties in New Mexico," Mel said. "They used the same species of bat you see in Austin, the Mexican

free-tails. They brought in the guy who invented napalm
to create the explosives."

"And that's how we won World War II," Hendrix said.

"It might have been more humane than the atom
bombs we ended up using," Mel said.

"Not to the bats," Hendrix offered.

"No, not to the bats. The point is the experiments
worked. They glued little tubes of napalm to the bats' legs
and set them off on timers."

"What could possibly go wrong?" Hendrix asked.

"Well, at one point, they did set the Carlsbad air base
on fire," she said.

"That must have been a setback." Hendrix chuckled.
"Imagine if something like that had happened with the
Manhattan Project up the road in Los Alamos."

"The fire didn't help," she said. "But what really did
the project in was the fact the researchers couldn't guaran-
tee the bat bombs would be ready for battle until 1945. So
the military pulled the plug."

"Roosevelt probably gave the order to spite his wife."

"Poor, misunderstood Eleanor," Mel said.

"You know, I did hear about something similar the
Russians deployed in World War II," Hendrix said. "They
trained dogs to run under German tanks with bombs
strapped to their backs. But when they tried it in combat,
the dogs ran back under the Russian tanks they'd been
trained on."

He arced his hands outward and made an explosion
sound.

Mel slugged him on the shoulder. "Rafe! That's awful."

"You didn't seem to care when it was bats exploding."

"Dogs aren't bats," she said. "Dogs are very special
creatures, many of whom have better personalities than
some humans I could name."

Hendrix pointed at himself. "Me? You're the veterinarian who plays favorites."

"All animals are created equal," Mel said. "Dogs and horses are just a little more equal than the others."

"Okay, Orwell, enough about exploding animals for one lifetime. You should get a dog."

"I told you, I don't take my work home with me," Mel said. "But if you got a dog, Rafe, I could come over and snuggle with it, take it for walks, give it free checkups. I saw a black Lab puppy yesterday . . ."

"I've got an animal for you," Hendrix said. He motioned her over to the telescope and showed her how to focus it to get the crispest image.

"What you're looking at right now, that's the first constellation my father showed me when I was six," Hendrix said. "He would take me to Cherry Springs State Park in central Pennsylvania, which is one of the darkest spots back east. When I moved to DC, I used to take Becca to the Washington and Jefferson National Forest in Virginia to show her what I'd learned from my pop. She loved it."

Mel stepped back from the telescope and rested a hand on his shoulder. "I'm sure she did, Rafe. What daughter wouldn't want that kind of special time with her dad?"

He let out a breath and swallowed hard. "It's okay," he said. "I want to show you this."

She nodded and brought her eye back to the scope.

"Is it one of the dippers?" she asked.

"Nope," he said. "That's the square of Pegasus, the body of the great winged horse. The four stars that make the square are Alpha, Beta, Gamma, and Alpha Andromedae."

"Sounds like a sorority house."

"It's one of forty-eight constellations charted by Ptolemy in the second century. And then a German guy gave them Greek letter designations in the 1600s. Back then, the good letters were all still available for star naming."

"Kind of like how most of the low football numbers have been retired in the NFL," she said.

"Pretty much, though the German guy reused the basic letters and appended the constellation names to them. Now the star at the lower right of the box, that's Alpha. If you follow a diagonal from there to the next two stars and then jog a bit up and to the right to a third star, those are his neck and muzzle."

"Not sure I'm following you, Rafe."

"Do you see the bright orange star?"

"I think so," she said. "Yes."

"That's Enif, the tip of the muzzle."

She nodded. "Enif is Enif. Where are the legs?"

"They're at the top right tip of the square," he said, leaning in toward her. "Two lines, one has three stars at about a forty-five-degree angle and the other a kind of dog-leg of four stars just below that."

"Or horse leg," she said. He caught a side view of her grin as it formed.

"Shit, Rafe, I can see it," she exclaimed. "It's a freaking upside-down horse."

After he showed her the wings, Hendrix led Mel inside, setting down the telescope and pointing toward the only light on in the small house, his bedside lamp, visible through the half-open door.

"Which star is that?" she asked.

"The one leading us home," he said.

That gun belongs up the ruffled sleeve of a riverboat gambler, Susie Preston thought as she looked down all four barrels of the derringer.

She'd been about to grab a pad of wall Post-its from the multipurpose room for tomorrow's writing lab session when a single tap on the counter had prompted her to turn around.

Susie had expected to see the janitor stopping to flirt, broom handle at attention, or maybe a student who'd fallen asleep in a study carrel. It happened a few times a year.

But the tap had come from one of those stubby silver barrels now demanding her attention.

Instead of thinking her way through the situation or reacting to it in a rational way, Susie free-associated, higher brain functions stunned into submission. *This was not like her, not at all,* a distant part of her noted, only to be subsumed by synaptic misfires.

She glanced down at her hands, unnaturally splayed fingers rigid. The distant voice inside her grew more insistent: *This is what panic feels like.*

From images of the Old West riverboat, her mind flitted to a phrase: "trigger warning." That was a big part of the school librarian's job now. You still matched books to student interests, yes, but you were always careful to serve them up with warnings about possibly traumatizing subject matter, like the side effects listings at the end of a drug ad: *One semigraphic rape scene may cause flashbacks and nightmares.*

That was the thing she hated about trigger warnings: they always turned into spoiler alerts.

Some cruelty to animals. Episodes of child neglect.

Multiple depictions of gun violence.

Which made her think of the multipurpose room. Of course she'd been rummaging in THE room. Too perfect.

She heard herself breathing, sucking in air in short bursts.

Tried to slow her mind again, failed.

While all these words and images tumbled through her consciousness in a handful of seconds, he stood there, expression neutral, not mocking, not sinister, not particularly troubled.

Her thoughts, she thought, were ricocheting.

She felt the sickening smile forming. It was nerves, she realized, bundles of them. Can't help it.

Enough, she told herself. Focus. She punctuated the unspoken word with a nod of her head.

Which remained intact, even after that sudden move.

A good sign, right?

I can do this, she thought.

She almost formed the words with her lips, a prayer of positive thinking.

Took one deep breath, calming.

"Can I help—" Susie started to say.

CHAPTER

5

HENDRIX WAS DREAMING of running down a forest trail with Mel and their dog when he awoke to her easing on top of him as the sun rose behind her tangled halo of hair. He'd heard the phrase before, but this time it hit him full force: She was a vision.

They made love silently, bodies in harmony, until she collapsed onto him with a long, rolling shudder. He wrapped his arms around her until she softened into him, warm breath tickling the hairs on his neck.

"I thought you wore me out last night, Rafe, but then I saw you this morning and you were just so damn cute I had to have my way with you one more time."

"I'm glad you did," he said as she disentangled herself and made for the bathroom.

"But now," she called out over her shoulder as she started the shower, "I have to go. Be a good boyfriend and make me toast and coffee for the road."

* * *

She texted him after checking into the conference.

"Beautiful hotel," it read. "Got here just in time. I'll call you tonight after the sessions."

He waited until nine and then called her. Voice mail.

"Hey there, wanted to hear your voice," he said. "Hope you're having fun."

He didn't know how to end the call. "I miss you," he said after a few beats.

She texted at eleven. "Ended up at a late dinner with a conference group and then too many drinks at the hotel bar. I'm drunk and crashing. I'll call you after my run in the morning."

"xo," he texted.

"xo," came the reply.

*   *   *

It was an unsettled night. Too drunk to talk felt like a weak excuse. He'd grumbled his way to bed and woken up in a cold sweat at three AM. The nightmare had returned. Death wasn't ready to let him go.

Hendrix stretched, dressed, and donned the headlamp for what turned out to be an uneventful run to the pie plate and back. He'd felt uneasy, though, like the farmer's idiot son might ambush him at every turn.

Still keyed up, Hendrix took a long shower as the sun rose. He made coffee, grabbed the newspaper, and followed his regular morning routine. After washing and drying the cup and recycling the paper, he still hadn't shaken the sense of dread.

At least Mel would be calling soon, he thought. He debated calling her first, but he didn't want to seem as needy as he felt. He decided to check the *Dallas Morning News* site for the latest headlines.

When the home page opened, a red banner filled most of his phone screen: "Woman shot at JFK death spot."

He scrolled to a photo of paramedics loading a stretcher into an ambulance next to the white X on Elm Street that marked the exact location where the President had been murdered.

He swiped away the browser and hit redial. The call went straight to voice mail.

Hendrix hung up, reopened the browser, clicked on the headline, and read as much of the story as he could manage.

A Fort Stockton woman was shot and killed just before 5 am today as she jogged across the white X that unofficially marks the spot on Elm Street where President John F. Kennedy was assassinated.

The rifle police believe was used in this morning's killing was recovered from the sixth floor of the Dallas County Administration Building in the same spot the gun used to murder the president was found when the building was called the Texas School Book Depository.

Investigators say the rifle in today's crime was the same make and model as the one Lee Harvey Oswald used to take the president's life on November 22, 1963, suggesting a grisly reenactment may have been the motive.

Security footage shows the woman crossing North Houston Street on Elm at 4:53 am with another person jogging beside her. Ten seconds later, the video shows the woman falling to the pavement as she passes the X in the middle of the street.

The other jogger, who was wearing a hooded sweatshirt, did not stop to assist the woman, perhaps in an effort to run to safety. Police are asking the surviving runner to come forward for questioning. The victim's name is being withheld pending notification of family.

Hendrix grabbed his keys and ran to the truck.

II

II

CHAPTER

6

B Y THE TIME he got to Mel's mother's house, state and local police were there. Mrs. Sanchez sat sobbing on the front porch as a trooper and a patrolman stood to either side.

He hadn't wanted to believe it, had refused to believe it, even as he'd raced into town. Faced with this cold confirmation, Hendrix pounded the dashboard so hard with his right hand that he cracked it.

* * *

Mrs. Sanchez spotted Hendrix when he was halfway up the front walkway.

"Oh, Rafael, they took her," she wailed. "They took her, *mija*."

The trooper tensed as Hendrix approached. "Ma'am, who is this?" he asked.

"That's Melody's boyfriend, Rafael," she said.

By the look on his face, Hendrix could tell the trooper knew who he was.

"You live here now?" he asked.

"Yes, sir," Hendrix said, extending his hand. The trooper shook it and the patrolman did the same.

"This is Rafael Hendrix," the trooper told the patrolman evenly. Tipping to the situation, the young cop nodded. His hand slipped onto his holstered service revolver.

"I'm guessing you'd like to have a word back at the station," Hendrix said.

"A word? With the world's most famous sniper whose girlfriend was just killed in a reenactment of history's most famous sniper attack?" the patrolman asked. "Hell yes, we'd like a word."

Hendrix looked at the veteran trooper and raised an eyebrow.

"Ma'am, you said one of your daughters is on the way?" the trooper asked Mel's mother, who was giving Hendrix a confused, wounded look.

"Yes," she said as she turned away from Hendrix. "That's her now."

Mel's older sister was rushing up the sidewalk.

"Well, then, ma'am, we'll leave you with our deepest condolences, and we'll make sure to update you on any developments in the case," the trooper said.

"I have a feeling there'll be developments soon," the patrolman said, narrowing his eyes at Hendrix.

The trooper shook his head. "Come on, Mr. Hendrix," he said, "you can ride with me."

* * *

Hendrix sat in the small interrogation room, hands on the table, waiting for the pissant local cop to make a move. He'd confiscated Hendrix's phone and left it sitting on his desk down the hall. That didn't bode well for a quick stop.

"You might as well tell us the whole story, Hendrix," the young officer said, leaning across the table far enough that he was putting himself in mortal danger.

The trooper stood in a corner of the room behind the patrolman. Hendrix caught his eye and the trooper shook his head. Not worth it.

Hendrix agreed. He kept his hands on the table, palms down, and did his best not to give in to the rage building inside him.

"Shouldn't you call your supervisor in on this?" Hendrix asked.

"The chief?" the patrolman said with a snort. "Naw, if it's Saturday morning, he's bass fishing. Wouldn't answer his phone even if he had a signal. Besides, I got this handled."

Perfect, Hendrix thought.

"We've got security video, Hendrix," the cop continued. "We'll get your phone records, and hers. No matter how careful you played this, you did something that'll trip you up. It'll go easier on everyone if you just lay it all out for us right here, right now."

"I'm going to say this once: I didn't kill Melody Sanchez," Hendrix said. "You're wasting time we don't have."

"Whose time am I wasting?" the cop asked.

The trooper looked up from under the brim of his hat like he thought it was a fair question.

"Look," Hendrix said. "Someone tried to kill me on the road up from Marathon last week. Shot up my truck and took off. Whoever did that may have been following me when I was with Mel."

"Who?" the cop asked.

"Melody Sanchez."

"Did you file a police report?" the patrolman demanded. "Someone ventilates my truck, I'm going to the authorities."

"I'm telling you now," Hendrix said. "I think whoever attacked me on the highway may have killed Melody to get revenge against me."

"That seems unlikely," the trooper offered.

Great, Hendrix thought. Now the reasonable one thinks I did it.

"There's a lot of people who blame me for the school bombing in DC because I disobeyed a direct order to stand down and took my shot to save the First Lady in the classroom next door," Hendrix said. "Grief can twist you up pretty good."

"You've got a point there," the trooper said.

"No, he doesn't!" the young cop said, slamming a fist on the table. "Shit, you're an infamous sniper—and a freaking sniper just killed your girlfriend. Coincidences like that don't happen in the real world."

Hendrix considered describing his run-in with the neighbors to give the officers someone else to investigate but thought better of it. He'd be cooling his heels until Monday if he told that story.

"I agree," Hendrix said. "It's a suspicious set of facts. But I was at my house in Fort Stockton last night."

"Can anyone vouch for that?" the trooper asked.

"No," Hendrix conceded.

"You know what I think happened?" the cop asked.

Hendrix rolled his eyes.

"Give me a snotty look like that again and I'll smack you to Tuesday," the young patrolman sputtered.

"What's the saying down here?" Hendrix replied. "You couldn't pour water out of a boot if the instructions were printed on the heel."

The cop's cheeks turned purple.

"Maybe we ought to wrap this up for now," the trooper said.

"In a minute," the patrolman snapped. "What I think went down was that you got run out of Washington, DC, and found yourself some sweet Mexican tail to pass the time here. But she poked a pinhole in your rubber and got herself pregnant. You were her lottery ticket, Hendrix, but you weren't going to let her cash it."

The trooper removed his hat. "Larry," he said, "that's enough."

As Larry turned to tell the trooper off, Hendrix flipped the table on its side, punched the cop in the throat, and pulled his service revolver out of the holster while he gasped for air. Hendrix kicked the table toward the trooper, thwarting his attempt to pull his own piece, and brought the butt of Larry's gun down on the local cop's left temple, knocking him cold.

"Hands," Hendrix said to the trooper, who raised them gingerly as he looked down the barrel of Larry's .357 and saw a full cylinder.

"I understand why you're riled," the trooper said. "Your girlfriend's been murdered, and this racist idiot wouldn't stop poking at you. This is the wrong play, Mr. Hendrix, but I do sympathize. I am genuinely sorry for your loss."

Hendrix nodded, but held the revolver steady. "Undo your gun belt with your left hand," he instructed. "Let it drop to the floor and then push it over to me with your foot, gently."

The trooper did as he was told.

"Where's your cell phone?" Hendrix asked.

The trooper hooked a thumb toward his shirt pocket.

"Leave it there," Hendrix said as he removed the cuffs from Larry's belt. "Walk over to the nearest chair, slowly."

"Gently, slowly, I get it," the trooper said. "I have nothing against you, and I'd be hard-pressed to think you would have pulled a stunt like that in Dallas, not after saving the First Lady the way you did, and the President's life even before she was the President. You're not a killer."

"Not at heart, no," Hendrix said. "But I have done it as a profession, and I won't hesitate to do it again. Now please have a seat and put your hands behind the chair."

The trooper complied. Hendrix had one cuff on him when Larry started to stir. Hendrix placed the barrel of the revolver against the trooper's temple—gently—and drew back the hammer before giving Larry a vicious kick to the face that shattered his nose and put him out again.

After Hendrix finished cuffing the trooper, he fished the phone out of his shirt pocket.

"Password," he said.

"It's one of those face things," the trooper said. "Just hold it up in front of me and I'll favor you with my best grin."

Once he got access, Hendrix dialed a number he never thought he'd call again.

"This is Rafe Hendrix," he said. "I need to speak to the President."

The trooper let out a low whistle.

"Yes," Hendrix said, "it's urgent."

* * *

"Slow down, Hendrix," the President said after he gave his account of recent events. "Let me run this back by you: You shot your neighbor's truck because he was going to kill a wolf, then you broke into his house and threatened to kill him and his son. Then some asshole in a *lucha libre* mask came gunning for you on the highway, and the next thing you know, your girlfriend's shot dead where Kennedy's head went back and to the left for the last time."

Hendrix winced. "It sounds crazy, but it's the truth."

"It sounds fucking deranged. And the real truth is, you can't stay out of trouble," the President said, voice rising. "You just beat the shit out of some local yokel and you're about five minutes from being gunned down in a holding cell when his fellow officers catch wind of what happened."

"It's Saturday morning in a small town, nobody else is here," Hendrix said.

"I'm here," the trooper said.

"Who the hell is that?" the President asked.

"That is the proverbial good guy with a gun, state trooper . . ."

"Corboy," he said.

"Put him on," the President demanded.

Hendrix held the phone to the trooper's ear.

"Yes, Madame President," he said. After he listened and nodded for a full minute, he added, "I understand. You have my word."

"What was that about?" Hendrix asked the President after she was finished with Corboy.

"I told him you're a good man, I trust you with my life, and he is to render you any needed assistance in this investigation."

"Thank you, Madame President," he said.

"Now we'd better get you out of there quick before you cost me any chance at reelection. Remember, I'm not that Monopoly guy."

"What Monopoly guy?"

"The cracker-ass rich guy on the Get Out of Jail Free card," she said. "You are on serious thin ice. Now retrieve your damn phone, keep your head down, and don't harass any more locals until I call you back with a plan."

"You going to try anything if I uncuff you?" Hendrix asked the trooper after the President hung up.

"Have I tried anything yet?"

"You were going to draw down on me."

"When I thought you might be ready to kill me, yes," the trooper said. "But we've reached an understanding, thanks to the President."

"She told you to render me any needed assistance, right?"

"She did."

"And you agreed."

"I did, and I do."

"Okay, I need you to keep Larry on ice for a couple of hours until I can get someplace safe," Hendrix said.

The trooper nodded. Hendrix uncuffed him, keeping the revolver on him as he did.

"I'm going to take your gun down the hall and leave it on Larry's desk when I pick up my phone," Hendrix said. "Keep Larry on a short leash until the FBI has a chance to talk to his chief."

"Count on it, Mr. Hendrix."

"I owe you, Corboy."

"I hope you find the sonofabitch that killed your friend."

"Whoever it is, he's playing games with me," Hendrix said. "I don't think he'll make it very hard for me to find him. Catching him may be another story."

*   *   *

After grabbing his phone from Larry's desk, Hendrix set the trooper's now-unloaded gun in its place. He emptied the chambers of Larry's .357 into the adjacent trash can and stashed the revolver in a potted plant outside the station break room. Let him hunt for it.

Hendrix walked out the front door of the station and realized his truck was still parked at Melody's mother's house. He didn't want to risk being spotted by whatever other members of law enforcement might be on scene, but he needed his vehicle. He walked to the corner and spotted Will Plummer's body shop a block north.

Plummer was at the counter. He smiled when Hendrix jingled the bell entering the shop.

"Rafe, good to see you," he said.

"Better to see you," Hendrix replied. "I need a favor."

Hendrix gave him the basics and Plummer agreed to pick up the truck. He drove them in his SUV within a few blocks of the house and parked. They exchanged keys and Hendrix drove back to the body shop. A few minutes later Plummer arrived in the truck.

"Mission accomplished," he said.

"Thank you," Hendrix said. He was about to leave but stopped at the door.

"What is it?" Plummer asked.

"When you were working on my truck, did anything suspicious happen at the shop?"

"Actually, yes," Plummer said after a beat. "We did have a creeper out on the lot one night. Security camera picked him up, but he was wearing a hoodie. We couldn't get an ID. He didn't steal anything, so I didn't go to the police."

"Do you still have the video?"

"I saved it to my hard drive in case he came back around," Plummer said, inviting Hendrix behind the counter.

They watched the video together, a couple of minutes of a shadowy figure casing the shop. At one point, he disappeared around the driver's side of Hendrix's truck, out of the camera's view, but they didn't see a door open.

As Plummer had said, the man wore a hoodie. It looked a lot like the one Melody's jogging companion had been wearing in Dallas, but most dark hoodies looked pretty much alike.

"Would you mind emailing me a copy of that video?" Hendrix asked.

"Will do," Plummer said. "But whatever you're involved in, please stay away from the automatic weapons this time."

* * *

Hendrix drove past the church on his way out of town, then circled the block and parked in front. He was done with Fort Stockton, even if he hadn't worn out his welcome, but he didn't want to leave without paying his respects to Melody Sanchez.

He walked through the empty nave toward the altar, where a table of votive candles in red glass holders was set out for remembrance. After dropping five dollars into the donation box, Hendrix chose a candle at the center of the table and lit it for Melody. Then he lit one for Becca.

If you could plot the course of your life on a map, it seemed to Hendrix that grief would be the glowing red circle all roads eventually intersected, linking the far-flung dots marking memorable moments of joy, pleasure, and satisfaction. After first experiencing it as an unpleasant hub you had to pass through on the way to and from happier emotional states—the O'Hare Airport of consciousness— grief became the final destination, destroyer of memories, terminus of hope.

He closed his eyes in search of a prayer and felt tears welling. He placed both hands on the table to steady him- self and leaned forward toward the warm light.

I will keep you in my heart, Hendrix thought as he wiped away tears. I'm sorry I put you in harm's way and couldn't protect you. But if what you told me is true, we'll meet again in a place where no harm can come to us.

What a gift it was to know you.

He stepped back to sit in the front pew and watch the candles burn down. He looked up at the mural of Jesus, so serene on the cross, so sure of his path. Hendrix hoped to get there someday.

*   *   *

He stopped at the house to grab some clothes, his shaving kit, his phone charger, his telescope, and the card from the President. His rifle and the nine were in the truck. He couldn't think of anything else he needed inside, so he locked up, got the toolbox from the shed, and started the truck.

But looking at the front door now, he recalled a line from the *Dallas Morning News* story about Mel's death. He called it up on his phone browser: "a grisly reenactment may have been the motive."

There had been four presidential assassinations in U.S. history. Hendrix had studied them in depth during his Secret Service training. On a hunch, he searched for recent news of murders at the sites of the other three. No hits on Lincoln or Garfield. But the McKinley search made the hairs on the back of his neck stand up. Two months earlier, a charity fundraiser had been gunned down in Buffalo, New York, on the same block where the President had been shot in 1901. The gun used was the same caliber as the one used to assassinate McKinley, and the story Hendrix found had speculated about a possible copycat element.

Hendrix widened the scope of his search to include other infamous political assassinations. He got hits on a recent killing at the site of Anton Cermak's murder in Miami Beach, some of which mentioned the parallel. There had also been a homicide at the Los Angeles school built on the site of the hotel where Bobby Kennedy had been killed in 1968. None of that coverage suggested a potential connection, but there were too many coincidences to ignore.

Hendrix dialed the White House and left a message for the President to call him back urgently. He was on the highway south to Big Bend National Park a half hour later when his phone rang.

"Wherever you are, Hendrix, I hope it's far away from Fort Stockton," the President said. "You've made folks there pretty angry, and Fox News is reporting you're a person of interest in Melody Sanchez's murder."

"I guess Larry woke up," Hendrix said.

"He got his nose reset and shared his story with the world."

"Well, shit, Madame President."

"Deep shit, Hendrix."

"It keeps getting deeper," he said. "I believe you may be in danger. I've found evidence there were three more potential assassination copycat killings in the last several months. If the FBI investigates, they'll probably find others."

"How are we just now learning about this?" the President demanded.

"They weren't as obvious as X marks the spot," Hendrix said. "The hotel where RFK was killed, there's a fancy school there now. A librarian was shot just outside the room built where Sirhan Sirhan did the deed. Same caliber bullet was used on the librarian, but it would be hard to make the connection otherwise.

"Similar story in Miami Beach," he said. "Two maintenance guys attacked in the park where FDR and Anton Cermak were shot. Again, same type of handgun was used to commit the copycat crime, and only one of the two victims died. Similar story in Buffalo at the McKinley assassination site. The guy has good attention to detail."

"And now he's escalated," the President said.

"It looks like he shot Melody Sanchez to get the world's attention," Hendrix said.

The President paused, taking it all in. "What if he killed your girlfriend to get your attention?" she asked. "And he committed the earlier crimes to make sure you'd get me involved once you discovered the pattern?"

"If that's the case, I'm sure your detail will recommend you stay in the White House until the end of your term," Hendrix said.

"Yep," the President replied. "But you know that ain't gonna happen."

"I do."

The President told Hendrix to sit tight while she briefed the FBI and Secret Service. An hour later, she called back.

"You were right, Hendrix. This has been happening all over the country. He's been planting murders like time bombs. Melody's killing was the detonator."

Hendrix pulled into a turnout and scanned his surroundings for hostiles. He felt like he was being watched.

"We're going on offense," the President said. "I'm putting together a group of FBI and Secret Service agents from the Joint Terrorism Task Force."

"What's my role?"

"Officially, you don't have one."

"This has to be connected to the bombing," Hendrix said.

"I agree," the President said. "It looks like someone with a gift for orchestrating mayhem is still very unhappy with us. But no one wants you anywhere near this."

"Except you, I hope," Hendrix said.

She laughed. "Hendrix, I was the first person to rule you out as an investigative resource. You're a trouble magnet. But if I leave you to your own devices, you'll just spring a hellacious mess on us at the worst possible moment. So I'm sending an FBI agent down there to babysit you. You can follow up on whatever leads seem promising and report the results to me. I am the beginning and end of your chain of command. Got it?"

"Understood, Madame President, but—"

"You work better alone? You don't need supervision? Stow it, Hendrix. This is your best and final offer. You get a highly competent minder who's been ordered to assist you while she keeps you out of trouble. Her name is Special Agent Hannah Sutton. Play nice."

"Where am I meeting her?"

"Dallas. Now let's get this fucking psycho."

CHAPTER

7

W HEN HENDRIX ENTERED the hotel lobby, he was
surprised to see the veterinary conference still going
on, but then he realized they probably hadn't even heard
Mel was an attendee. Since she was killed miles away, it
might not matter if they did know.

That was a lesson he'd learned during his leaves from
Afghanistan and in the surreal months after the bombing: You could be going through unspeakable hell, but
the world just kept turning for everyone else. Forget out
of sight, out of mind. With mass shootings nearly every
day, people saw the carnage playing out on their giant TV
screens just long enough to download another game to
their phones. Distraction trumped compassion.

It was seven and the bar was starting to fill with a lively
Saturday crowd. Hendrix found an open seat near the service station at the far end, a photo of Mel at the ready on
his phone.

The bartender gave him a nod of welcome as he set
pints in front of two patrons closer to the entrance. He

walked half the length of the bar toward Hendrix, who pointed at the tap and raised an index finger.

While the bartender pulled the pint, a cocktail waitress stepped up to the service station with an empty tray.

"Looks like a good night," Hendrix said.

The server held her right hand out flat and waggled it. "Eh," she said. "Pre-dinner crowd, they're in a hurry and they're bad tippers. I'm always happier once the serious drinkers settle in. Round after round of 'hit me again' and they're usually feeling generous by the time they stumble back to their rooms at closing time."

The bartender set a beer in front of Hendrix. He raised the glass in appreciation and took a sip while the waitress read off her order.

"I love working with Jake," she said after the bartender moved off to get her drinks together. "He's fast and friendly, two critical qualities when I have to deal with the early birds."

"Well, I'm a good tipper who's easy to please and in no hurry to be anywhere," Hendrix said.

"I knew I liked you," she said. Hendrix saw that the bartender was almost finished with her orders, so he pulled out his phone and swiped open the screen.

"I was supposed to meet my wife here an hour ago, but I got delayed," he said as he showed her the photo. "You didn't happen to see her leave in a huff, did you?"

The server took a good look. "No," she said, "but is she here for the veterinary conference?"

"Yes," Hendrix said. "She came in yesterday and I'm meeting her for the rest of the weekend."

"She hasn't been in tonight, but she was here for several hours last night with three other veterinarians," the server said, pointing out a large banquet along the back wall. "Fun group. All women, so don't get jealous."

Hendrix looked around the room and saw several tables where patrons were wearing name tags or had conference tote bags leaned against chair legs.

"Are any of the other women here now?" he asked.

The server picked up her full tray. "I don't think so, but I'll take a closer look when I make my rounds."

Hendrix thanked her and dropped a twenty on the tray as she turned to leave.

"I heard you say you're looking for your wife," the bartender said as he emptied the overflow tray under the tap.

Hendrix showed him the photo. The bartender nodded.

"Jill usually clocks out a half-hour before close," he said, pointing at the server. "After she left last night, your wife's group was the only table left. When I told them it was last call, it looked like they were all going to head off to their rooms, but one of the women brought your wife over here for a final round."

"Did you catch any of the conversation?" Hendrix asked.

"Not really," the bartender said. "I have quite a bit of cleaning and prep work to do at close, and they were huddled up. Honestly, it looked like they were making plans. Fast friends for sure. Maybe they knew each other from other conferences. The Texas veterinarian world is probably a pretty small one."

"That's true. She says she sees a lot of familiar faces at these things," Hendrix said, leaning into his cover story.

A customer was signaling the bartender for another round. "Good luck finding your wife," he said as Hendrix stood to leave. "You should check the room if you haven't already. And if she turns back up here, I'll let her know. She seems like a nice lady."

Hendrix forced a smile and dropped a twenty on the bar. As he walked out, he caught Jill's eye. She shook her head. None of the other women from last night were here. Time to check in and see if the special agent had arrived.

The woman at the front desk said she hadn't been on duty Friday, so Hendrix didn't ask her about Melody Sanchez. It would have been an awkward conversation, anyway. If he continued to play the role of late-arriving husband, the clerk would be wary about giving him Mel's room number, let alone a spare key. Instead, he asked if they had any rooms for the night.

"Just a couple," she said.

"Well, I only need one," he replied.

"I guess it works out," she said as she took his credit card and driver's license. She was halfway through checking him in when she stopped and looked up from her screen to give him a once-over.

"I thought you seemed familiar," she said without a hint of anxiety. "Welcome to Dallas, Mr. Hendrix."

Apparently not a Fox News watcher, he thought as he took the key card, tapped it once on the reception desk, and headed to the elevators.

While he waited, his phone began buzzing. It was a DC number.

"Hendrix," he said.

"Special Agent Sutton," said the voice on the other end of the line.

"Are you in Dallas?" he asked.

"Just landed," she said. "I assume you're at the victim's hotel."

"Yes, gathering as much intel as I can before the trail runs cold."

"Makes sense. I'm sorry I couldn't get in earlier."

"What time will you be here?"

"I'm staying at an airport hotel tonight. We can connect in the morning."

"All right," he said. "I need you to have the Bureau pull all available video from this place first thing, If the locals haven't gotten to it. We want interior and exterior, including the bar."

"On it," Sutton said. "And Hendrix, I've been briefed on your connection to Dr. Sanchez. I'm sorry for your loss."

"Thank you, Agent Sutton."

With that, Hendrix was left with nothing to do until morning except try to calm his racing mind.

*   *   *

After lying for several hours under the Egyptian cotton sheets on the memory foam bed in the perfectly cooled hotel room that felt like a palace in comparison to his most recent home, Hendrix tossed the overstuffed goose-down pillow at the mini bar, changed into running shorts and T-shirt, tucked his key card into his wallet, and hit the four AM streets of Dallas to retrace Mel's likely route to the Grassy Knoll.

There would not have been many pedestrians for Mel and her jogging partner to encounter on their predawn run. But there might be decent surveillance video from the shops they'd passed. He'd have Sutton interview the managers after she secured whatever video was available in the hotel.

As he neared a major intersection, Hendrix spotted a security cruiser in the lot of a big-box electronics store. There was an older man behind the wheel, working on a large sandwich as he watched the street.

Hendrix cut right and jogged across the lot toward the man, who rolled his window down mid-bite and said, "Don't you come any closer, now."

Hendrix stopped and held his hands out, palms forward. "I'm not here to cause you trouble," he said. "I just want to ask you a question."

"Well, you can ask it from right there, I suppose," the man said.

"Were you parked here yesterday at about this time?"

"This is my normal shift, and this is my normal meal-time," he replied. "I'm a creature of habit, so this is also where I normally park. So, yes, I was here. Who's asking?"

"I'm looking into the murder of the jogger near the book depository," Hendrix said. "I think she and her running partner might have come by here and I'm wondering if you perhaps saw them."

The man placed his sub sandwich on the dashboard and brushed shredded lettuce off his rent-a-cop uniform. "I might have," the man said. "But you'll need to be more specific about just who you are before we talk further. You don't look like a detective."

"Can I come over?" Hendrix asked.

The man held his left hand out the window and beckoned him to approach.

"Got any ID?" the man asked after Hendrix had covered the distance between them.

Hendrix slowly reached into the pocket of his shorts and fished out his wallet. He removed three twenties and handed them to the man, who nodded as he took the bills, seemingly relieved that his questioner understood the transactional nature of the interview.

"Did you see them?"

The security guard nodded again.

"What can you tell me about the man in the dark hoodie?"

"Not a whole lot, except it wasn't a man in that hoodie."

"How do you know that?"

"There was a nice breeze, so I had my window down," he said. "It wasn't stultifying like tonight. I heard them talking as they ran by."

"What did they say?"

"That, I don't know. They were too far away for me to make out the words. But the woman who got shot, she said something that made the other jogger laugh. It was definitely a woman's laugh."

Hendrix nodded. "Anything else?"

"No, but I did think it was odd," the security guard said.

"What was odd?"

"Like I said, there was a breeze, but it wasn't exactly chilly," he said. "So I wondered why the hell she had her hood up."

*   *   *

As Hendrix made his way back to the hotel—he didn't think it was a good idea to show up at the crime scene unannounced—he chewed over the new intel.

It made sense Mel's jogging partner was a woman, given that the bartender and server said she was with female conference attendees. The plan the bartender thought she was making with the woman who brought her up to the bar almost had to be a meet-up for the early morning run.

And what the guard had said about the hoodie—that it made no sense for the woman to cover her head given the weather—left Hendrix with little doubt she had knowingly led Mel to slaughter.

He returned to his room and set the coffee pot to brew before taking a quick shower. He and Special Agent Sutton needed to pick up this woman's trail today. It might already be too late, but Hendrix figured there were too many cameras and other variables, like the security guard watching the world go by on his meal break, for her not to leave some trace.

After he dressed, Hendrix poured himself a cup of coffee. It was good, but he noted that even at this fancy hotel, guests had to make do with wax-paper Starbucks cups.

He set his cup down and called Sutton.

"You need to get over here," he said.

"I'm in the lobby," she replied.

"I'll be right down." He was glad Sutton was taking the assignment seriously. He hoped she was good in the field.

* * *

When Hendrix exited the elevator, she waved him over to the reception desk.

"This is Rafe Hendrix," she said to the man standing on the other side of the counter. His badge read Winston Strong, General Manager.

"We're honored to have you here," Strong said, offering his hand for a firm shake. "You probably get this a lot, but you're a true hero."

"Thank you," Hendrix said, without adding he seldom got the hero treatment and on the rare occasions he did, it was typically from gay folks of color like Winston Strong appeared to be.

"Thank you for giving us an assist here, Mr. Strong," Hendrix said.

"You're very welcome," the manager said. "And please, call me Win. That goes for you, too, Special Agent Sutton. Now, you asked about the security footage."

"Yes," she said. "We'd like to get a download of everything you have from Thursday afternoon through yesterday."

"That's going to be a lot to go through," Strong said.

"We've got analysts back in DC who do this for a living," Sutton replied. "We'll tell them to start with the bar on Friday night and the lobby and main entrance footage covering the hours after that until dawn. Hopefully that'll be enough to give us an ID on this mystery jogger and then we can review the rest of the video for additional intel."

Strong nodded. "And once you make the ID, I'm sure you'll want to talk with whoever checked the mystery jogger in as well as the bar staff, the maid who serviced the room, and anyone else who crossed their path."

"You got it, Win," Sutton said. "You're a natural."

The manager smiled. "I watch a lot of *NCIS* reruns when I visit my mom for Sunday dinner."

"Anything else we should get Win going on?" Sutton asked.

"I think that covers it," Hendrix said. "But if the Dallas PD comes looking for the footage, please hold off on delivering it to them until we've had a chance to examine it."

"You get first crack," Strong said. "I know how these turf battles go. The feds always win them in the end, but they can eat up precious time."

* * *

"Mark Harmon making my job easier once again," Sutton said as they emerged from the main entrance and walked to her rental car.

She had a crisp, no-nonsense stride that matched her sartorial choices: white cotton blouse, tousled brown hair touching the collar, light blue linen pants, sensible flats that played down her height, which Hendrix pegged at five nine.

Sutton appeared to be in fighting shape—no surprise for an FBI field agent—with toned arms that likely took work to maintain as she approached forty, if Hendrix's own midlife workout experience was any guide. She wore minimal makeup on a face as pleasant to look at as it was hard to read. And no jewelry beyond the small diamond studs in her ears.

She looked like an overworked middle manager heading back to the office after a too-short lunch break and looking forward to an evening of too much wine. A classic stress fest. Hendrix decided to keep that conclusion to himself.

Sutton drove the route Hendrix had run a few hours ago. He wrote down the names of the shops they passed on the notepad from his room.

"We'll need to check for footage at all of these," Hendrix said.

Sutton sighed. "I know. These investigations are such a grind. But it just takes one hit to break things open."

Hendrix told her about his encounter with the security guard.

"Guy like that, give him sixty bucks and he'll tell you Dr. Sanchez was jogging with the Duchess of York if that's what he thinks you want to hear," Sutton said.

"You're probably right," Hendrix said. "But I didn't peg him as a bullshit artist."

"No, just a mall cop looking for bribes," she replied. "Unimpeachable."

"It tracks with what I learned from the hotel bartender and a cocktail server who saw Mel with three other conference attendees Friday night," Hendrix said.

They were stopped at a red light. Hannah Sutton looked directly at him for the first time. "You have been busy."

"She was important to me."

Sutton nodded and focused again on traffic as the light turned green.

"I was told you'd be trouble," she said.

"Only for the killer and his accomplice," Hendrix said.

Sutton nodded. "If we both stay this focused and methodical, we might be the ones who bring them to justice."

"Your lips to God's ears," he said.

"I assure you, God's got nothing on the full investigative powers of the FBI and the JTT."

*   *   *

Sutton parked a block from the crime scene. They got out of the car and sat on the hood to watch. The scene was cordoned, and technicians were working in both the depository building and on the street near the X, taking pictures, measuring distances, processing it in full.

"They got the low-hanging fruit yesterday," Sutton said. "Weapon, shell casings, blood samples, fingerprints, any possible DNA from the shooter."

"Stray rounds?" Hendrix asked.

Sutton shook her head. "Just the two head shots. She wasn't running fast, but he must be pretty good to two-tap a moving target at that distance."

Hendrix's breath caught.

"I'm sorry," she said. "That was insensitive. I'm not used to working a case with someone who was close to the victim. I'll do better."

He nodded. "Not your fault. And your insights are useful. Please don't hold back."

Sutton asked Hendrix for the notepad and stepped away to call in the names and addresses of the shops for video retrieval.

He looked up at the sixth floor of the building formerly known as the Texas School Book Depository. It was a ninety-yard shot.

Hendrix had taken accurate shots from that distance in Afghanistan, including some at moving targets as he braced himself against the open doorway of a Blackhawk taking evasive maneuvers to avoid small-arms fire and RPGs.

Oswald had been no slouch—he'd scored a rating of sharpshooter at two hundred yards with an M1 in the Marine Corps—but Hendrix had the benefit of intensive Special Forces training and the finest armaments the Pentagon's bloated budget could provide.

Hendrix thought back to his Secret Service training covering past assassinations. If the killer had used a setup similar to the 1940 surplus Italian infantry rifle and 1960s 4× scope Oswald had employed to shoot Kennedy, it would indeed take decent marksmanship to make the first head shot.

To Sutton's point, though, it was the second shot, especially given the light breeze Saturday morning, that had required real skill. The shooter would have had to work the bolt action to chamber a second 6.5 mm round and then lead Mel with the crosshairs as she stumbled forward, hitting her again.

The mental image of his girlfriend bleeding out on the pavement was too much. Hendrix turned away from the crime scene and doubled over, heaving up an acrid mixture of coffee and stomach acid. There wasn't much to empty—he hadn't eaten since yesterday—but it left his throat raw.

After wiping his mouth with his right sleeve, Hendrix turned back to see Hannah Sutton offering him water. He accepted the bottle and used it to wash his mouth out before drinking the rest.

He stared down at the pavement and crumpled the plastic bottle. He felt as if he couldn't move. He'd expended all his nervous energy in setting his part of the investigation into motion, but he had run straight into a wall. He needed sleep. He needed food. He needed distance from this nightmare. His legs buckled.

Sutton took him by the arm and led him to the car.

"It's too much," she said. "I'm taking you to the hotel."

He nodded. His head felt muzzy.

"The President said you'd be babysitting me," he said. "I thought she was joking."

*   *   *

"You got this?" Sutton asked when they reached his room.

Hendrix slid the key out of his pocket and held it in front of the pad until the lock released. Sutton worked the handle and pushed the door open without letting go of Hendrix's arm.

The curtains were still drawn, and the room felt like a cool, dark oasis. He sat down heavily on the bed and kicked off his shoes.

"Get some sleep and call me when you wake up— tomorrow morning," Sutton said. "I'll work all these video leads in the meantime, and we can review everything I turn up over a decent breakfast."

He nodded and watched as she walked to the door, too exhausted to speak.

"Running yourself ragged isn't going to help find your girlfriend's killer," she said as she left.

He was on his back and asleep before the door clicked shut.

*   *   *

Hendrix woke up disoriented and chilled. He'd passed out atop the covers, and the air conditioning had settled into his bones. With the heavy curtains closed, he had no idea what time it was.

He half-turned to look over his shoulder at the bedside clock: 7:12. He stood and walked to the window, careful not to move too quickly and lose his balance. He pulled the curtains and was momentarily blinded by the intense morning sun. He'd slept nearly eighteen hours.

After splashing water on his face, Hendrix called Hannah Sutton.

"Feeling better?" she asked.

"Not sure," he said. "I don't think I've ever slept that long."

"Your body finally decided to stop following unreasonable orders," she said.

"Seems that way."

"Hungry?"

"Very."

"I'm downstairs in the restaurant. They've got a full breakfast menu. Plenty of options for you while we go over the latest developments."

*   *   *

Hendrix took a hot shower that killed the air-conditioner chill. He'd set the coffee maker to brew beforehand, but as he dressed, he realized he needed to get some food in him before having his first cup.

The sleep had gotten him halfway back to feeling human. Eggs, hash browns—and then coffee—should take care of the rest.

Alone on the elevator, he examined himself in the mirrored panel. "Keep your head in the game," he told his reflection. Enough of this PTSD circuit-overload bullshit, he thought. There'd be plenty of time to collapse once they found Mel's killer.

*   *   *

He drenched the over-easy eggs and crispy potatoes in hot sauce and wolfed them down as Hannah Sutton watched with apparent concern.

"Pace yourself," she said.

He gave his fork a rest and took a long draw on the coffee. "Where are we on the video?" he asked.

"Good news and bad," she said. "Nothing promising from the shops along the route, and the bar camera is nonfunctional."

"Shit," he said. "What's the good news?"

"Front-desk camera was working fine," she said. "DC office is reviewing the full footage. And the bartender is fast-forwarding through the most likely time frames with our friend Mr. NCIS in the manager's office as we speak. If our mystery woman picked the key up herself, we should have a warm trail to follow soon."

Hendrix spotted Winston Strong walking toward their table as if Sutton had conjured him. His expression was grim.

"No luck?" Hendrix asked.

Strong shook his head. "We skipped all the way back to Tuesday," he said. "She was never at the registration desk. I'm sorry. We did get a few seconds of them from the entrance camera when they started their run, but the, uh, person of interest has the hoodie pulled down to obscure her face."

"We appreciate your help, Win," Sutton said. "That means our phantom jogger was never a guest of the hotel."

"Or she had an accomplice who handled the check-in," Hendrix said.

"We'll get a sketch artist to meet with the bartender and circulate it," Sutton said.

"We need to track down the other two women who were at that table," Hendrix said. "Maybe one of them saw something that will help us find the suspect. They and the cocktail server can at least help with the sketch."

"The team is following up on credit card receipts from Friday night," Sutton said. "Unless the other two were in on it, they should be relatively easy to track down."

"We're here to help in any way you need," Strong said. "The conference attendees checked out this morning, but we'll have registration information on any who stayed here."

"Thank you, Win," Sutton said.

"Wait a minute," Hendrix said as the manager turned to leave. "If the entrance camera was recording, and the woman came into the hotel the night before to meet up with Melody at the bar, you should have footage of her coming and going without a hoodie."

"Good call," Sutton said.

"I'll load the Friday night footage and go through it with the bartender right now," Strong said.

"We'll be here," Hendrix said.

* * *

Thirty minutes later, Hendrix was on his third cup of coffee and antsy to get going.

Sutton had gone to the lobby to call in for an update on the investigation and to see if there was a sketch artist available.

When Winston Strong returned, he had the bartender in tow.

"Anything?" Hendrix asked.

The bartender looked confused. "I thought you were the victim's husband," he said.

"It's complicated," Hendrix said.

"Tell him what you told me," the general manager said.

Reluctantly, the bartender laid it out. "We saw the woman you're looking for come in the main entrance just before happy hour. I recognized her yellow blouse."

"You didn't recognize her face?" Hendrix asked.

The bartender shook his head. "She was wearing a scarf wrapped over the top of her head and dark oversized glasses, like a celebrity avoiding paparazzi."

"Or a woman cheating on her husband trying not to be recognized," Strong said. "We do see quite a bit of that."

Or like Jackie O., Hendrix thought.

He thanked the men for their help and paid the check. He almost bumped into Sutton coming back into the restaurant as he was leaving, lost in thought.

"What's up?" she asked.

"We're going to need that sketch artist," he said.

*   *   *

"I've got an idea," Sutton said as they walked toward the atrium entrance. "Dallas is crawling with investigators. We've taken things here as far as we can. The killer and his accomplice are long gone."

"I'm listening," Hendrix said.

"While the Dallas team follows these leads, we could try to pick up the killer's trail at one of his earlier re-creations."

Hendrix nodded. "Now that we know what we're looking at, we might find something the initial investigation missed."

"And we have the resources to be more thorough than the locals," Sutton said.

"Where was his most recent murder we know of before this?"

"Los Angeles."

"The school librarian," Hendrix said.

"Yes," Sutton said. "Playing the role of Bobby Kennedy."

"Does the JTT have any planes available?" Hendrix asked.

"When the President sent me to work with you, she gave strict orders that we stay off the radar," Sutton said. "We sure as hell can't show up on a flight manifest of the Joint Terrorism Taskforce."

"How long's the drive?"

"If we trade off, we'll be there by this time tomorrow."

"We can take my truck," Hendrix said, "but there's something I want to check first."

After Sutton grabbed her overnight bag from the rental, she found Hendrix on his back, shining his phone flashlight under the truck.

"Worried about IEDs?" she asked.

"After you lead convoys in Afghanistan, you're always worried about bombs," he said. "But I'm looking for a tracker."

"What makes you think someone's tracking you?"

"I took the truck to a body shop a couple weeks ago after a maniac in a Mexican wrestling mask shot it up on the highway," Hendrix explained. "The shop owner said someone was prowling the lot one night when it was parked there. Someone was surveilling me enough to know who my girlfriend was. I assumed it was a tail, but I saw video of the prowler on Saturday just before I drove here. Similar hoodie pulled down low. I think it might have been our mystery woman keeping electronic tabs on me."

"That would explain how they knew where she was going for the weekend," Sutton said.

"Exactly." Hendrix slid halfway under the chassis. He groped his way along the frame until his hand touched something out of place in the wheel well. It was a small metal box attached with a magnet.

Hendrix pried the box loose with a flat-head screw-driver, then picked it up by two corners with his thumb and forefinger to preserve any prints. After inching out from under the truck, he dropped the box into a fast-food bag left over from his drive to Dallas and gave it to Sutton.

"Not up to crime lab standards, but it'll do," she said while he brushed himself off. "I'll hand this off to the team. Do you want to have them check your phone?"

"No, I've had it on me pretty much this entire time, except for the hour it spent on a police officer's desk in Fort Stockton Friday morning."

"I heard about that, Hendrix. We don't need any repeats in LA."

"Agreed," he said. "I'll gas up and get us some water and snacks while you drop off the tracker."

"Meet you back here in an hour," she said. "First shift's yours. You ought to be rested enough to go coast to coast."

Hendrix called the President to give her an update, but she wasn't available. He left a message that the babysitter was better than expected and he'd behaved so well she was taking him on a field trip. If she wanted to know where, she had to call him back.

8

"IF WE TAKE I-30 to I-20 and I-10 through Phoenix, it's a straight shot," Hendrix said. "Twenty hours of triple-trailer semis, drug mules, and assholes in BMWs. Boring as hell and twice as hot, but the cell service will be good."

"Speaking of boring, someone should teach you how to shop for road-trip snacks," Hannah Sutton said as Hendrix merged onto the westbound interstate out of Dallas. "Goldfish crackers, pepperoni sticks, and a twelve-pack of store-brand water? Who eats like this?"

"I was in a hurry," Hendrix said. "Besides, there's more than that. Check the bottom of the bag."

"Mentos?" she asked as she pulled out a tube of the chewy mint-flavored candy. "These are stale when they put them in the package."

"Sorry," he said. "You can show me how it's done when we make our first gas stop."

"You bet I will, Hendrix. We're talking everything from cheddar-caramel popcorn to yogurt smoothies."

"I'll stick to the basics, plus plenty of black coffee," he said. "But you have fun."

"You like donuts with your coffee, Hendrix?"

"Sure."

"Here's something that'll blow your mind: donut holes aren't real," she said. "They're a purely conceptual snack."

"How so?" he asked. "They taste real enough."

"When they make donuts, they're shaped exactly as you see them in the bakery case. They're little inner tubes of dough. They aren't solid discs with the middles carved out."

"I'm aware of that," he said.

"So what the hell is a donut hole then?" she demanded. "It's not a donut remnant. It's not a 'use the whole buffalo' kind of situation. It's just a little round ball of dough cooked separately in hot oil. It's riding on the donut's coattails. And calling it a hole? The hole is part of the donut, right? A ball of dough can no more be described as a hole than you can call your ass your elbow."

Hendrix shook his head in wonder. "You've given me a lot to think about," he said.

There wasn't much late-morning traffic and the road was good. Hendrix was able to cruise between eighty-five and ninety for most of the first leg. He hoped they wouldn't get pulled over before they reached the New Mexico border. He wasn't sure how well the Fort Stockton police station mess had been cleaned up, and he didn't want to find out.

*   *   *

They were twenty-five miles from New Mexico when the state police cruiser came down the on-ramp they'd just passed at ninety mph.

"Shit," Hendrix said, motioning with his head as he took his foot off the gas.

Sutton leaned to her right to see the car bearing down on them.

"No lights," she said.

"Just wait until he runs my plates."

Sure enough, the trooper hit the lights and siren less than a minute later. Hendrix had already slowed to sixty-five; now he signaled and pulled over onto the wide shoulder.

"I wonder how long he'll sweat us," she said.

But the trooper parked behind the truck and got out right away.

"Why's he taking off his hat?" Sutton asked.

Hendrix chuckled. "It's so I won't back over him or shoot him." He rolled down his window and waved the trooper forward.

"Come on, Corboy," he said, "I won't bite."

"After seeing how you operate, I thought the careful approach would be best," the trooper said as he walked up to Hendrix's door.

"Trooper Corboy, meet Special Agent Hannah Sutton of the FBI."

"This is the poor guy you roped into that mess at the Fort Stockton police station?"

"The very same, ma'am," the trooper said. "Pleased to make your acquaintance. If this guy's bothering you, let me know."

"I appreciate that, trooper," she said. "But if he bothers me, I'll make sure he regrets it."

"You just happened to be patrolling this stretch of road?" Hendrix asked.

Corboy pointed at the OnStar console above the rearview mirror. "Little birdie told me you were nearby."

"You took down my plate at Mrs. Sanchez's house."

Corboy nodded. "You're not the only one who knows how to do his job."

"I don't even subscribe to OnStar," Hendrix said.

"The only way to stop it from tracking you is to tear it out by the wires," the trooper said.

"I take it this isn't a social call."

"No, sir, I'm afraid not," Corboy said. "I came to warn you that the officer you roughed up has some very nasty friends, part of the Proud Boys movement. They're looking for you."

"I'm done with Texas, anyway," Hendrix said.

"I thought so," the trooper said. "But those sonsabitches are spread far and wide. I don't imagine they'll be looking for you quite as hard elsewhere, but you should keep an eye out."

"Always," Hendrix said. "Thanks for tracking me down."

"If I can track you, Larry can too," the trooper said. "He wouldn't have any trouble getting a warrant from a local judge after what you did to him."

I should have finished the job, Hendrix thought.

"Any breaks in the case?" Corboy asked.

"We know the person who was jogging with Melody Sanchez is a woman, but that's about it," Hendrix said. "We're heading to Los Angeles to try to pick up the killer's trail at one of his earlier crime scenes. Maybe we'll find his accomplice, too."

"Good luck, Hendrix."

"Rafe." He offered his hand and the trooper shook it.

"Chuck," Corboy said as he pulled a card out of his shirt pocket and handed it to Hendrix. "I promised the President I'd give you whatever support you need. Call me anytime."

Hendrix nodded. Corboy tipped his wide-brimmed hat toward Sutton and put it back on his head as he walked to his patrol car.

"Look at you making friends," Sutton said. She pulled Corboy's card out of the cupholder where Hendrix had set it. "Could come in handy if we need someone to follow up on leads back channel."

"All right, Sutton," Hendrix said as he unbuckled his seat belt. "New Mexico is all yours."

*   *   *

"Can I ask about your family?" Sutton said after she'd been behind the wheel half an hour.

Hendrix turned from staring out the passenger window, but he kept his eyes on the road rolling under the hood.

"Yes, you can ask," he said. He pulled a bottle of water out of the bag and took a long slug.

"Are you from military?" she asked.

He nodded. "My dad did four years in the Army just before and after I was born. He was active in the Reserves for a dozen years after that."

"Did he encourage you to enlist?"

"Not exactly," Hendrix said. "He'd have been happy to see me become an astronomer or get a good office job, especially since he knew I'd be sent into a war zone. No one thought Afghanistan would take twenty years to lose, but it was still pretty hot when I signed up. With my family's service background and my football accomplishments, I was able to get into Ranger School. Special Forces just sounded right to me. I wanted adventure, and I wanted to be a badass."

"Do you regret it?"

"It's hard to regret doing something you're suited for," Hendrix said. "I wouldn't call myself an elite killing machine, but I had a good mix of physical and analytical skills that were well honed with proper training. If I didn't think about it too much, there were times over there when I took great pride in doing the job. I wish I'd gotten to do it in the service of beating the Nazis and saving the world for democracy, but the Taliban were, are, and always will be nasty shitheads. They hate women, they hate modernity, and most of all, they hate the West. But we didn't do any lasting good over there. And we all knew it."

"That's pretty cynical, Hendrix," Sutton said.

He laughed. "I'll give you cynical. Our base was tasked with keeping one supply road open. One. That was our sole mission while I was there. Our caravans got our share of trucks through, but no sooner would we finish a run than those fuckers would blow up the road."

"Keeping an essential supply route open sounds important," she said.

"Except those supply trucks were carrying materials to rebuild the road," he said. "Every time it got blown up— and some of our guys along with it—Uncle Sam would put out big contracts to repair the road. The local guys who took the contracts, they'd pay off the Taliban so they'd let them do the work."

"So your job was to keep the road from blowing up just long enough to get the materials through for the next rebuild . . . when the protection money would give the enemy enough money to buy more explosives to blow up the road."

"You got it," Hendrix said. "We were paying the Taliban to kill us. It was a real-life game of Frogger, but we never got to the other side of the road."

Sutton whistled. "Kafka would be proud."

"I would have had a lot more fun sniping Nazis, all things being equal."

"And then you came home and started a family."

Hendrix didn't answer.

"Okay, enough on that subject, clearly," she said. "I hope you at least get to see your little boy sometimes. What is he now, five?"

Hendrix turned toward her. "Like you said, enough."

"I'm sorry," she said. "I don't have children, so I can't imagine. I had an aunt who lost a son before I was born. When I was growing up, she'd tell me how much I would have enjoyed my cousin, and then she'd say, 'When you bury a child, you bury yourself.' I was nine or ten. It terrified me."

"Let's gas up at the next truck stop," Hendrix said. "I need to piss."

"And I need to shut the fuck up," Sutton said. "Okay, gas, a stretch, a piss, some good junk food, and we slam the door on this subject. Sound good?"

Hendrix nodded. "I'm ready for my next shift," he said.

*   *   *

Twelve hours into the drive, he was so tired the road looked like it was floating in front of his high beams. Hendrix nudged the dozing Sutton.

"You need to switch?" she asked, rubbing her eyes.

"Soon, but I'd rather not do it in the middle of pitch-black nowhere," he replied.

"Misery loves company, I guess."

"I thought some conversation might wake me up," he said.

"Want to go over the case?"

"I've been doing that in my head for the last hundred miles. You mentioned you don't have kids."

"That's right."

"That's the sum total of what I know about your life outside the Bureau," Hendrix said.

"What do you want to know?"

"Where'd you grow up?"

"The District."

"Were your parents in government?"

"My dad sold insurance and my mom stayed home to raise me," Sutton said.

"Sounds like you grew up in a time warp."

"Only they encouraged my interest in law enforcement," she said. "I got the 'women can be anything they want to be' message regularly from both of them."

"Why the Bureau?"

"I met a recruiter at a high school job fair, of all things," she said. "I mean, they didn't hire me at seventeen. It was a cross between speed dating and career day. I hit it off with the woman the FBI sent. She wasn't much older than me, and this had to be a shit assignment they handed to the newbie, but she saw something in me. We kept in touch; she rose in the ranks. When I graduated from college, she recruited me for real. Ten years later, here I am."

"Do you see your parents often?"

Sutton shook her head. "Couple of times a year. They retired and moved to Florida, the Villages. I think they turned into swingers. It's the horniest retirement community in America. I hate it there."

"Are you married?"

"To the job."

Hendrix nodded. "I was too. It just took me too long to realize it." He yawned and opened his eyes as wide as possible, but it was a losing battle.

"Pull over," she said. "I'll do the last leg. We'll be in LA in eight hours."

He eased the truck onto the shoulder and parked. He left it running so any car that might happen by wouldn't hit them. If not for the truck's lights, Hendrix and Sutton would have a hard time seeing well enough to get out and switch places.

Hendrix walked behind the truck and continued east along the shoulder, shaking out his arms and moving his head from side to side to loosen up for the final drive.

"Don't go too far," Sutton called out as she climbed into the cab.

He was about to answer when headlights burned to life less than a quarter mile back

"Someone's been running dark," he said.

"Get back here, Hendrix," she shouted as automatic rifle fire started kicking up rocks just out of range.

"Go!" he said. "Get clear and call for backup." As Sutton fishtailed onto the freeway, Hendrix tucked and rolled into the scrub just past the shoulder. There was no cover that he could see—not that he could see more than a few feet ahead of him. He crawled on his stomach, hoping to get far enough off the road that he'd be hard to find.

When he saw a spotlight beam playing on a nearby stand of stubby brush, Hendrix froze.

A few seconds later, the light zeroed in on him.

"Rafe Hendrix, you're under arrest," said a man who sounded like he was walking toward his position. "Sit up and show me your hands."

"Is that you, Larry?" Hendrix asked.

"Officer Farnham to you, shit bag."

The light moved out of Hendrix's eyes as Larry Farnham's buddy used it to light the path.

"Hey," Farnham called back to the truck. "Keep that light on him."

In the moments he'd been submerged back into darkness, Hendrix had felt around and found a flat rock that fit into the palm of his right hand. In his left, he held a handful of dirt.

"You don't have jurisdiction in California, Larry," Hendrix said. "Why don't you scoot on back to Fort Stockton before my partner calls for backup."

Farnham snorted. "What do you think of that plan, Jack?"

"Not much," the man with the searchlight replied.

It was the farmer's son. Vengeance would be theirs, Hendrix thought, if they weren't such irredeemable dipshits.

When Officer Farnham was about five steps away, Hendrix rolled hard to his left out of the search beam and then kept going in a semicircle. Larry took a pot shot with his service revolver and missed as Hendrix jumped up and threw dirt into his eyes from two feet away.

Then Hendrix swung his left hand and connected with the cop's temple, knocking him cold with the rock.

As the searchlight found them again, Hendrix fell in front of Farnham, keeping the cop between him and the farmer's idiot son. He scooped up the revolver and clubbed Farnham on the other temple to keep him out for the duration.

Hendrix chanced a dash toward where he'd pulled the truck over but had to throw himself flat when the kid showered the area with bullets from his assault rifle.

The kid's problem was he couldn't work the spotlight and aim the gun at the same time, so as long as Hendrix stayed outside the now-stationary beam, he was a blind target.

But if Hendrix circled back closer to the truck to take out the kid, he'd be cut to pieces.

"Stand up, you stinking coward," the kid bellowed. "You sneak into my house and duct tape me in my own damn bed and now you won't stand and fight."

Junior punctuated his rant by ripping several rounds in Hendrix's vicinity.

It might be a standoff for the moment. But the kid had the high ground and superior weaponry, which would be decisive when the sun started to come up in the next thirty minutes or so.

Hendrix was doping out a plan when he heard his truck roaring back toward them at full throttle, lights off. As soon as the kid turned the spotlight on the road to pick it up. Hendrix leaped up and ran toward him. The farmer's son unloaded most of a clip at the truck as it sped closer and Sutton returned fire as she steered with her right hand.

By the time the kid thought to swing the light back into the scrub, it was too late. Hendrix was fifty feet away and the kid was exposed in the truck bed.

Hendrix unloaded the remaining five shots from Farnham's revolver at center mass. The bullets lifted the kid up an inch or so as they blew him backward out onto the concrete.

Sutton had stopped in the middle of the road about seventy-five yards away. She came running as Hendrix checked the body. Dead.

"Thanks for coming back," Hendrix said.

"You okay?" Sutton asked.

"I'm sure as hell awake now," he replied.

*　*　*

At five AM, Sutton called the incident in to FBI headquarters.

"Great thing about Pacific time: it's the crack of dawn here, but my colleagues are all clocking in," she said after hanging up.

"What's the upshot?" Hendrix asked.

"A team's been dispatched to deal with the locals and help contain the situation."

"But the whole world knows about my run-in with Larry at the Fort Stockton police department."

Sutton nodded. "That's why I said contain. There's no way the media won't connect you with this. So the Bureau will say they're looking to speak with you and will provide further updates after that happens."

"That'll buy us maybe a day," Hendrix said.

"Wish I could disagree with that."

"Fucking Larry and his Proud Boy buddies."

"Let's keep things in perspective, Hendrix. You took out two assholes affiliated with that particular group, and you'd already crossed both of them. There's no posse out to get you. You'll be back in DC under protective custody by midweek."

"With no overt help from a President hoping to win a second term."

"Let's just focus on the Bobby Kennedy re-creation and see if we can turn up anything useful today," Sutton said. "There are dozens of agents on the Melody Sanchez case. Even if you are sidelined, they'll follow up on anything we give them."

CHAPTER

9

As the sun rose over the mountains in the truck's rearview, Hendrix inched along the rolling parking lot of westbound I-10 to central Los Angeles. He exited at Koreatown and navigated to the Robert F. Kennedy Community Schools on Catalina Street, the most expensive public-school complex in U.S. history.

They were close to Hollywood and would hit Santa Monica and the Pacific if they continued west, but he detected no hint of the ocean in the smoke-tinged air. A scattering of improbably tall royal palms and the Art Deco confection of the Wiltern Theatre, clad in lime-green terra cotta, were the only signs of glamor. The workaday character of the neighborhood, its strip malls, bus stops, and small office complexes, suited Hendrix's mood. He was here for answers, not a tan.

The crime scene had long since reopened to students. Hendrix and Sutton followed the colorful RFK murals into the library and checked the supply room that stood where he'd been shot during his 1968 campaign appearance. Hendrix hoped the killer had left a clue that could be understood by someone who knew the murder was no random act of violence but found only reams of copier paper and boxes of pens and pencils.

"Dry hole," he said.

"We'll get the LA team over here to reprocess the scene." Sutton said as they pulled out of the lot.

They had an appointment to see the detective in charge of investigating the librarian's murder. The precinct house was nearby. Hendrix parked the truck at an open meter halfway down the block.

"You must be our friends from the FBI," the detective said as they walked into the lobby.

"Thanks for waiting here for us," Sutton said.

"Hal Montoya," he said, shifting a manila folder to his left hand so he could shake hands with his right. "It's such a nice day, I thought we could chat in the park across the street. There's a food truck with great coffee, much better than the sludge upstairs, anyway."

Hendrix thought about reminding him this wasn't a social call. Instead, he introduced himself and followed the detective to the food truck, ordered a cup of black coffee that singed his hands through the protective cardboard band, and joined Montoya and Sutton at a nearby picnic table.

Two months had passed without a break in the case, and Hendrix got the vibe this guy wasn't staying up late going over the evidence.

"School shootings aren't exactly unique in LA," Montoya offered. "In this case, because she was singled out, our theory is the shooter knew her. Maybe an ex-lover or stalker."

"Any suspects fit that bill?" Sutton asked.

"No," Montoya admitted.

"Hell of a theory," Hendrix said.

"Sorry, we haven't had much sleep," Sutton said, shooting Hendrix a sharp look.

"I get it," Montoya said, seemingly unruffled. "We didn't explore the Bobby Kennedy angle. There are references to him everywhere there, you saw it. But this seemed completely unrelated."

"It was part of our Secret Service training, walking through assassinations down to the caliber of weapons and the exact spots where the victims fell," Hendrix said. "The connection wouldn't be obvious to most people at this point."

"Even if it was, domestic perp is always a better bet than copycat assassin," Montoya offered.

Hendrix nodded. "But now that you do know, does it put anything you saw in a different light?"

Montoya thought it over. "No living eyewitnesses, no one we talked to saw the shooter going in or coming out," he said. "We processed for prints, reviewed the security footage, interviewed her friends and family . . . nothing jumps out because we didn't find much to go on. The only thing that looks different now is the caliber of the handgun matches the one used by Sirhan Sirhan. And where does that get us?"

"What's in the folder?" Hendrix asked.

"Crime scene photos," the detective said, sliding it across the table. "I also printed out screen caps from the school security video showing vehicles in the parking lot at the time of the shooting."

Hendrix flipped to those. "Not too many cars that late in the afternoon," he said. "Did you track down the owners?"

Montoya nodded. "A couple of teachers, an assistant principal, a janitor, and the soccer coach."

Hendrix studied the photos. "What about her car?" he asked.

The detective looked puzzled, but then closed his eyes and nodded.

"We didn't find any keys on the victim," Montoya said.

"That didn't seem strange to you?" Sutton asked.

"Of course it did," Montoya said. "I may not be a junior G Man, but I've been doing this for fifteen years. We searched her apartment thinking the shooter may have taken her keys and tossed the place, but there was no sign of entry."

"If he had keys, there wouldn't be," Hendrix said.

"True," the detective said. "But she kept the place neat, and there was no indication he'd gone through her dresser looking for valuables."

"Or trophies," Sutton offered.

"So you didn't find her car?" Hendrix asked.

Montoya shook his head. "Without any keys, I don't think anyone thought to check for a vehicle."

"Maybe if you'd been doing this for twenty years instead of fifteen, you'd have thought to do a basic registration check," Hendrix said.

"Okay," Montoya said. "I deserve that. Come back to my desk and we'll run a records search."

*   *   *

Hendrix was so angry he didn't trust himself to say another word. Sutton did the talking, looking over Montoya's shoulder as he ran the victim's information through the California Secretary of State's database.

The librarian had owned a Honda Accord. The registration had expired less than a month ago, five weeks after she'd been murdered. They ran a search across all state law enforcement databases and found it had been abandoned in San Bernardino, where it now sat at the police impound lot.

Sutton wrote down the pertinent information and thanked Montoya for his help. Hendrix snorted.

"Look, I get it," Montoya said. "I'm sorry."

"You're an embarrassment," Hendrix said. "If I find out we could have brought this guy in earlier based on evidence in that car, I'll be seeing you again, Detective, and it won't be for a cup of coffee."

*   *   *

"Why didn't you tell him what you really thought?" Sutton asked as Hendrix bulled his way through the thickening midday traffic on the 405 south.

"He's lucky I didn't take his head off," Hendrix said. "A rookie could have figured that out."

"A rookie wouldn't be so used to phoning it in," she said.

Hendrix gripped the wheel so tightly that his fingers started to go numb.

"At least we have a real lead to follow," she said.

"True. Coming to LA was a good idea."

"You're welcome, Hendrix," she said.

He took a deep breath and eased his foot off the gas. "I owe you one, Sutton."

"Nobody wants this guy more than you do," she said. "But I'm a close second."

*   *   *

After stopping at a drugstore for a box of latex gloves, they found the Accord in a corner of the impound lot.

"It's been sitting out here for weeks," Hendrix said. "Any exterior physical evidence will be long gone."

Sutton pulled on a pair of gloves and tried the driver's side door. It was unlocked.

"Hey," she said, "things are looking up."

Being careful not to disturb any prints or fibers that might be revealed once the FBI techs arrived to process the scene, they looked at the cup holders, glove box, and floor mats for any items the killer might have left behind, but the car was depressingly clean.

"She lived up to the librarian stereotype," Sutton said.

"What time do the techs arrive?" Hendrix asked.

"They said they'd be here early afternoon, so could be any time now," she said.

"Let's step back and let them do their work. I don't want us to . . ."

He stopped as Hannah Sutton leaned in on the driver's side, studying the spot where the top half of the seat joined to the bottom half.

"What is it?" he asked.

Sutton emerged with a small white register slip.

"UPS Store," she said. "It's a receipt for a mailbox rental."

Hendrix clenched his right fist and felt his throat constricting. "Where?" he asked.

"Phoenix."

"Let's go," he said.

* * *

Hendrix's phone rang as soon as they got back to the truck.

"Madame President," Hendrix said.

"What the fuck did you do to that police officer on the freeway, Hendrix?" she asked. "He's in a coma. No such luck for your neighbor."

"Ambush," Hendrix said. "Trooper Corboy warned us on our way to LA that they were gunning for us."

"Was one of them the guy with the *lucha libre* mask?" the President asked.

"I think that's our Dallas shooter," Hendrix said.

"Is there anyone who doesn't want you dead?"

"Besides you?"

"I'm still trying to decide, Hendrix. And why LA?"

"We were taking a look at the RFK copycat murder," Hendrix said. "We turned up a lead, a mailbox in Arizona."

"Have Sutton call it in and then get your ass back to DC," the President said. "You're officially wanted for questioning in that freeway death. Your freelance investigating days are over."

"I'll head back tomorrow," Hendrix said. "As soon as we check this lead. I'm not going to cause you any more trouble."

"Don't make promises we both know you'll never be able to keep, Hendrix." The line went dead.

He hit the steering wheel with a fist.

"Sounds like that went well," Sutton said.

"I'm surprised the Bureau hasn't asked you directly to bring me in," he said.

"They have, Hendrix. I told them we're on our way back to DC and keeping our heads down in the meantime. I didn't mention we'd be making a pit stop in Arizona."

"Time's up, then," Hendrix said.

"As the song says, we've got tonight," Sutton said. "So let's walk through it. There's no way a school librarian in Los Angeles drives to Phoenix to rent a mailbox."

"Yeah," Hendrix said as they headed east on I-10, back the way they'd come. "We've got this fucker. He just doesn't know it yet."

"But why the hell would he steal her car and abandon it in San Bernardino after shooting her in the library?" she asked. "He got in and out of the school clean. Why not fade away?"

"Maybe he heard a janitor coming down the hallway and had to leave by a different door than he'd planned," Hendrix said. "He'd done his homework, had her under surveillance, knew what she drove, where she parked, and grabbed her keys because the Honda was closest to that door."

Sutton shook her head. "Then wouldn't they have found his car nearby?"

"Maybe he came back for it after he ditched her car," Hendrix said.

"That's not a crazy hypothesis," she said. "But it's not quite as elegant as I'd expect this guy to be."

"Why do you think he took the car?" Hendrix asked.

"That's what bothers me. I don't have a good theory. Except maybe he wanted to fool the locals but then make it easy for anyone taking a closer look after Dallas to find it."

"That crossed my mind, too," Hendrix said. "Like the President said, Dallas was designed to get my attention, and these earlier murders ensured she'd get pulled into the investigation when I started making connections."

"Which would mean we're driving into a trap," she said.

"I hope so," Hendrix said. "Because that means the killer will be there."

"It's a five-hour drive," she said. "The store should still be open when we get there."

Hendrix mashed the gas pedal and his truck responded with a reassuring jolt of acceleration.

"Are there any Mentos left?" he asked.

*   *   *

They caught the owner of the UPS Store franchise as she was locking up for the evening. Once Sutton satisfied the woman with her FBI credentials, she opened back up and invited them in.

"We see the occasional postal inspector," the owner said as she fired up the computer in her small office. "No surprise that some people rent mailboxes with less than pure motives. But I've never had a visit from the FBI."

"You've finally hit the big time," Sutton said.

The woman chuckled as she called up the information on the rented mailbox.

"Bill Smith," she said. "Is that anybody's real name?"

"Not anybody who's renting a mailbox at the UPS Store, I'd guess," Sutton said.

"Well, if his ID was fake, at least the address he gave was real," the owner said.

*   *   *

It was a drab three-story apartment building in a seedy section of Scottsdale, a block off an arterial street dotted with pawn shops, check cashing outlets, gas stations, and fast food joints.

An orange notice was affixed to the entry door. The building had been seized for delinquent taxes and was up for sale in foreclosure. Hendrix and Sutton sat in the truck and watched for signs of life as the last sparks of sunset disappeared into the Sonoran Desert.

"Looks buttoned up," he said. "No lights, no broken locks or jimmied windows."

"If there are squatters in there, they're keeping a low profile," Sutton said.

"If he's in there, he's watching us from behind the blinds," Hendrix replied.

"Let's come back in the morning with a full team," she said.

"I'll be in a holding cell if we do that," he said.

"True, but I can lead them in and report back to you. Better than barging in with no backup and getting yourself killed."

Hendrix opened his door and got out of the truck. "You're all the backup I need, Sutton. If you're willing to come."

"Okay, Hendrix, but if we end up dead, I'm going to kick your ass."

*   *   *

Sutton kept watch while Hendrix picked the lock. It was a Home Depot special, and he was in within ten seconds. She stepped in after him and eased the door closed.

They waited for their eyes to adjust to the fading light. The mailbox rental agreement showed Bill Smith in the third-floor rear apartment. Sutton moved toward the open stairway in the middle of the small common area, but Hendrix placed a hand on her shoulder.

"I'll take point," he whispered, pulling the nine-millimeter from his waistband.

She nodded and pulled out her service weapon as he ascended to the first landing. Seeing no threats, he turned and motioned her up as he made his way to the second floor.

No light, no movement, no signs of life. Hendrix repeated his recon on the next landing and proceeded to the third floor. No activity. He crept to the door at the end of the hall and placed a hand on the knob. It turned readily.

Hendrix stepped to the side and pushed the door open. The apartment's living area and open kitchen were cleaned out. No furniture, just a breakfast bar, fridge, sink, and stove.

Hendrix stepped inside, arms extended, gun ready.

When he felt the needle in his neck, he didn't have time to turn back and fire before he lost consciousness.

CHAPTER

10

PAIN IS INFORMATION.
    There was so much of it now that it was hard for Hendrix to make sense of it. The inputs threatened to overwhelm the system.

Which wouldn't be the worst outcome, as long as the loss of consciousness wasn't permanent.

And he'd finally met the guy in the *lucha libre* mask.

He was a professional interrogator who knew how to keep his subject down but not quite out. Finest training CIA money could buy.

He'd started with some waterboarding, like a chef trotting out a signature dish as a welcome to the regulars.

There were no questions to accompany the simulated drowning, which meant either this was the softening-up phase of a lengthy interrogation, or he already had all the information he needed and just wanted to have a little fun with his victim before finishing him off.

Hendrix decided the best way to survive the panic was to welcome the death this technique convinced your amygdala was imminent. Welcoming death came naturally to Hendrix these days. Relaxing into the flood of water through the towel wasn't quite possible, but asking for it helped keep his muscles from locking up and lowered the volume and intensity of his gasping, puking screams.

No words were exchanged during the torture session's opening phase. If the interrogator wasn't going to interrogate, then the victim wasn't going to plead for his life, Hendrix decided. Not yet, anyway.

The waterboarding had been, what, two hours ago?

Hard to tell with precision. Although Hendrix was not allowed to go unconscious, he had been in a mental twilight several times as the torture ebbed and flowed. Mostly flowed.

The pain, then, was the only solid information he had. While his torturer had stepped away to get another implement ready, Hendrix took stock of what the pain was telling him.

Aching jaw from the four or five solid blows of the chisel that had been shoved into his mouth to crack out three lower left-side teeth.

Lacerated tongue, collateral damage when he had stuck it in the bloody hole where one of the teeth had been and failed to pull it back in time to avoid the chisel's return.

Dislocated left elbow after his arm had been put into a winch apparatus that ratcheted tighter and tighter until the bone felt like it was about to splinter.

At least three cracked ribs on that side as well, courtesy of a rubber-headed mallet swung with a gusto that indicated emotional release.

So this was personal for the torturer. And now it was personal for Hendrix.

He could feel the blood drying his torn shirt to his chest where his right nipple had been torn mostly off with a pair of pliers. He wished those had been used on his teeth instead of the chisel.

Which made him think: The implements were all regular hardware store purchases.

Even the pruning shears, which were small enough not to have required a trip to a home and garden store.

The shears were what had put him close to blackout when the torturer used them to snip off the smallest two toes on his left foot.

He pushed away the image by focusing on what the tools could tell him. This was an improvised operation. Or at least that was how it was supposed to look.

No power tools. Hendrix looked at the portable floodlights facing him and the chair he was cuffed to. No cords. Battery powered.

Which suggested a remote or abandoned location without electricity. All the better to keep anyone from hearing the screams.

There were no other sounds, human, animal, or mechanical.

Was Sutton being held elsewhere? Had she escaped from the Scottsdale apartment building? More likely she had been incapacitated or killed. If this was all as personally directed toward Hendrix as it felt, probably the latter. Tie off the loose end. He hoped he was wrong.

It was hot in the windowless room. What he could make out past the bright lights were gray concrete walls. Maybe an old storage room.

The single door, which lay about twelve feet behind the lights, was metal. It was open a crack, but not wide enough for him to assess the thickness or to admit any breeze that might stir.

Hendrix blinked the sweat out of his eyes and turned, gingerly, first to the left and then to the right. Both wrists were cuffed tight to the back of the metal chair. His right ankle had a little play, but the cuff on the left was ratcheted tight enough to sting when he turned in that direction.

The chair wasn't bolted down, so he could topple himself over, but he didn't see what that would get him. Better to stay calm and wait for a higher-percentage opening.

If the torturer had left him here to die, he'd have to throw himself sideways at some point and try to inch his way out of the room. He'd make that call just before he couldn't help pissing himself. For now, his bladder was holding out.

For all he had endured, Hendrix reflected that the injuries had left him fully ambulatory. With the missing toes and cracked ribs, he wouldn't be entering any 5Ks, but this seemed like the work of someone who wanted to make a point, rather than someone building up to the kill.

That could change in the next round, but Hendrix decided to hang onto the silver lining as long as possible. He hadn't even been maimed in a way that would be easily spotted, no eyes gouged out and hanging down his cheek or chopped off fingers or ears.

Small favors.

Another hour or so passed and still no sign of the man.

It was unlikely he would go to all the trouble of tearing Hendrix down without ever saying a word, especially if this was about punishment or revenge.

But give it another couple hours and Hendrix would have to make a try for the—

"I hope you haven't drifted off," the torturer said as he entered the room, revealing a nondescript dark hallway before he stepped inside and closed the door. He was still wearing the wrestling mask.

"Ah, good, you're awake."

Hendrix gave a slight nod. Now that the man was talking, he might explain what this was about and what fate awaited him. Either way, Hendrix was ready to get it over with, even if it meant watching fire erupt from the barrel of a gun.

"I admire your calm resolve," the man said as he turned off one of the portable lights and began disassembling it and returning the pieces to a molded plastic case.

"I didn't expect it from someone who has such a hard time following basic protocols. If you had only shown that level of discipline and restraint when our lives first intersected, we would not be meeting like this today.

"In fact," the man continued, pointing at his own chest, "this person, this . . . tool of vengeance would not exist if you had been able to follow one simple order. I had put all of this well behind me. I was once again a normal member of society, a human being capable of giving and receiving love. I never would have sacrificed that willingly. You pulled the monster back out of me that day. Every one of the deaths since then is on your hands. But there is only one death that matters to me. In that, we are joined."

"Two," Hendrix snarled.

The torturer paused, then nodded. "For you, it is two now, isn't it? Sadly, that's just the start."

The man took a deep, resigned breath. He slipped a small black penlight from his pocket, clicked it on, and held it in his mouth. He turned off the other portable light and began disassembling it in the same way he had the first.

The bobbing penlight illuminated the man's work breaking down the second portable lamp. When he had finished boxing it up, he hefted both cases by their handles and carried them into the hall. He closed the door behind him, leaving blackness in his wake.

Hendrix was relieved not to have the floodlights trained on his face. Turning them off had also cooled the room down a degree or two.

He was still in a great deal of pain, but this was information he had already processed and dissociated himself from to the extent possible. He wasn't bleeding out. His lungs were not punctured. This was bearable.

He wanted, desperately, to sleep, to relegate the injuries to the waking world for an hour or two. But first he needed to process what he had just heard.

This was about the children killed in the bomb blast. Correction: It was about one child. The child the torturer had lost along with his reclaimed humanity.

No one like him had shown up on the lists of parents and guardians during the investigation that looked for connections between the victims' families and the suicide bombers.

But Hendrix knew this type. Ex-spook, had done terrible things to people half a world away, had become woven into the fabric of the very terror he was sent to fight against.

Of course the torturer would be furious at Hendrix for ignoring an order. The only way this man could live with whatever damage his "enhanced interrogation" techniques had done during the war was by reminding himself he was only a link in the chain of command. "I was just following orders" was the lie so many of history's monsters had told themselves.

After all his dirty work was done, the torturer had probably taken retirement at twenty years, perhaps with a bonus tied to a secret commendation. He'd then walled off the horror by immersing himself in the lives of the family he had told himself he'd been out there protecting with a grim series of rendition flights to dark and unnamed places for simulated drownings and electric shock treatments. He had tried to elicit the information needed to stop the next attacks and bring the perpetrators of the first one to justice. That he and the other torturers had mostly failed in that effort likely did not enhance his emotional stability.

So the torturer had staked his salvation on one little kid, probably a grandchild, maybe a nephew or niece. That chance at redemption had been blown away at the school that day.

When Hendrix had taken the shot, setting into motion a sequence of events that awakened a horseman of the Apocalypse.

That vengeful rider had now come for him, not at a gallop but at a determined, steady trot. The journey had taken two full years. Hendrix shook his head at the single-minded focus it had taken to put this plot into play.

If this was the end, he thought, it was almost just. He was the only person the torturer could hold accountable for his devastating loss.

Hendrix would fight back if he got the chance, no question. But if he didn't succeed, his death at least would have a meaning he could understand and accept.

As the hours wore on, Hendrix nodded off. He wasn't sure for how long, but it wasn't long enough. He jerked awake as the door opened and the torturer entered, still masked, shining the penlight along the floor to illuminate his path.

In his other hand, he held a baggie of ice. As he drew closer, the torturer casually tossed it into Hendrix's lap. He shined the penlight on the baggie long enough to reveal that it also held Hendrix's amputated toes.

"I thought you might be missing those," the torturer said. "I'm not sure they can be reattached. If not, you can keep them in a jar as a reminder, or feed them to your dog, if you have one."

Hendrix thought about his last night with Mel and winced.

"I've given you plenty of time to think about what I told you earlier," the man continued. "You're smart, and I'm confident you now understand why I . . ." He gestured toward the baggie, which had started to leak onto Hendrix's crotch.

"I'm not going to kill you," the torturer said. "Not today. But I am far from done with you. No physical pain I could inflict would come close to giving my loved one a full measure of justice.

"But you have another child, Mr. Hendrix, up in Michigan. Just turned five?"

Hendrix strained against the cuffs, drawing blood from his left wrist. Parental desperation could give you the strength to lift a car off your kid, right? Not this time.

"It's ironic that I've seen your boy more recently than you have," the man continued from behind the black mask with cartoonish orange lightning bolts running down each side. "David is a bright, handsome child. His stepfather is as loving and nurturing as you would hope. Even coaches your son's soccer team. A strong role model.

"David would have a fine life ahead of him," the man said. "But I'm not going to let that happen."

Hendrix bounced the chair on the concrete, but that was good only for a loud scrape. The torturer looked at him with what appeared to be a pitying smile.

But now it was Hendrix's turn to speak.

"No," he growled.

He put as much menace and resolve into the word as he could muster, like a man giving a rabid dog a last chance to back down before putting a bullet in his brain.

"I respectfully disagree," the man said, playing the penlight across Hendrix's face. "I'll make sure you're on hand to see David's promising life cut short."

Hendrix felt fresh blood tricking down his wrist.

"You're right to be angry with me," he told the torturer. "It was my fault. I disobeyed a direct order, and those kids died. I am sorry. I can never make it right. I know that. Take me instead. End this. That's what I would do if the positions were reversed."

The man slowly shook his head. "One, the situation would never be reversed," he said. "I understand the critical importance of chain of command. Two, I did think about hunting you down, killing you, and then walking away. That would have been infinitely easier than the project I have undertaken. But it would also leave the scale out of balance—putting you out of your misery while leaving me trapped in mine. There are still people who love me, but it isn't enough.

"And what else have I had to do with my time besides setting this plan into motion? It hasn't exactly kept me out of trouble, but it's an intellectually stimulating hobby. You can take some solace in that. I may wait months or even years to finish the job. Thinking of your anguish makes it easier to be patient."

In becoming his mortal adversary, this man had gone to a dark land far beyond reason. Hendrix decided to respond in kind.

"If you let me live, I will find you and I will kill you," he said.

The man laughed. "Yes, you will find me. I'm sure of that. But look how well that turned out this time."

The man clicked off the penlight and stepped forward in the pitch black. A moment later, Hendrix felt hot breath on his left ear and the sting of a needle entering his neck.

"You'll find a way out of here," the man said as Hendrix lost consciousness. "If you remember your military training."

*   *   *

When Hendrix came to several hours later, he giggled. Something was tickling his foot.

"Davey?" he said.

They had a game. When Hendrix got home from the White House early enough. He would scoop his son up in both arms. Davey would wriggle onto his back until he was being cradled. And then he would squeal as Hendrix swung him back and forth while counting out "a one, a two . . ."

"A three!" Davey would yell as Hendrix softly tossed him onto the cushions of their overstuffed couch. Then the toddler would roll onto his stomach and say, "I sleeping, I sleeping." This was Hendrix's cue to join Davey on the couch and tickle him from his toes to the backs of his ears until his son erupted in a fit of laughter.

Sometimes, Davey would roll off the couch and tickle Hendrix's feet through his socks. "Tickle Daddy," he'd say. "Tickle Daddy!"

"All right, Davey, all right," Hendrix said now.

He snapped back to reality. Still bound to the chair, Hendrix opened his eyes and looked down to see a scraggly hump-backed rat licking the congealed blood from the stumps of his severed toes.

Horrified, Hendrix kicked the rat away. Even with his limited range of motion, he got his foot far enough under it to launch it across the room, where it thudded against the concrete wall. After about fifteen seconds, the stunned rat stood, fixed Hendrix with a beady-eyed stare out of a 1930s gangster movie, turned, and stalked out the partially open door.

Hendrix shuddered, which sent a wave of pain through his body. Nothing ticklish about that.

He had no idea how long he'd been out. The room was empty except for Hendrix, the aluminum chair, and a portable cooler placed to the right of the door.

Hendrix tested his bonds: one pair of cuffs encircled each ankle and one pair threaded through the chair's crossbars and closed around his wrists. No dice.

There were no sounds of humanity, no car horns, no chatting passersby. The torturer had said he wanted Hendrix to watch him kill his son. There was no reason to doubt the man's intent. Which meant that either he'd send help anonymously or he'd take the chance Hendrix would figure out a way to escape, as he'd said when he'd inserted the hypo into his neck.

He gathered as much strength as he could and swallowed several times to get some saliva going.

"Hey!" Hendrix shouted. "Help! Someone help! I'm trapped in this room!"

He might as well have been on Mars.

All over but the shouting, Hendrix thought. And now that's over too.

He almost passed out from the exertion, but then bit his tongue with the side of his mouth that still had all its teeth. That gave him enough of a jolt to consider his next move.

Hendrix realized he had to rule out the possibility of a rescue, planned or unplanned. Because if none materialized soon, the only question would be how long until someone discovered his body. Maybe the building would be demolished with him in it and no one would ever know what happened to him. Or maybe some kids looking for a place to party would smell his putrefied body on the way in and tip off the police.

His mind was drifting. He had to focus on getting out of the building. What had the torturer said? Remember your military training.

Although he'd never endured anything this stressful in Afghanistan, he realized the fifty-six days of hell known as Army Ranger School had best prepared him for this day. He'd lost twenty pounds, limited to two MREs a day even as the instructors pushed his body beyond its known limits. Long walks in heavy boots, strapped with a sixty-pound pack. Endless sit-ups and push-ups. Grueling runs on rugged terrain. Hand-to-hand combat with no referees. Live-fire drills at two AM.

The beginning, in Fort Benning, had been a shock to the system, but it was nothing compared to the three-week Mountain Phase, when they were thrown into the wilderness in small groups and fought to survive over twenty exhausting days and freezing nights of patrols, combat simulations, and infiltration exercises that included free-climbing eighteen feet up a sheer rock ledge for a recon drill. He'd barely slept. In Army parlance, Hendrix was smoked. But he'd stuck with it as dozens of students washed out. He'd envied them as much as he hated them.

And then came the Florida Phase, ten days of punishing, fast-paced patrol exercises in a bug-infested swamp. He had been one of the 102 members of his class to enter the last week. Only ninety-six made it out alive, and Hendrix had nearly been the seventh casualty.

The day had started with a predawn small-boat exercise on a stretch of the Yellow River that passed through Eglin Air Force Base near Pensacola. Heavy rains had left it at flood stage, and they'd passed by airmen humping sandbags onto the banks. It was a cloudy day, with temperatures in the mid-sixties. They caught glimpses of the midafternoon sun arcing downward as they split into three companies. The members of Company B, Hendrix's group, and Company C jumped out of the boats into a swamp that seemed to radiate malevolence, from its boot-sucking mud to the chest-high waters that ended just under the chins of the shorter soldiers on his team.

The trainers leading Company A decided the water was too cold and deep to proceed with the exercise and returned their charges to camp. That made the ensuing investigation especially uncomfortable for the leaders of the other two companies.

The water was brisk, in the low fifties, but Hendrix and the sixty other soldiers stuck in that swamp soon got used to the temperature. The exercise had been scheduled to last three hours, following Army hypothermia protocols, but through a cascading series of operational stresses, he and most of the others in his company were in the water twice that long.

The creek had been the killer. It was four feet deeper than the swamp waters it cut through. They built a rope bridge to cross it, which ate up ninety minutes. Hendrix had just finished tying a support rope to a cypress tree when the soldier next to him whispered that he was numb all over.

"I don't want to wash out," he told Hendrix, "but I can't feel my limbs."

Hendrix called over one of the instructors observing from a nearby zodiac, who in turn huddled with two colleagues. After a heated exchange in which the two junior instructors pleaded with the hard-ass exercise leader to cut the day short, they called in a chopper for evac. The medics took two other soldiers complaining of similar numbness. Those three survived.

The first time Hendrix was scared that day was when he caught a brief panicked look on the face of a junior instructor. He'd spent full days on and in the water kayaking with his parents all through childhood, but those had been summer outings on warm days with plenty of breaks on the banks of whatever river they were floating. This was different.

The evacuations, which required two round trips by the chopper, ate up two more hours. Hendrix would never forget the chill from the rotors as the stricken were hauled out of the water in harnesses. By the time the remaining soldiers crossed the rope bridge, they'd been in the water longer than the guidelines allowed. But they Rangered up and moved out, slogging through the swamp toward higher ground. An hour later, three more soldiers were diagnosed with hypothermia and medevaced to the base hospital. They didn't make it through the night.

At ten PM, more than seven hours after they'd entered the muck, the rest of the soldiers heaved themselves onto dry ground, enveloped by a thick, clammy fog Hendrix swore he could feel piercing his skin and coiling around his vital organs. Another soldier collapsed nearby. Hendrix and two other students carried him to the nearest road for ambulance transport. He died en route to the emergency room.

As Hendrix rubbed his arms and felt that his skin was the texture of corduroy from the goose bumps, he had one thought: He wanted to see the stars again before he died. He and his two comrades fell asleep waiting for the rescue. Only Hendrix had awakened when the transport truck crawled by, trying to spot them through the fog. Hendrix attempted to stand, but his legs faltered, and he fell backward into the ditch. So he flopped over and used his arms to pull himself onto the gravel, dead legs dragging behind him, then fished his flashlight out of a side pocket and beamed an SOS pattern down the road. Miraculously, the truck stopped and backed up to pull them aboard.

He and the remaining soldiers survived the open-air truck transport back to base. The next morning, they learned the death toll, which included one soldier who'd drowned in the swamp less than a thousand yards from dry land. It was the deadliest day in Ranger School history. When the incident made national news a few weeks later, Hendrix was lauded as a hero for his desperate crawl to safety, a bright spot in an otherwise bleak story. It would have been easy for the torturer to find as he plotted his revenge. To a man, Hendrix thought then, they'd known what they had signed up for. At graduation a week later, Hendrix held the insignia of a dead colleague as he and the remaining soldiers recited the Ranger creed.

As he prepared himself to leave his concrete torture chamber now, Hendrix repeated the last sentence in a hoarse whisper: "Readily will I display the intestinal fortitude required to fight on to the Ranger objective and complete the mission, though I be the lone survivor."

At least today he wasn't wet and cold, Hendrix thought as he saw the rat scurry past the doorway out in the hall, undoubtedly waiting for another crack at his bloody foot. That was not going to happen. If he could survive the worst punishment Ranger School had ever dished out, he would get through this.

He didn't have enough leverage to scoot forward in the chair. Which left only one escape option. He'd have to tip the chair over onto its side and push himself across the floor by flexing his knees.

The thought exhausted him. If he gave up, no one would ever know. But then he closed his eyes and saw Davey's sweet face.

He'd have to tip himself to the right, so he didn't land on his injured ribs. He calmed his breathing and started rocking from side to side until he generated enough momentum to heave himself over. His long legs and torso helped.

His right shoulder took the brunt of the blow, which made him wince. But he preferred the stinger to landing on his dislocated elbow, and he hadn't injured himself further.

From this vantage, Hendrix could see out the cracked-open door into the hall, where a slash of sunlight bisected the floor. Daytime. But was it the end of the same day he'd been tortured? More likely the next morning or even afternoon.

If his toes were in that cooler, it's possible they could be reattached. If they were still on ice in the baggie, he had up to twenty-four hours. Even more reason to get the hell out of the room now. The torturer was a master of psychological manipulation. Maybe he'd left the cooler to motivate Hendrix to escape. Whether the toes were still in there was a question he didn't dwell on.

He took several deep breaths and began making his way toward the door by bringing his knees up as far as they would go and then pushing out and down. Each time he did, he was able to move a few inches closer to the door.

He developed a decent rhythm and added a shoulder shimmy to the process, herky-jerking himself to the door in about ten minutes. It would have gone faster, but he had to rest after every push.

Hendrix's throat was so dry he could no longer swallow. If he could open the cooler, he would gladly sacrifice his toes for the chance to suck on an ice cube. But it was a model that required pressing in large plastic buttons on both ends of the curved handle to roll the top open. He'd die before he pulled that off with his hands cuffed to the chair.

Hendrix bumped himself into position to scoot through the doorway. Thirty minutes later, he made it to the end of the hall, which led to a short stairway. He stared at the four concrete steps for several minutes, gathering strength and trying to hang on to his sanity.

"Just fucking do it already," he said.

With those inspiring words echoing off the walls, Hendrix scooted around so that his legs were extended over the top step. He was still on his right side.

Using only the shoulder shimmy, he inched his way toward the tipping point. He had a moment of triumph when the chair landed upright on all four legs as it thunked onto the floor at the base of the stairs.

But the momentum kept the chair going so that it tipped over again. This time, Hendrix landed on his left side. The pain in his ribs was so intense he blacked out. When he swam back to consciousness, he was glad not to see any rats feasting on him. Savor the small victories.

Unable to flip over onto his right side, Hendrix willed away the excruciating pain in his rib cage as he made slow progress toward the exit door, which was propped partway open with a large rock.

A half hour later, he was outside. The asphalt parking lot was sticky from the midday sun. It burned and tore at Hendrix's cheek as he pushed his way across it. The thirst was like nothing he'd ever experienced.

"Fuck you, Phoenix," he said as he was overtaken by delirium. "You're too close to the sun."

H ENDRIX AWOKE IN a hospital bed.
His head felt like a bottle of aspirin with a few pills rattling around under a giant wad of cotton. He watched the rising sun out the window and felt himself drifting off again.

Something.

Something.

Something he needed to remember.

A plastic pitcher of ice water and a short glass sat on the side table to his left. He reached across his body with his right hand and felt the tug of compression tape across his chest. Not good, he thought.

As Hendrix poured the water, he examined the IV taped to the top of his left hand and the bag of clear fluid dripping into it. Saline? A smaller bag hanging next to it was empty. Painkiller? That would explain why he was having to grasp so hard at every thought.

As he sipped the water, he learned what he could about the condition of his body. Compression tape meant cracked ribs. How badly cracked was hard to figure with the painkiller keeping him comfortable. His left cheek was bandaged. Something was wrong with his jaw on that side. He probed his mouth with his tongue, and felt some kind of appliance, maybe a temporary bridge, where several teeth used to be. The news wasn't getting any better.

His left elbow was swathed in an air cast. He put down the water and used his right hand to tug loose the sheet. He couldn't see much with a gown covering him to the knees. He pulled harder on the sheet and got a look at his left shin and foot. The area around the two smallest toes was mounded in gauze. He tried a wiggle but couldn't feel anything.

Hendrix poured another glass of water and pushed the call button. A few minutes later, two women entered. One was a nurse. She said good morning and started checking his blood pressure and tending to the IV.

"You must have one hell of a story to tell, Mr. Hendrix," the other woman said. She was holding a chart.

"I'm still trying to remember it," he said.

"I'm Dr. Taylor, the surgeon who worked on your foot."

"I was trying to figure out the state of play there," he said.

"Then I have some good news. You were picked up by the EMTs yesterday after someone made an anonymous 911 call. Given that you were found cuffed to a chair, they called in the police as they transported you. The responding officers found the cooler in the room where you were apparently held. Once they saw the contents, they raced it here. I was able to reattach both toes. I'm here to check the blood flow."

Hendrix puffed his cheeks and blew out a long breath. The jumble of words from the doctor alarmed him. Cuffed to a chair. Toes in a cooler. What the fuck had happened to him?

"We've got you on some serious painkillers, Mr. Hendrix," the doctor said. "Take it slow. If everything's not coming back to you yet, just rest a while longer and I promise you it will. You endured a significant amount of trauma yesterday. Your body and mind need time to heal."

"That's good advice," the nurse said as she hung another small bag of clear liquid, this one full, on the IV stand and secured his line to it. "Leave everything to us and we'll have you out of here in a week."

Hendrix nodded. Something, though. Something important he needed to remember.

"Was anyone else there?"

"When you were found?" the doctor replied as she lifted up the gauze and examined his foot. "No."

He closed his eyes and rubbed his face with his right hand.

"I'm sorry we couldn't save the three teeth you lost, Mr. Hendrix. They were in the cooler, too, but the window was closed by the time you arrived. When you get implants, you won't be able to tell the difference."

He gestured at his foot. "What about those?"

"Your toes look good," the doctor said as she replaced the dressing. "You might lose some sensation, but there's a good chance you'll fully recover that in time. The main thing is to protect it from infection. Your other injuries are minor. Two cracked ribs. That elbow is hyperextended, but it isn't broken. And the burn and abrasion on your cheek should clear up in a few days. We even sewed up your right nipple."

"Where was I found?"

"In an abandoned warehouse a few miles west of Scottsdale," the doctor said. "Or outside the warehouse, I should say, in the parking lot. The EMTs said it looked like you wriggled out of the building bound to that chair.

They said it didn't seem possible you were able to get as far as you did, that you must be in great shape and maybe have some survival training in your background. Once we identified you, we knew they were right about that."

Hendrix nodded. It felt like everyone knew more about his situation than he did.

"When you passed out, the asphalt burned your cheek like you'd touched the element of an oven," the doctor said as she leaned over his face and replaced the dressing. "Luckily, once you stopped moving, the spot under your head cooled down enough to stop baking you."

"That was yesterday?" he asked.

The doctor nodded. "They wheeled you into my surgery just after three thirty. Judging by the burn, you probably crawled into the parking lot during the hottest part of the day, maybe around one. The road that passes the warehouse doesn't get much traffic, but someone must have driven by and noticed you within a couple hours of your escape."

"And the call was anonymous?"

"Mmm hmm," the doctor said as she finished checking her notes. "The police are trying to track down the caller to see if they're connected to what happened to you."

"You talked to them?"

"Yes, the ones who brought your toes waited for me to finish the surgery," she said. "As you can imagine, they are keenly interested in finding out what happened to you. They asked me to let them know as soon as you were conscious today."

"Did you?"

"Not yet. An interrogation, even a friendly one, wouldn't be good for you right now. For heaven's sake, you don't even remember what happened yet, so what good would it do anyone?"

Interrogation. When she said that word, disjointed images rapid-fired in his brain: A bright light shining in his eyes. Davey on the couch. A rat with a bad attitude.

He reached over to the tube delivering a fresh round of painkillers and pulled it loose from the cannula. The nurse overcame her surprise quickly enough to grab it and keep it from draining onto the floor.

"It's starting to come back," Hendrix said. "I need to clear my head. There's something important. I just can't quite grab onto it yet."

"Okay," the doctor said. "You're going to be in a lot of pain when this wears off, but if you know something that will help the police catch whoever did this, it might be worth it. I want you to stay in this bed in the meantime and get rehydrated. The big bag is saline. You need that."

"Deal," he said. "I appreciate it, Doc."

"You're welcome," she said. "But as soon as you remember what you need to, the nurse is going to hook you up to the small bag again and give you more rest."

Hendrix nodded and raised his right hand in farewell as she and the nurse departed.

He remembered everything now, but he couldn't tell them that. Getting questioned by the cops would only slow him down. He rolled halfway onto his left side and pulled himself up on the rail far enough to reach the phone on the nightstand next to the head of the bed, just behind the wheeled table that held the water pitcher.

A note taped to the base of the phone read, "Dial 0 for operator and 8 for outside line. Local calls only." Hendrix picked up the receiver, punched 0 and asked the operator to please connect him to a person he had to reach in Washington, DC. He promised he would only pass along the number of the hospital and have the person call him back. Then he gave the operator Hannah Sutton's cell number.

By the fifth ring, he was giving up hope. But then Sutton stepped out of the bathroom.

"I thought they were never going to leave," she said. "We need to get you the fuck out of here."

"Wait," he said as he cradled the phone. "My son—"

"He's fine, Hendrix," Sutton said. "The Detroit field office is keeping a close eye on both him and your ex without revealing their presence. They're safe. With any luck, they won't get dragged into this mess."

Hendrix closed his eyes and gave thanks. "What happened to you?" he asked. "How did you get away?"

"I got a hypo in the neck as soon as I walked into that apartment," Sutton said. "I saw you knocked out on the floor as I was falling onto it myself. I woke up yesterday in the bed of your truck next to your wallet, keys, and cell phone. They didn't take any of my things, either. When I got into the cab, there was a burner in the cupholder with a note saying to keep it charged and turned on at all times or David dies. That's when I called the Detroit office. On my own phone, of course."

Hendrix didn't feel sharp enough to figure out why the torturer had bothered to leave Sutton alive. After all, he'd murdered several innocent bystanders at the assassination sites. Why leave a loose thread like Sutton, especially one who was trying to stop his plot before his vengeance against Hendrix was complete.

"What is it?" Sutton asked.

Hendrix closed his eyes for a long moment. "Sorry. I'm still pretty fuzzy. Do you have the burner on you?"

"Yes, just in case he called overnight. But he didn't, and there's no record of any previous calls in or out."

"How did you find me?"

"That part was easy. First, I went back into the apartment to see if you were still there. It was empty. No sign of our friend. Then I started up the truck and was about to call for backup when I heard a news report about a man found in the parking lot of an abandoned warehouse unconscious and cuffed to a chair. I figured that had to be you. I called three hospitals before I finally hit this one. They said you were in surgery and wouldn't be able to see visitors until today, maybe later. So I waited until the third-shift change last night, snuck in, and waited for you to wake up."

"You're pretty good at this," he said.

"You think so? It's a miracle both of us lived through the ambush," she said. "You should have listened to me when I asked you to wait until we could get a full team on site."

Hendrix shook his head. "Our guy would be in the wind before we got anywhere close," he said. "This was the only way to make contact."

"You're paying a high price for that," Sutton said.

"Not as high as the one he's going to pay."

She nodded. "Can you walk?"

"I don't think so," he admitted.

She handed him his clothes. "I found these in the closet. Get dressed and I'll be right back."

Sutton returned wearing scrubs and pushing a wheelchair upon which sat several boxes of gauze and a tube of antibiotic gel. She unplugged the saline drip and eased the IV out of the top of Hendrix's hand. Even with whatever remained of the painkillers in his system, it stung like a son of a bitch.

Sutton squirted a small glob of the gel onto the IV site and bandaged it. She helped Hendrix into the chair and wrapped his head in a couple layers of gauze, leaving enough space around his mouth to let him breathe freely.

"Revenge of the Mummy," she said as she wheeled him into the hall. There was no one at the nurse's station, and they made it onto the elevator without incident. Hendrix could only see indistinct shapes through the gauze, but he heard a man say "Let me get that" as they neared the entrance.

"Our doorman was one of the officers waiting to question you," Sutton said as she wheeled him across the parking lot to his truck.

"I'll make it up to him somehow," Hendrix said.

She helped him into the passenger seat, pushed the wheelchair against a lamppost, and hopped into the cab. They were back on the freeway before Hendrix could finish removing the gauze from his head.

"Where are we going?" he asked.

"I want to check in with the Phoenix FBI office and bring them into the fold."

"No," Hendrix said. "If we spook him, he'll go to ground again. We need to track him down ourselves."

"What's the play?" Sutton asked.

"Thanks to you, my family's safe in Michigan," Hendrix said. "If he shows up there, the Bureau will take him down. Which means we head back to DC. He may still live there, and from the way he set this all up, he's likely going to take a shot at the President. He wants to make me suffer before he kills me, but he just wants her dead."

"Okay, Hendrix," she said. "Get some rest and I'll try to avoid the potholes."

When they stopped for food and gas a few hours later, Sutton spotted a medical supply store and went in to buy Hendrix a boot to protect his foot.

While she was inside, Hendrix's phone rang. It was the White House switchboard. A few moments later, he was speaking with the President.

"Why aren't you back here?" she demanded.

"We are en route, Madame President," he said. The painkillers had worn off and he was in no mood to be dressed down by his closest friend.

"I heard a pretty fucking strange report from the DNI today about you being pulled out of a warehouse cuffed to a chair."

"Our friend in the *lucha libre* mask set a trap for me, and I obliged him by walking into it."

"On purpose?"

"You know how in baseball they have that thing called the unintentional intentional walk?" Hendrix asked.

"I'm familiar with it," the President said. "I hate it. It's wishy-washy."

"I hoped I could somehow get the jump on him, but I knew the odds were he'd take me down. Either way, I had to see him."

"What did you learn?"

"He only talked about me, but I think he's after you too. He was close to a child who died in the bombing, and he wants to make me pay by killing Davey in front of me."

"Jesus."

"Sutton's got the Detroit field office on high alert. But I think it's a two-for-one deal with this guy. I gave Sutton as much of a description as I could, including the biographical information he shared, and the Bureau is running it all down. We could have an ID on him by the time we get back."

"She's still with you?"

"She sprung me from the hospital before the local cops could question me," Hendrix said.

"Good," the President replied.

"Madame President, this guy tortured me like a professional. He's got to be CIA. He's before our time, but I'll bet he was in Afghanistan and probably all the black sites after 9/11. Ask the DNI to see what he can turn up."

"That war, seems like it'll never be over. Never should have started in the first place. Shit, we found bin Laden in Pakistan and he was a Saudi motherfucker backed by his people to the hilt. But we can't upset the balance in Kashmir, and we can't stop the oil fields from flowing for even a day. There's nothing anyone wants or needs from Afghanistan, so let's turn it into a parking lot and then bug out after twenty years. God, I hate this world sometimes, Hendrix."

Sutton emerged from the store and held up a large bag.

"At least we're amputation buddies," Hendrix told the President. "That sick bastard cut off two toes on my left foot."

"The big ones?" she asked. "Because that will fuck with your balance."

"No, the small ones," he said.

"The small ones?" the President said with a snort. "You lost two chiclets and you think that has anything to do with me losing a whole foot and half my leg? You're an asshole, Hendrix. Amputation buddies. Shit. Get your ass back here and I'll have the White House physician stack up some nice soft pillows to rest your foot on."

She hung up so fast she didn't hear Hendrix chuckle.

"Who was that?" Sutton asked as she climbed into the truck and passed him the bag.

"The President wanted to know why we're not back yet."

"We'd best get moving then," she said.

CHAPTER

12

ONE UNEVENTFUL PIT stop and nine hours later, Sutton pulled into a mammoth truck plaza west of Tucumcari, New Mexico. The sun had set a couple of hours back and the high desert climate was favoring them with a cool fall evening.

While Sutton went into the deserted travel center for food and Tylenol, Hendrix babysat the truck. Realizing he had to piss, he opened the passenger door and fumbled with the medical boot until he got it locked on. Good to give it a test run, anyway, he thought as he hobbled around the back of the truck to remove the hose nozzle from the gas tank.

As he did, Hendrix caught movement in the shadows to his right. A sawed-off prick in a western shirt complete with shiny snaps and shit-kicker boots gave him a nasty grin as he advanced into the light.

"Can I help you?" Hendrix asked.

"Nope," the man said. "We've got some unfinished business with you from Fort Stockton. But you don't need to lift a finger."

Hendrix looked up at the round mirror hanging from the top of the pumps to help motorists avoid back-up collisions. Two more assholes were coming in from his left.

"You mean, like this finger?" Hendrix asked as he pointed the gas nozzle at the first man, who was now three feet away, and soaked him from hat to heel in mid-grade.

"Fuck, ow, fuck!" the man yelled, clawing at his eyes, which had taken a direct hit.

Hendrix turned and repeated the move on the other two, drenching the lead attacker, but only grazing one pant leg of the third man, who was peeling off to the far side of the pump island.

Without waiting to see what that thug was up to, Hendrix turned back to the pump and hit the alarm button.

"What happened?" came a staticky drawl over the pump speaker.

"We've got a bad spill on pump 53," Hendrix said. "Someone drove off with the nozzle in their tank."

"Not again," came the exasperated response. "Jimmy'll be out to shut it down. You should get clear and gas up at a different island."

Before Hendrix could respond, the third man made his play, looping the hose from the other side of the pump around Hendrix's neck.

He tried to spin loose, but between the slick puddle of gas and the medical boot, he was only able to turn partly away from the pump before nearly falling to the ground.

Pressing his advantage, the assailant pulled the hose tight, pinning Hendrix against the pump again and sending a stinger through his cracked rib cage. He was in no condition to fight one asshole, let alone three, but now here came the other two dripping with as much anger as gasoline.

Hendrix still had the nozzle in his hand, and he let loose another stream toward both men, which made them jump back. But the third kept pulling the other hose tighter, grinding Hendrix's back into the credit card reader sticking out of the pump.

Hendrix pointed the nozzle up and over his right shoulder and made it rain on the other side. That loosened the man's grip on the hose. But it gave the other two enough of an opening to rush Hendrix, who dropped to the ground as they converged on the spot where he'd been pinned to the pump. He let go of the nozzle and rolled under the truck before they could correct course.

He had escaped for the moment, but as he watched the three sets of feet spaced around the truck, he realized he was trapped, marinating in a pool of gas with no way to defend himself.

"What the fuck is this?" a man's voice growled from just beyond the circle of attackers.

Hendrix took a chance. "Jimmy, is that you?"

After a pause, the man said, "It is. Who are you and why are you under that truck?"

"Call the police, Jimmy," Hendrix said in as stern a tone as he could muster. "These hoodlums are fixing to blow up the plaza."

"Holy shit!" Jimmy exclaimed. Hendrix watched the man's booted feet turn back toward the main building and take off at a fast trot.

"You'll be dead before the cops get here," one attacker said.

"Maybe so," Hendrix said, "but I'm taking you assholes with me."

"Big talk," another one said.

"My Zippo will do all the talking," Hendrix said. "Poke a head under here and I'll send this place sky high."

"You're bluffing," the third attacker said.

He was right, but Hendrix could tell by the quaver in the man's voice that he wasn't confident in his conclusion.

One of the men on the driver's side went down as a gunshot rang out. He landed on his side, facing Hendrix, his shocked expression fading as he died from the head wound.

The man who'd been standing next to the dead guy ran into the darkness.

"You, stop right there." Sutton was speaking to the third man, the one on the passenger side, who'd slipped trying to get away.

"You all right, Hendrix?" she asked.

"I've been better," he said.

"Ease out on the driver's side," she said. "I've got this asshole."

Hendrix rolled out and stood slowly, using his good foot and his right arm to do it. He watched across the hood as Sutton kept her gun on the third man's temple.

"Not your lucky day," she said. "Why the fuck do you go around calling yourselves Proud Boys? You're a total disgrace."

"Yes, ma'am," he whined. "Things got out of hand, but we weren't . . ."

"Gonna kill him?" she asked with a snort. "Of course you were. Avenging your peckerwood police officer friend, covering yourselves in enough glory to make up for the fact you haven't seen a pussy up close since the day you came out of your mama."

The man swallowed hard and turned red under the harsh fluorescent lights. They could hear sirens approaching.

"Give me your fucking keys and point out your vehicle," Sutton said.

The man complied, handing over a keychain with a metal 88 hanging from it and gesturing toward a late 2010s

Camaro parked fifty yards away, near the area where tired truckers pulled in for naps.

"On your knees," Sutton said as Hendrix opened the driver's side door and grabbed his phone and the burner along with the nine-millimeter stashed in the center console.

"Got everything?" she asked.

"Almost," Hendrix said as he hobbled around back. He popped the tailgate, grabbed the telescope case and started for the Camaro.

He was surprised to hear another shot a few seconds later. He turned back to see Sutton walking around the rear of the truck and heading toward him as she holstered her service weapon.

"You don't really have a lighter, do you?" she asked.

"No," he said.

"I do," Sutton said as she spun the wheel on a small plastic Bic and tossed it toward the front of the truck before running to Hendrix and tackling him.

The first explosion was jaw-rattling, but the ones that came after, as every pump island on their side of the empty plaza went up in rapid succession, were almost enough to give him a concussion.

Before he could clear his head, Sutton was helping him to his feet and into the Camaro.

"Let's see those shitheads follow us now," she said as she dropped into second gear and fishtailed out of the truck stop, away from the procession of police vehicles lighting up the road behind them.

"What the hell was that?" Hendrix demanded as Sutton gunned the Camaro eastbound onto a frontage road running parallel to the freeway.

"You mean saving your life?" she asked.

"I mean executing that man while he was on the ground surrendering to you. They don't teach that at Quantico."

"Shit, Hendrix, haven't you heard? We're the cops, writ large. We are a tribe apart. We make our own laws, harsh ones, and the people rightly fear us."

"You can't believe that," he said.

"Isn't that why these freaks are out to get you? You broke the first rule, treating a fellow member of law enforcement like one of the unwashed."

"Larry? He'll live," Hendrix said. "Besides, he had it coming."

"And that yahoo with the Hitler keychain didn't? Aren't you sick of following those outmoded rules of engagement? I would happily kill every Proud Boy in their sleep if I had the opportunity. They are a cancer on our society."

"Civil war seems extreme," Hendrix said.

"It is extreme," she agreed. "But those fuckers are the ones who declared it. The sooner we acknowledge that, the faster we can push them back into the dank holes they crawled out of."

"I saw this in Afghanistan," Hendrix said. "Guys who crossed the line from self-defense into murder because they decided there were no innocents to defend. Their only goal was to survive, and they couldn't be too careful. So they'd blow away an unarmed family out for a drive because they might be suicide bombers. I'm talking little kids in the back seat, Sutton. You need to pull yourself away from the darkness."

Sutton snorted. "That wasn't a child I shot. That was a Nazi who wanted to kill you."

Hendrix shook his head, which was a mistake. Jesus, he hurt all over. Okay, he'd misjudged Sutton's character, but this wasn't a fight he was going to win. The intensity of the argument took his last reserve of energy. He eased his head back into the headrest and gave in to sleep.

* * *

The dream took Hendrix back to the day, about a month before the Blackhawk attack, when Wyetta Johnson was leading a platoon to investigate a local fabric shop an informant claimed was a front for a bomb-making workshop.

"We're not here to shop," Hendrix reminded the platoon as they assembled around the doorway.

"Not unless they have my favorite sale," Johnson said.

"Which one's that, L.T.?" a corporal asked.

"Bras half off," she replied to a round of appreciative laughter.

The joke had the intended tension-breaking effect. But one of the newbies was that bad combination of scared, dumb, and trigger-happy. He'd been ready to waste the family that owned the shop, including three kids under ten, as soon as they'd come to the front counter.

The newbie had racked his rifle and pointed it at the woman standing behind the register. The man next to her, her husband, looked like he was about to do something desperate, which was just what the newbie wanted.

Hendrix was sure the scene was going to end with brains on the wall. But then Johnson stepped between the newbie and the counter. It was a tight enough squeeze that the barrel of his rifle brushed against her cheek as she moved into place.

"Lower your weapon and wait for us in the Hummer," she told the newbie.

"These are hostiles and they're helping the insurgents kill everyone they see in an American uniform," he said without moving the rifle. "You might be blind to it, but the rest of us aren't."

The newbie shut the fuck up when he felt the barrel of Hendrix's nine-millimeter against his right temple.

"One more word and you die where you stand," Hendrix said.

The newbie lowered his weapon and left to wait in the Hummer.

Johnson turned to the platoon and said two words: "Charlie Mike." Continue Mission.

"Hooah," they replied softly before completing a search of the premises, which came up clean.

On the way out, Johnson apologized to the woman, slipping several hundred dollars into her hand.

Hendrix held the door open for his L.T. "I had it under control, showboat," she said, slamming her shoulder into his arm as she passed.

"You're welcome," Hendrix replied.

After they returned to base and got the newbie reassigned, Hendrix and Johnson got very, very drunk. It was the only bender they'd gone on together, in-country or out. Hendrix thought they'd both deserved it.

That was a world and a lifetime away, and yet the seeds of Wyetta Johnson's political rise had been planted that day.

In the early stages of the marriage, when the sex was still great and Judy's resentment toward his checked-out parenting hadn't had time to build, Hendrix had reconnected with Johnson. She had just been elected to Congress and he'd sent her a congratulatory note: "You're the biggest star I see now."

That outreach led to monthly lunches and occasional couples' dinners, though their wives never warmed to each other. Judy told Hendrix she didn't enjoy how "earthy" the language got between him and Johnson. Johnson told Hendrix her wife, Cleo, thought Judy was as pretentious as she was judgmental. When Hendrix asked Johnson if she agreed with that assessment, she'd shrugged. The dinners stopped.

And then the Senate seat had opened up unexpectedly in Illinois. Johnson had been appointed by the governor to fill the last year of the term and was given a clear shot in the primary to retain it. She did so while establishing a national reputation as a refreshing straight shooter, dubbed by NBC News as the Democratic reincarnation of John McCain.

"I don't think you can be reincarnated as someone when you were alive before they died," she told Hendrix over celebratory drinks. "And I don't know how thrilled John would be to look in the mirror and see a gay Black woman staring back, but you know what, Rafael? I will take it."

Her star still rising, Wyetta Johnson ran for President midway through her second Senate term. Thanks to questions about the "CM" tattoo she'd gotten on her left wrist after finishing physical therapy and adapting to her prosthetic leg, Charlie Mike became her campaign slogan. Hendrix didn't think of himself as sentimental, but hearing that phrase chanted by thousands of citizens at her televised campaign rallies—and a few times in person when he rotated into her protection detail after she became the nominee—gave him goose bumps.

Continue Mission was core to Johnson's beliefs. She saw elective office as the best way to support and build on everything she'd fought for in Afghanistan, and the progress she'd made as a community organizer in Chicago.

The message was as effective with voters as it was simple to remember. She won in a squeaker of an election the right wing charged the Democrats with stealing when they'd made Puerto Rico a state in the previous administration's second term.

Looking for people she could trust, the President-elect had tapped Hendrix to lead her Secret Service detail and named the medic with the Pashtun hookup White House physician. With decent majorities in both the House and Senate, Johnson had a good run in advancing what was widely seen as a sensibly moderate policy agenda. It looked like they might all live happily ever after.

Until the bombing.

* * *

Hendrix's eyes popped open. He wiped sweat from his brow and glanced at the dashboard clock. He'd slept for half an hour. Sutton had opened the car's windows and sunroof to cut the stench of gasoline.

"We need to ditch these clothes before we get pulled over," Hendrix said. "Reeking of gas after a truck stop explodes is a quick ticket to a dark cell."

"That wasn't much of a nap," Sutton said. "But you're right. We need to get rid of this car, too. One of those assholes got away and I'm sure he can describe his fascist friend's bitchin' Camaro."

"How far are we from Texas?" Hendrix asked.

"About forty-five minutes."

Hendrix found Corboy on his recent calls list and hit redial.

"Every time I hear from you, it's trouble," the trooper said.

"It's lucky you like me," Hendrix said.

"It's lucky the President ordered me to help you," he replied. "But even that has its limits. You're cashing in the last of your chips with this call."

"Understood."

"Okay, then," Corboy said. "What do you need?"

"A clean car and a change of clothes for me and Agent Sutton."

* * *

They met Trooper Corboy on the front lawn of his immaculately kept ranch-style home on the outskirts of Amarillo.

Sutton handed over the keys to the Camaro and Corboy pointed at a beat-up silver Prius parked up the block.

"I'll be surprised if we make it out of Texas in that thing," Sutton said.

"I don't want to hear it," Corboy said. "This is the longest-tenured abandoned vehicle in the nearest state impound lot. That means no one's looking for it, and the boys there say it runs fine. As long as it gets you clear of Amarillo, I'll call that mission accomplished."

He handed Sutton the keys and a duffel bag full of clothes.

"There's a truck stop with showers at the first freeway exit east of here," the trooper said. "Try not to blow it up."

Hendrix closed his eyes and sighed.

"Yeah, I know," Corboy said. "And from what I know, this wasn't a clear-cut case of self-defense like that freeway ambush. You better hope there's a presidential pardon waiting for you."

"Charles, where are your manners," came a voice from the open front door.

"Linda, please," Corboy called back.

"Don't 'please' me, Charles, invite them in."

"We don't want to intrude," Hendrix said as the trooper's wife marched down the short walkway.

"Oh, hush, you're as bad as Charles," she said. "Linda Corboy."

"Rafe Hendrix," he said. "And this is Special Agent Hannah Sutton of the FBI."

"That explains it," Linda Corboy said. "Charles is always complaining about the FBI and ICE. The locals hate the staties and the staties hate the feds. It's like high school. Rafe, step into the light. Oh no, you are in rough shape. Both of you, come on inside, shower, change your clothes, and I'll look at those injuries."

"Linda's a nurse," Corboy said, apparently resigned to this change of plan.

"We appreciate it, Linda," Sutton said. "These fumes are giving me a terrible headache."

After they'd cleaned up, Linda Corboy insisted on feeding them hot beef sandwiches, mashed potatoes, and gravy.

"This is an excellent meal, ma'am," Hendrix said as he finished his second tall glass of iced tea.

"So much for the leftovers," the trooper said.

"Oh, hush," Linda Corboy said. She turned to Sutton. "He loves cold beef sandwiches on white bread with a gallon of mayo. He looks forward to the leftovers more than the meal they came from. But he never sulks for long. True, blue Chuck Corboy, the most even-keeled cop you'll ever meet."

"I do love those sandwiches," he said.

"Guess what, honey? I saved some beef out in the fridge just for you." She leaned over and kissed him on the nose. "Now, Rafe, come over to the recliner where I can train the lamp on you."

Hendrix was sore in places he didn't remember feeling before. He shuffled the half-dozen steps from the dining room table to the recliner and slumped into it. It was so comfortable, he started to nod off.

Linda Corboy pulled a stool up next to the chair, sat down, and snapped her fingers. When Hendrix opened his eyes, he saw her undoing the straps of the boot, which she had cleaned remarkably well while he'd been in the shower.

"We need to change these bandages," she said. "If you put pressure on these toes, they're going to pop right off and then bye-bye little piggies. Stay off your feet as much as possible, elevate and change these bandages using plenty of antibiotic ointment twice a day. Do all that and you'll be good as new in a couple of months. How's the compression tape?"

"Holding up," Hendrix said.

"Good. Your elbow doesn't look like much more than a bad strain. In fact, it all looks a little worse than it is. You're lucky. Now why don't I make up the couch for you and get agent Sutton checked into the Corboy guest suite?"

"Linda," the trooper said with alarm as he returned from clearing dishes.

"Thank you for your hospitality," Hendrix said, "but your husband's right. We've overstayed our welcome."

The trooper came over to help Hendrix out of the chair. "You get pulled over, you weren't here," he whispered.

"Quit telling secrets," Linda Corboy said. She gave Hendrix a sandwich bag containing ten pills. "Oxycodone for when the road gets too rough. Don't take more than three of these a day, and don't mix 'em with alcohol."

Hendrix nodded. "Thank you, ma'am."

Corboy handed him off to Sutton, who helped him out the door and up the block. She got him seated in the Prius, grabbed their things from the Camaro, and bid their hosts farewell while Hendrix watched from the passenger seat. He hoped he'd see the trooper again when this was all over.

If it was ever over.

III

13

THEY MADE GOOD time through the Panhandle and across Oklahoma. The Prius was peppy, and Sutton was steady at the wheel. After taking one of the pills at midnight, Hendrix was in and out until daybreak.

"You slept through Arkansas," Sutton said when he leaned forward to grab a bottle of water. "Good choice."

They had Tennessee and Virginia ahead of them. "Twelve hours to the District," he said. "Want me to take a shift?"

"As long as you're not addled on Oxy, I could use some rest," she said.

They stopped at a rural gas station, pumped a few gallons into the tank, and enjoyed homemade biscuit and bacon sandwiches. Small pleasures in the eye of the storm.

Hendrix eased himself behind the wheel, glided the seat back, and situated his booted left foot on the dead pedal. Linda Corboy had been right. He wasn't doing so bad. He was overdue for a dressing change on his toes, but he shuddered at completing the task in a gas station bathroom. It would keep until DC. He hoped.

Sutton was out before Hendrix got back on the freeway, leaving him alone with his thoughts, a dangerous place to be these days. He set the cruise control to seventy-five and watched the mile markers melt away in the light traffic.

The cruise control made him think of the torturer. Smug, locked on the course he'd set for Hendrix, and planning to finish him and his son whenever it suited him.

They had to flush him out, take away his advantage. If they could rattle him and disrupt his time line, they had a chance of bringing him to justice. The tools of a torturer were no good if the torturer wasn't in control.

Hendrix was eager to hear if the Secret Service had turned up anything to give credence to his thought that this lunatic was targeting the President in parallel. That would be a start.

They could revisit the other murder sites and see if they could turn up new leads like they had in Los Angeles. But given how things had turned out in Phoenix, Hendrix was convinced the evidence pointing there was planted. The torturer was meticulous in his approach. It was unlikely he'd left a trail they could pick up elsewhere.

Absent a Secret Service breakthrough, all they had was the burner phone, which hadn't rung yet and might be just a way for the torturer to track them. The DNI would assemble a profile of the man based on the sketchy description Hendrix had provided, but the torturer likely anticipated any personal details he shared in that concrete room would be passed along to the authorities. The man must have felt confident his identity would elude at least an initial round of investigation.

Whatever the torturer had done to make himself tough to find, he had to know they'd get to him once they reinterviewed the families of every bombing victim.

Which meant there had to be a tight time line on the killer's end game. Weeks, not months, as the saying so often went in Washington when officials tried to demonstrate they were acting to address the latest hot-button issue.

With the investigative resources of the federal government, a full revisit of the bombing probe would take no more than a month. The torturer wouldn't cut it too close, though, so figure he'd make his play in two to three weeks. Which left them maybe a week to get smart or lucky enough to catch him before the reveal.

One advantage Hendrix and Sutton had was the ability to be nimble. On their toes, he started to add. Well, it was still true metaphorically, if not in reality. While the official investigators processed scenes and developed profiles, they could test hunches and . . .

"Sutton, are you awake?" he asked.

"For you, sure," she grumbled.

After stretching her arms and taking a swig of water, Sutton said, "Back to the land of the living. You need me to take a shift?"

"I want to run something by you," he said.

"Shoot."

"Why hasn't he re-created Lincoln and Garfield?" Hendrix asked.

Sutton nodded, thinking it over. "Maybe he's saving them for last."

"Maybe. But he set off all the tripwires in Dallas. He's got our attention, so all he'd be doing is risking capture at this point with the other two."

"Makes sense," she said.

"But what if he already did try one or both—and failed for some reason?" Hendrix continued. "History's full of botched assassination plots. The guy's good, but he's human. He could fuck up just like any of us."

"He's been careful," Sutton said.

"Won't hurt to check it out," Hendrix said. "Once we get a decent rest, you take Lincoln in the morning. I'll take Garfield."

"What am I looking for?" she asked.

"An attempted killing that echoes the assassination. That would have been unlikely to go unnoticed at Ford's Theatre, but let's be thorough."

"That's why you're taking Garfield? You don't think I'm up to the task, you old control freak?"

"It's not that," Hendrix said. "Well, I will concede the control issues. But I always enjoy the National Gallery of Art, and this is a good excuse for a visit."

"I thought Garfield was shot at a train station," Sutton said.

Hendrix nodded. "The Baltimore & Potomac station. It was on the southwest corner of Sixth Street and what's now Constitution Avenue. Teddy Roosevelt had it torn down in 1908 after the feds took control of the property. It now houses the west building of the National Gallery."

"Maybe the killer thought a re-creation wouldn't track with the media or law enforcement since the station no longer exists," Sutton said.

"True, but that didn't stop him in LA."

"Garfield was a long time ago," she countered.

"Only twenty years before McKinley, and he re-created that in Buffalo with a new building in place there as well," Hendrix said. "He's revisited two of the big four presidential assassinations. It's odd he'd skip the others, but it also doesn't make sense that he'd wait until now to do them."

"You're right," Sutton said. "Garfield didn't die right away, though. Maybe our guy doesn't count it as an assassination. The doctors basically killed him by sticking their dirty fingers in his wounds until he contracted a deadly infection."

"You make good points, and at least one of them is probably right. But it's been years since I've seen Rubens's *Daniel in the Lions' Den*. I spent a lot of time in front of that one after the bombing, looking for some commiseration and inspiration. I'm ready to reconnect with it."

"I didn't peg you as an art lover," she said.

That made him think of the evasive driving instructor's punchline to his grisly story about the Bogotá money-laundering bust gone bad.

"My ex-wife owned a gallery," he said. "Some of it rubbed off."

*   *   *

At two AM, they decided to catch some rest before heading into the District. Hendrix found a Holiday Inn Express outside the Beltway, booked two rooms, and made a plan to meet Sutton in the breakfast bar at seven AM. He wouldn't be doing any early morning runs for a while—if ever, depending on how well he recovered. He'd have to figure out a different way of dealing with the nightmares.

Taking out the bogeyman would be a good start.

CHAPTER

14

A FTER BREAKFAST, SUTTON let Hendrix take the
Prius.

"I'll Uber over to Ford's Theatre and then head to my
place to grab my car," she said.

"Call me if you turn anything up," he said.

"I can't imagine the press corps would have overlooked
a murder attempt at the nation's most infamous theater,
but you never know."

She was pissed, but Hendrix stood firm. He wanted
her on the sidelines after the stunt she'd pulled in Tucumcari. It was eating at him. She could be useful in ticking off
this box, and then they'd see.

Besides, if there was going to be any action, Hendrix
wanted it for himself, and Garfield was much more likely
to lead there, and ultimately to David.

* * *

The office of the gallery's HR director was small and spare.
Oddly, there was no art on the walls.

"If I worked here, I'd hang something new from the archives every week," he said.

"If only it were that easy," she said. "I could maybe put up a poster from the gift shop, if I paid for it first."

"Not even an employee discount?"

"Ten percent." Her initial smile, as spare as the room, was gone. "What's this about, Mr. Hendrix? You were a bit cryptic on the phone."

"Looking for a needle in a haystack."

"For Monet, you need to visit the Art Institute in Chicago."

Hendrix nodded. "You are probably aware President Garfield was assassinated on this block."

"I thought that one was solved."

"That one was. I'm looking for a copycat."

"No one's been shot here," she said.

"Right. We're checking to see if there was a botched attempt, something we may have missed."

She paused, then shook her head.

He stood. "Sorry to waste your time. I'll be in the main gallery looking for haystacks if you think of anything."

As he turned to leave, she said, "I wish you had come last week, when it might have done some good."

He placed his hands on the back of the chair and waited.

"Latrice Turner. We thought it was a mugging."

"Take me through it," he said.

"Latrice came back from her lunch break one Tuesday afternoon about four months ago in considerable distress. When she got to the security station, she was shaking. The guard brought her here immediately."

"Did you know her?"

"Not well. She had worked here for ten years, associate curator, well-liked, quiet, didn't make waves."

"Good federal employee."

"Yes. But with a healthy suspicion of the police."

He nodded. "Latrice."

"Right. So when she asked me not to call it in, I understood."

"Easier for you, too," Hendrix said.

She winced. "I should have insisted. None of it added up."

"Can you please call her in now so I can get the details firsthand?"

"I wish I could. Latrice . . . killed herself two days ago. Took some pills, then slit her wrists in the bathtub."

"Did she live alone?" Hendrix asked.

"Single mom. Her sixteen-year-old son found her when he got home from school. I don't understand how someone could do that."

"Maybe she didn't."

"That's what I'm wondering now," the HR director said.

"What happened the day she was accosted?" Hendrix asked.

"Like I said, none of it added up. Younger woman mugged by an older man in broad daylight. And it wasn't even a mugging. He didn't take her purse."

"Sexual assault?"

"Never touched her. He was walking behind her, and she heard a loud click. She turned around, and he was pointing a pistol at her. Old."

"You mentioned he was older."

"Yes, Latrice said he was probably mid-sixties, gray hair, clean-shaven, dark sunglasses. But the pistol was even older. It was a revolver with a very short barrel. She said it almost disappeared inside his hand."

"Big man?"

"Yes, but also a small gun."

"What did he do when she stopped?" Hendrix asked.

"He told her to turn around and keep walking. So she did, thinking her life was about to end. When she got inside, she looked back, and he was gone."

"That's when the guard brought her to you."

"Yes. He didn't see anything, but she was so distraught he thought it best to have her talk with me."

"How did you leave it?"

"The more we talked, the more she became convinced it would be pointless to involve the police. Worse than that, she said, if it somehow made headlines, it might lead him to track her down and finish the job."

"Smart lady," Hendrix said.

"For the last four months, I would have said we both played it smart. But now . . ."

"Maybe there were other issues in her life, depression," Hendrix offered.

"Maybe. How was Garfield killed?"

"A desperate lawyer was upset the President wouldn't see him about a job in the administration. So he showed up at the train station and shot Garfield twice in the back with a gun just like the one Latrice described."

"Shit."

"Yeah."

"Do you think he tracked her down at her house?"

"That's a distinct possibility."

"You'll find him?" she asked.

"I will."

"Will I hear about it?"

"This is the best lead I've gotten on a very difficult case," Hendrix said. "I'll let you know what we find."

"I'm not going to be able to sleep tonight."

"I know the feeling. Reach out to her son, see what you can do for him. It'll help with the guilt."

*　*　*

Losing his parents young was bigger than any gut punch Hendrix had endured in Afghanistan, he reflected as he waited for the elevator back to the lobby. Doug and Marjorie had always been fit and active, so it had been almost impossible for Hendrix to wrap his head around both of them dying in a boating misadventure. They had taken that trip through the Pennsylvania Grand Canyon many times together, but investigators concluded a combination of age—they were in their late fifties, which didn't seem that old to Hendrix—and high water had gotten the best of them. They'd lost a step and it had cost them their lives.

His parents' dog, Charlie, had managed to swim to safety after a whipsaw current capsized their kayaks and pinned them underwater against a boulder. The tour leader had adopted Charlie after first letting him go to the county shelter. It was the least he could do, Hendrix thought at the time. He was glad Charlie was yappy and hyperactive. He hoped the dog drove the guide nuts.

His mom had taught Hendrix to kayak on calm lake waters in a tandem when he was six. His dad had coached his Pop Warner football team and prepared Hendrix to be a quarterback, instilling a sense of easy leadership in him as he entered his teens and maintained his agility even as he shot up to full height.

Hendrix's ability to evade tackles while selecting targets for his passes had cemented his status as varsity starter in high school. After a decent sophomore season, he led the team to a state championship junior year before suffering a heartbreaking loss in the conference finals as a senior.

In that game, on the last snap he'd ever taken, Hendrix's team was ahead by one and pinned to the five-yard line with under two minutes to play. He had stepped back into the end zone as he timed his most reliable receiver racing up the sideline to the twenty. The left tackle, a sophomore with a wicked spin move off the line, blindsided Hendrix for a safety before he could get the throw off, turning a one-point victory into a one-point defeat.

When he'd left the locker room after a long, hot shower that included an ill-advised head butt of the tiled wall, Hendrix found his dad beaming in the parking lot. He'd seen how his son had gone to the opposing sideline after the final whistle and congratulated the young tackle for the spectacular game-winning play.

"Seeing you do that made me prouder than I was when you took home the trophy last year," his dad had said as he wrapped Hendrix in a bear hug. "Don't lose that sense of decency."

The lessons Hendrix learned on that team, and the ones from his father that had gotten him there, he carried into adulthood. What his dad called his grace in the pocket had saved his life more than once in Afghanistan. He hoped Latrice Turner had given her son enough guidance to get him through his teens. He wished the kid luck.

* * *

Hendrix called Sutton from the lobby. "We got a hit at the National Gallery," he said.

"That's great. What did you find out?"

"He fucked up, Sutton."

"How?"

"Misfire. Four months ago. Victim saw him and survived."

"What kind of description did she provide?"

"Pretty sketchy, unfortunately. And now she's dead. We missed her by a few days. She apparently killed herself."

"Then how do you have a description?" Sutton asked. "Did she leave a note?"

He paused.

"I'll give you the whole story when we meet up. Right now I need you to drop the Ford's Theatre angle and help me nail this prick."

"Absolutely. Whatever you need."

"Run a search through every database you have access to, put together a list of gunsmiths and dealers who handle antique firearms. We're looking for someone who could fashion rounds for a .442 Webley. That ammunition hasn't been made for decades, so it would have to be a hand-crimped .45 round, probably."

"That was also the handgun Custer carried," Sutton said.

"Really? That would make for quite an ad campaign: the gun of choice for incompetent lieutenant colonels and presidential assassins."

"I'll fire up the computer and put together an inter-view list."

"Thanks. We can make the rounds together if the list turns out to be as short as I think it will."

"Roger that. You want to meet in the District for din-ner?" she asked.

"Not tonight," Hendrix said. "I have a couple of per-sonal errands to run."

"Got it. It's been a while since you were back here."

"Never thought I'd see it again, to be honest."

"Life's full of twists and turns, Hendrix."

15

He GRABBED A cup of coffee at an outdoor café and watched the serious people who ran the Western world walk by on their way to their next PowerPoint policy presentations and lobbyist meetings.

Why hadn't he answered Sutton's questions about the victim's description of the killer? Instinct. He no longer trusted her.

The nagging feeling had started after he'd been abducted in Scottsdale. Sutton's story, that she'd been knocked out but left otherwise unharmed while he was being tortured in the abandoned warehouse, didn't track with what they knew about the killer.

Leaving Sutton alive was sloppy or uncharacteristically sentimental for a man who'd been killing innocent women and men across the country for months. Hendrix had chalked it up to possible fear of discovery in the act. Maybe someone had been walking nearby and the killer had to leave faster than he'd planned. That had seemed as likely as anything else.

But then Sutton had turned into an executioner at the truck stop in New Mexico. And she'd kept pushing him away from the Garfield investigation, throwing out reason after reason why the lead wasn't worth following. It wasn't a question of prioritization. They didn't have much to go on, which was why he thought of such a long-shot play in the first place. He was trying to shake something— anything—loose. Why would she oppose that?

Now there was the death of Latrice Turner to factor in. If it was murder, why did the killer wait four months to finish the job? There was only one reason that made sense: He was going to let Latrice live, figuring it was riskier to kill her if she had reported the first attempt on her life to the police. But when he discovered she might become part of this investigation, he had to act. The killer couldn't let Hendrix talk to the one living victim who could pick him out of a lineup.

Barring ongoing surveillance Hendrix had missed— which was quite possible, he had to admit, given the tracker he'd found under his truck—the only way the killer would know the heat was on was if someone told him. And there was only one person in a position to do that.

Sutton was staying at her own place in the District. He wouldn't see her until tomorrow morning, unless she brought him in to follow up on gun dealer leads this afternoon. Whatever was going on, he'd press her on it the next time they met.

Hendrix finished his coffee and set out for a place he'd vowed never to visit again.

* * *

The storage unit was a narrow closet, one of dozens in the long hallways of the climate-controlled warehouse where people kept the things they didn't need but couldn't throw away.

He punched in the four-digit access code and retrieved the two white bank boxes he'd stashed there when he'd cleaned out the house. Hendrix could not bear the thought of sending Becca's keepsakes to a landfill. It made no sense, but he felt that by paying for this storage locker in perpetuity, he would somehow be honoring her memory, keeping a small part of his daughter alive.

And now here he was in one of the conference rooms the facility offered customers to review stored financial documents and the like. The two boxes sat on the table side by side like children's coffins. He drew in a sharp breath and lifted the lid on the one to his left.

Inside, he saw Becca's jewelry box. It held a few pairs of earrings and a charm bracelet she had stopped wearing the year before she died. For a while, Hendrix had bought her a new charm as a present for every special occasion, which was a blessing for a dad. But he remembered with a wince the one he gave her that last Valentine's Day, when she had rolled her eyes and said, "Dad, I stopped wearing that a month ago. Didn't you notice?" Of course, her mom had noticed.

He moved on through the rest of the box, which held a couple of stuffed animals Becca had not been able to part with, a science fair ribbon she was proud of, and the snow globes from their vacations. Those had remained a popular gift option until the end.

Hendrix closed the lid and blinked his eyes, which felt hot. The fluorescent lighting was harsh. He was tearing up. He sat down heavily in the cloth-covered swivel chair and lowered his face onto his hands, which were knotted in a prayer position. He focused on his breathing. In a few minutes, he was functional again, barely.

He almost returned the boxes to the storage locker without further exploration. But he felt Becca's presence here in a way he hadn't since he'd left the District, and he did not want her to think he was a quitter.

The box on the right held what he had come to find—Becca's diary and several loose and framed photos she had kept on her dresser and a bulletin board near her nightstand.

He skimmed the diary and realized this was the first time he had opened it. He had not wanted to invade Becca's privacy when she was alive, and he could not bring himself to read her words in the weeks after her death.

Her entries, rendered in loopy script, were sporadic. They contained no secrets or alarming revelations. She mostly wrote about trips they had taken, trips she wanted to take, and her plans for the future, each one more painful for Hendrix to read than the last. In school-related entries, she mentioned a couple of classmates, first names, nothing in-depth. He took pictures of those pages.

He went through the photos next, giving himself a few beats with each solo portrait or family photo before setting them back in the box. The pictures recorded her face filling out as her childhood progressed, but the bright eyes and wide-open smile remained the same throughout.

When he was finished, there were three photos laid out on the table. One was a class picture from her last school year. Another was a snapshot of Becca and three other girls at a birthday party. The final one showed her with a larger group of kids and two counselors in the on-site after-school program she attended on afternoons when her mom worked a full day at the gallery.

Hendrix had handled his share of drop-offs, but he had never done pick-ups. It was hard enough getting away from the White House for science fairs, music recitals, and other special functions. As a result, none of the kids or after-school counselors were familiar to him. But a couple of the girls were in both the birthday party and after-school pictures, and the photos had been important enough for her to pin to the bulletin board.

He stacked the two boxes to return to the storage unit, placing the three loose photos on top. He started to pick up the boxes but thought better of it. He arrayed the three group photos as they had been before and scanned them into his phone. Then he scrolled through his list of contacts until he came to his ex. He typed "We need to talk" and hit send.

* * *

Back in the car, Hendrix checked the time and was surprised to discover it was only three PM. He'd packed a lot of emotionally charged moments into the day already. He needed a break.

Instead, his phone rang. He answered without looking at the screen.

"Judy, I'm sorry to bother you, but it's important," he said. "Thank you for calling."

"Not Judy," Sutton said after a long pause. "Get your head back in the game. We've got an emergency."

"What happened?" Hendrix asked.

"I fucked up," she said. "I got a promising hit on a gunsmith. He was nearby, and I knew you had personal business, so I checked the lead out solo."

Hendrix gripped the steering wheel. "I told you we'd go together."

"I know, I know. I'm sorry. And now it's gone sideways."

"Where are you?"

"Strip mall parking lot half a mile from the guy's house watching squad cars and fire trucks go by."

"Are you hurt?"

"No," she said. "But when I asked him about the Webley rounds, he went for the Glock on his hip. I threw myself to the side, drew my piece and emptied it at him as I retreated out the door."

"Did you hit him?"

"Not sure, but it doesn't matter."

"Why?"

"One of the rounds hit his gunpowder cache and sent the whole place up. I barely cleared the blast radius."

"Jesus."

"So either he's a textbook wacko gun nut who sees every fed as the enemy, or I guessed right on the first try."

"Not that it does us any good now," Hendrix said.

"No. I'm sorry. This could have been the big break."

His phone beeped. This time it was his ex.

"I need to take this," he said. "Get yourself home and we'll regroup in the morning."

He ended the call and accepted the new one.

"Hello?" he said. No answer. He wondered if he'd accidentally hung up on her, but then he heard breathing.

"Hello," Judy said finally. "This had better be important."

"Life and death," he said.

He filled her in on what he knew about the threat.

"Oh, my God, it never ends," she said. "We'll all be killed by maniacs."

"I promise you I will not let that happen," he said.

She snorted.

"This guy has a connection to one of Becca's classmates," Hendrix continued. "Judging by his age, he's probably her grandfather, but he was somehow missed in the investigation, because no one in the files fits his profile."

"What does that have to do with me?" Judy asked.

"He knew enough about Becca to make me wonder if she might have been friends with his granddaughter."

"Did any of her classmates come to mind?" she asked.

"No, right," Hendrix said. "I didn't know who her friends were. I'm sorry about that. But I know you did keep track of her friendships and talked to the other moms at pickup."

"I didn't 'keep track.' I didn't have a spreadsheet of friends in case I might need to access the information someday," Judy said. "I took an interest. That's what parents are supposed to do. I asked about her life and I listened to her answers. I arranged play dates. I parented her, goddammit."

He took a breath. "You did. And you did a fantastic job of it, so good that I punted on it without even feeling guilty."

"How do you feel now?" she asked.

"I have more regrets about my parenting than I could get through on one phone charge."

"What do you want from me? Forgiveness?"

"No," Hendrix said. "Losing Becca was unforgivable. I know that. I don't want to repeat that mistake with David. I may not be in his life, but I never stopped loving both of you, and I would do anything to protect you. I need to send you a couple of photos and have you share anything you remember about the other girls in them. It might lead me to this killer before he comes after you."

"Are you having us watched?"

He hesitated. "We've asked the local FBI office to report anything unusual."

"We?"

"I'm working the case with a partner."

"Send me the photos," Judy said. "I'll tell you anything I know."

"Please tell David I love him, if you think it's appropriate," Hendrix said.

"No, it's not appropriate," she said. "He's moved on. He knows he had another father, but I don't think he remembers much about you at this point. We should keep it that way."

She hung up before he could respond.

He texted Judy the photos and headed back to a nearby electronics store to buy a decent camera. He wanted to get some surreptitious photos of Hannah Sutton on her way into their breakfast meeting tomorrow and send them to the President to verify her ID with the FBI. He decided he'd send them to Judy as well in case Sutton turned out to have some connection to the school.

When he got back to the hotel, he checked his texts. No word yet from Judy on Becca's school photos. Not a big surprise, given that the call with his ex couldn't have gone much worse. But if Judy was going to cut off communication, he hoped she'd at least wait until after she told him if she recognized any of the kids.

A T 7:43 AM, after another restless night, Hendrix found a good spot behind a jungle gym in the play lot across from the diner where he was meeting Sutton for breakfast at eight. He steadied the Nikon on the tripod, positioning himself for what could be the most important shot he'd taken in years.

At 7:57, he spotted Sutton walking up the sidewalk from the south and began shooting. As she entered the diner, he reviewed the sequence and saw several sharply focused, full-faced frames. Maybe some of his sniper skills were transferrable.

Using his phone as a hot spot, he connected the camera to Wi-Fi and sent the best three photos of Sutton to the President and his ex.

Judy texted back as he was packing up the rig. Finally, he thought.

But as he read the message, he felt the blood drain from his face: "Why are you sending me photos of my neighbor?"

He dropped the tripod case and took off at a hop-along trot, swinging his medical boot as fast as he could without falling over, barely dodging a commuter on an electric scooter as he crossed the street and almost knocking over a mom unfolding a stroller just outside the diner door.

She was gone, of course. His ex's phone was undoubtedly tapped, and the killer had tipped Sutton off that her cover was blown.

Hendrix loped out the back door and checked the alley. No dice.

He texted his ex: Grab David and get to the FBI office. Now.

No response.

He called her number. It went straight to voice mail.

He froze. Sutton had told him she'd called in the protective alert on Judy and David to the FBI, and he'd taken her word for it.

Something snapped inside him. Hendrix grabbed the shiny metal garbage can next to the door and began slamming it against the brick wall. He saw his reflection in the window, wild-eyed and covered with trash. His ribs ached and he let loose a guttural roar as he flung the battered can at a nearby dumpster.

As Hendrix limped out of the alley, he heard the door open and a voice shout, "Hey!" He kept going without turning back. They had his son. They had Judy.

They might already be dead.

He'd failed his family once again.

Hendrix made it back to the Prius without being arrested. He pulled himself into the driver's seat and rested his head against the steering wheel until his breathing calmed. He picked up his phone and called the White House.

* * *

"Madame President, thank you for taking my call," Hendrix said when he called back for an update an hour later.

He'd returned to the hotel, showered, and changed. He still felt like a pinned butterfly.

"I'm sorry I don't have better news about Judy and your Davey," the President said. "There was no trace of them at the house. We've got the entire FBI field office and plenty of locals following leads."

"What happened to the agent you sent to help me?"

"The real Hannah Sutton? We scrambled the Dallas team right after you called. They found Sutton's phone in a dumpster near Love Field about an hour ago. She's presumed dead. It's like Afghanistan all over again."

"Any ID on the impostor?"

"Nothing yet. She was living next door to your ex for several months, but the place has been scrubbed and she used an alias there as well. We'll track her down." She paused. "And your family."

"Thank you," Hendrix said. "I'm following a couple of leads too. I'll keep the investigators looped in."

"The FBI director briefed me on Latrice Turner. They found a puncture mark on her neck and traces of a sedative in her system. You were right. It was a hit. The ATF is investigating the gunsmith. Not much left of him to sift through, but they're treating it as a homicide."

"Madame President, you don't by any chance have an event coming up at Ford's Theatre, do you?"

"No, like most presidents since 1865, I'm a little apprehensive about visiting."

"Good. Stay as far away from it as possible over the next few days."

"My only travel this week is to throw out the first pitch at the Orioles-Nationals game Saturday."

"Flying or driving?"

"We'll take Marine One to Camden."

"Watch your six."

"Always, Lieutenant. See you on the other side."

* * *

He spotted the after-care counselor from Becca's school and waved her to his table at the back of the Starbucks.

"I'm Ellen Reynolds," she said as she took a seat across from him. She looked the same as she had in the photo, shoulder-length blonde hair, intelligent blue eyes, early thirties. He sensed a kindness in her he guessed kids would connect to easily. Adults, too, for that matter.

"Thank you for meeting me," he said.

She nodded. "I have a few things I need to tell you before we get started."

Hendrix braced himself. In the months after the bombing, several families and school staff members had reached out to excoriate him for his role in the tragedy.

"First of all, please know that Becca was loved by her classmates and all of us counselors in the after-care program. She was funny, bright, and empathetic. She intervened to stop bullying and even enlisted the other kids to help clean up the space at the end of the day. She was a gem."

"Thank you for saying that," he said. "She had this picture of you and her classmates on the bulletin board in her room."

He slid it across the table, and she looked at it intently, tapping a couple of the faces with a finger.

"I would do anything to go back to that time," she said.

"Me too."

They let the silence settle.

"The other thing I wanted to tell you is something you may have never heard."

"By all means."

She looked him in the eyes and said, slowly, "It wasn't your fault."

He shook his head. "I—"

"Please, let me finish. I understand you didn't follow the order to stand down. But if you had not acted, I am certain the first bomber would have taken out the other classroom. More people would have died. No one would have been saved. You made the best choice in an impossible situation."

"You're right," he responded. "That is a minority opinion."

"It's the right one from where I sit," Ellen Reynolds said.

"Thank you."

"Now what can I do to help?" she asked.

"Tell me what you know about the other girls in that photo. Was my daughter close to any of them?"

"Oh, yes," she said. "You didn't know that?"

He lowered his head. "There was a lot I didn't know."

"When you're protecting the President and his family, there are sacrifices. You need to give yourself a break."

"I appreciate the thought. What about the girls?"

"Dana—the girl with the long brown hair, here—she was your daughter's best friend."

"And they were in the after-school program together?"

"Most days. Sometimes your wife would get done at the gallery early enough so Becca could skip it. Dana's mom had to work until five, so Dana was usually there until closing. She missed your daughter on the days she was gone."

"Did Dana's dad ever pick her up?"

"No, he wasn't in the picture."

"Anyone else?"

She took up the photo and considered it. "A couple of times a month, her grandfather picked her up early to take her out on a special adventure. That's the way he put it. 'Ready for your special adventure?'"

Hendrix pulled out his phone and showed her one of the photos he had taken of the Sutton impostor outside the coffee shop.

"Oh!" she said. "That's Dana's mom."

*   *   *

"I was just briefed by the FBI director in person," the President said. "After I gave them the name you got from that teacher, he came running all the way to the Oval to loop me in face to face. Now why do you think that is, Hendrix?"

"Fuck," he said. "She's one of theirs."

"You should have seen the look on his face," she said. "He saw his career flashing in front of his eyes. Reminded me of your first week in-country when that IED took out the next Hummer in the convoy outside of Kabul."

"Scared shitless."

"Yep. It wasn't some crazy soccer mom who took out Sutton and kidnapped your family, it was Special Agent Nancy Marks. She's been on medical leave for six months. Back issues, supposedly."

"They didn't keep very good track of her," Hendrix said.

"I made that point to the director," the President said. "Forcefully."

"I can imagine."

"It gets better. Dana's grandpa, our serial assassin, he's ex Agency. Glenn Marks, interrogation specialist. He was waterboarding when waterboarding was cool. Took early retirement in 2007 after six years in all the hot spots."

"They haven't found him yet?" Hendrix asked.

"Nope," the President said. "Glenn and Nancy's last known addresses were scrubbed clean. Forensics is going over them again, but don't get your hopes up. There are bulletins out for both of them nationwide, Interpol, the works. That's where I'm putting my money."

"They know their cover is blown," Hendrix said. "We won't hear from them again until they make whatever play they're planning with Davey."

A silence hung between them.

"Hell of a thing, Hendrix," she said. "The first female, Black, gay, junkie President, and the bombing was the act of Russian separatists. The white supremacists must have been embarrassed to be shown up like that."

"Hard to tell if they were blushing under their hoods," Hendrix said.

"I'm sure they'll take their turn at bat before my first term is up. If we survive the fallout from this."

"Speaking of which, you need to cancel the first pitch in Baltimore tomorrow."

"I need to, huh? You giving me orders now? I have out-ranked you every minute we have known each other, you realize, on multiple fucking continents."

"Yes, Madame President, you need to hole up in the White House bunker until I bring this maniac and his daughter to ground."

"I will kill those assholes myself if they hurt your precious boy."

"I appreciate the sentiment. But you should be getting updates from inside the—"

"Have you ever been in that bunker?"

"You know I have."

"Not pleasant, Hendrix. Not even when you were there with me playing gin rummy for matchsticks waiting for the all-clear—just like we used to do in our tent back in Hell Man, come to think of it."

"The fries from the White House mess are much better than what we had in-country," Hendrix said.

"You can dress it up as much as you please, Hendrix. End of the day, a basement is a basement is a basement. I don't do basements."

"Don't do this."

"But a ballpark, now that's a cathedral," she said. "That's what you and I were fighting for, right? Baseball, hot dogs, foamy cups of watery-ass beer. That's America. And I am there for it."

"What does the head of your detail have to say about this plan?" Hendrix asked.

"Not much. When I give her the hard eye, she swallows whatever she was going to say, unlike you. I told her this morning the first pitch is on and I trust her to keep me safe."

"If she can't stand up to you, is she up to the job?"

"She is," the President said. "Amanda is an exceptional agent. She . . . hold on a second. She's calling me now."

He waited for two minutes and was about to hang up when the President came back on the line.

"Like I was saying, Hendrix, Amanda Perlutsky knows her shit."

"Did she find Davey?"

"I'm sorry, no."

"What then?"

"Amanda's on the way to pick you up. She'll explain everything when she gets there. It's a game-changer. I think we've got a real chance to get your boy back safe."

"Jesus. Okay. What about you?"

"We had agents all over the stadium yesterday and they've maintained a secure perimeter," the President said. "Between that, you, and Amanda, I feel well covered."

"Is she taking me to the White House?" Hendrix asked.

"Amanda's coming back, but not with you. What she's carrying cannot be linked to this administration. Not yet."

"Understood."

"But if this shithead somehow manages to make his play tomorrow, it could give us the edge we need."

"I like the sound of that."

"Me too. See you at the ball game, Hendrix. I'll wave to you from the mound."

* * *

Less than a minute later, Amanda Perlutsky, head of the President's Secret Service detail, pulled up in what appeared to be her personal vehicle, a late-model Ford Explorer. The glass had such a heavy tint he couldn't confirm it was her until she lowered the passenger window.

"Get in," she said. The window was already back up by the time his ass hit the seat, and the Explorer had jack-rabbited two blocks before he got buckled in.

He was about to ask Perlutsky to bring him up to speed when he glanced at the rearview mirror and saw the unconscious Nancy Marks—who he'd only known as Hannah Sutton—laid out across the back seat.

17

Nancy Marks had been picked up by DC police at the Arlington Cemetery Metro station, apparently on her way to Reagan National. Perlutsky had sped over from the White House to take her into custody from the station's holding room, sedated her, and then picked up Hendrix en route to Baltimore. The plan was the President's idea to flush out Glenn Marks and save David. It was a longshot, but it was the only shot they had.

The Secret Service's Baltimore safe house—actually a safe studio apartment—was two clicks from Camden Yards.

After Perlutsky left, Hendrix sat at the small kitchen table and thought about all she had told him as he memorized the route map and watched for signs of life from Nancy Marks.

The Service had locked down the streets he'd be using to get inside the ballpark, and they'd be blacking out the security cameras for fifteen minutes at one AM to give him time to get into position unseen.

It was a solid setup, but there was no Plan B other than get the President to safety if everything went south.

And good fucking luck with that, Hendrix thought. He couldn't dwell on that scenario, though, because it would also mean his son was already dead.

Although the Secret Service and FBI now knew the killer's identity, thanks to Ellen Reynolds, Glenn Marks had covered his trail well. The only thing connecting Hendrix to him now was the burner phone.

He walked the three steps to the breakfast bar where he'd plugged the burner in to make sure it was on and charged. It was, and he hadn't missed any calls.

Hendrix ran cold water from the tap and filled his glass. He looked across the room to the living area, where Nancy was out on the couch. He still caught himself thinking of her as Hannah Sutton. Whatever she was calling herself now, she'd start to rouse soon, if she wasn't already awake and listening.

He sat down at the kitchen table and watched her for several minutes. No signs of stirring.

He texted his ex, but got no response, as expected. If the FBI had found them, they would have let him know and this entire operation would be playing out much differently.

Six hours to go time. Most of the prep work would come after he got into position. He cast a rueful glance at the bed, where the rifle case awaited inspection. He'd get to it, but not yet. The worst aspect of this operation was that he would not be able to take it to the range and sight it in. Perlutsky had assured him it was calibrated to his specifications. It was the same model he was used to, though his Secret Service–issued rifle was still in a federal evidence locker from the bombing investigation.

He finished the water and picked up his own phone. Perlutsky was confident Glenn Marks would make his play at the game, because of the Baltimore Plot, which she had sketched out for him on the drive to the safe house.

Hendrix punched "Baltimore Plot" into his mobile browser and read through an account of the conspiracy. It gave him chilling flashbacks to the Capitol insurrection that had attempted to derail the electoral vote certification and assassinate the sitting Vice President two administrations back.

Hendrix had thought Glenn Marks was building up to replicating the Lincoln assassination, and maybe he would have if the circumstances had been different. But the Baltimore Plot was an even better callback in many respects. It would still give the prick his big Lincoln finish, but with an unexpected twist for a twenty-first-century audience.

Though it was barely remembered now compared with Lincoln's eventual assassination at Ford's Theatre, the Baltimore Plot had made plenty of nasty headlines in 1861.

With Lincoln's election in the fall of 1860 speeding up the push for Southern secession, it looked like Maryland, a slave state and hotbed of Confederate sentiment, might leave the Union before he took office the following March. That was a big problem, as almost all rail routes from Illinois to DC passed through Baltimore.

In January 1861, the president of the Philadelphia, Wilmington, and Baltimore Railroad asked Allan Pinkerton to look for seditious plots. Pinkerton's agents spent the better part of February gathering intelligence in Baltimore while he presented himself there as a Southern stockbroker eager to support the Confederate cause.

Lincoln started his twelve-day trek to Washington from Springfield, Illinois, on February 11. The next morning, Pinkerton got confirmation of a plot, led by a hotel barber named Cypriano Ferrandini, to assassinate Lincoln in Baltimore. That evening, still in his undercover role, Pinkerton was introduced to Ferrandini at the hotel bar.

"Never, never shall Lincoln be President," the barber told the detective. "He must die—and die he shall."

On Wednesday, February 20, one of Pinkerton's agents was invited to a meeting of plotters at the house of a secessionist sympathizer. In the candle-lit drawing room, Ferrandini directed his twenty-two guests to each choose a folded slip of paper from a wooden box. They were not to open their slip until they had left the meeting.

One of the ballots bore a red mark. The man who drew that ballot was to assassinate Lincoln after his train arrived at Calvert Street Station at twelve thirty PM on February 23.

On the morning of February 21, Pinkerton headed to Philadelphia to meet Lincoln's party, which was en route from New York. The detective met with the railroad president in his room at 6:45 PM.

There, Pinkerton outlined the plot. The best way to foil it, he explained, was to send the President-elect's train into Baltimore on schedule, while secretly spiriting Lincoln through the city earlier, on a different train.

They decided to send Lincoln ahead that very night on the eleven PM train. But they weren't able to meet with the President-elect at his hotel until ten fifteen. Pinkerton laid out the plot and the plan to thwart it. Lincoln took in the details with evident sadness but no sign of alarm.

As the clock marked the last few minutes to eleven, Lincoln rose from his chair. When the President-elect began to speak, Pinkerton's mood shifted from relief to alarm.

"I cannot go tonight," Lincoln told the detective. "I have promised to raise the flag over Independence Hall tomorrow morning, and to visit the legislature at Harrisburg in the afternoon. Beyond that I have no engagements. Any plan that may be adopted that will enable me to fulfill these promises I will accede to, and you can inform me what is concluded upon tomorrow."

With that, Lincoln left Pinkerton to scramble for an alternate solution. The detective spent the rest of the night working up a new plan to safeguard the President-elect. At eight AM Friday, one day before Lincoln's date with death in Baltimore, Pinkerton shared the revised time line.

The President-elect boarded the Lincoln Special at nine thirty AM as scheduled. He got off the train in Harrisburg at one thirty PM to meet with the governor, a Republican supporter. Lincoln told him of the plot and the plan to thwart it. Lincoln then sat for dinner at Jones House with the governor and other VIPs at five PM. At 5:45, the President-elect rose from the table and told the other diners he was tired and turning in early.

With that, Lincoln and the governor went to a room upstairs. There, the President-elect donned an overcoat he had brought with him from Springfield and a soft wool hat a friend had given him in New York. He also had a shawl he could use to shield his face. At that point, Lincoln later recalled, he left through the back door and "joined my friends without being recognized by strangers, for I was not the same man."

Hendrix flashed back to the Secret Service hustling Vice President Mike Pence across a hallway moments before the Capitol insurrectionists rounded the corner looking to kill him.

The best plots were the ones you disrupted well before the President or VP were in harm's way, he reflected. The worst were the ones where you had to make split-second decisions while the conspiracy played out in real time. As with Lincoln in Baltimore, Pence in the Capitol—and the First Lady at the school. He wished he'd had the luxury of even one day to thwart that one, like Pinkerton had—or hell, even an hour.

This time, he felt like he imagined Pinkerton must have in 1861—concerned, rushed, but ahead of the game. In control.

Lincoln was taken by carriage to board the secret Lincoln Special in Harrisburg and then travel a punishing 250 miles overnight on a route that required two additional train changes, starting with the regular eleven PM passenger train in Philadelphia. Meanwhile, the official inaugural train would keep its normal schedule with the other passengers, including Lincoln's wife, Mary Todd, aboard.

As Lincoln left Harrisburg, Pinkerton had the telegraph line to Baltimore cut so that no one who knew about the change of plans could wire ahead to the conspirators. Meanwhile, the governor turned away visitors who wished to see Lincoln at his mansion, telling them the President-elect was resting.

The two-car special sped on to Philadelphia without incident. Lincoln's final two trains were regular passenger runs. To make sure both of those trains kept to their schedules, the railway president told the crew of each that an urgent courier package would be onboard and that it must reach DC by the next day. The Philadelphia train was to delay departure if needed to secure the package. Pinkerton then created an elaborate decoy parcel marked "Very important—to be delivered without fail by eleven o'clock train." Meanwhile, Lincoln was to be taken incognito to a sleeping car.

When the special arrived in Philadelphia, Lincoln rode by carriage to another station three miles away. There, he boarded the eleven PM to Baltimore with two minutes to spare, after walking across the platform stooped over and hanging on to Pinkerton's left arm to disguise his height and keep his famous face out of sight.

That's where the plan was at its shakiest. Pinkerton had directed his top female agent to reserve four berths on the sleeper car out of Philadelphia. But how would Lincoln make his way through the train without being spotted by other passengers—especially with only a curtain separating the final passenger car from the sleeper?

The agent bribed a conductor, telling him she was traveling with her invalid brother and needed peace and quiet. The conductor stationed himself at the head of the last passenger car before the sleeper and made sure it stayed empty.

Hendrix admired the savvy operational improvisation displayed by Pinkerton and his team. He hoped he wouldn't have to make any last-minute changes to his plan, but he knew even as the thought entered his mind that it would be a miracle if this setup went off as they'd sketched it out.

Lincoln ducked into one of the sleeping compartments and tried to get some rest during the five-hour trip to Baltimore, but he was too tall to fit into the berth. His restless ride continued.

After the Philadelphia train entered Baltimore's President Street Station at three thirty AM, Lincoln's sleeper car was unhitched and pulled by a team of horses the additional mile to Camden Street Station. Except for the creaking of the train carriage and the breathing of the horses, "Darkness and silence reigned over all," Pinkerton later said.

Lincoln was supposed to spend no more than forty-five minutes in Baltimore, but the final train was late. Passengers began gathering at Camden for the morning departures. With dawn fast approaching, Pinkerton realized Lincoln might soon be at the mercy of a hostile crowd with only the detective himself and one bodyguard to protect him.

Just before daybreak, the train arrived, and Lincoln's car was coupled to it for the last leg. The President-elect and his small party arrived in Washington, DC, at six AM. The plot was thwarted.

But even with all that investigative and operational excellence, Pinkerton and Lincoln were ridiculed for what was seen as a cowardly overreaction to a phantom threat. Just like the fellow-traveling members of Congress who downplayed the seriousness of the 2021 Capitol insurrection that had placed their colleagues and the sitting Vice President in mortal danger, so had Confederate sympathizers turned Lincoln's successful effort to avoid violent confrontation in Baltimore against him.

A hundred and sixty years between those conspiracies, Hendrix thought, and the exact same strain of white supremacist malcontents had run a similar playbook to keep a legally elected President from taking office. After they were thwarted, they employed the same smoke and mirrors to downplay the seriousness of the plots, absolve themselves of responsibility, and cast the victims as false-flag agitators.

Nothing changes, Hendrix thought. We repeat the same mistakes.

"Not tomorrow," he said.

But what better way for Glenn Marks to end his assassination rampage than by killing the current President in the same city where Lincoln had dodged a bullet? And then making Hendrix watch while he killed his son as a bonus.

Especially given the desperate actions Nancy Marks had taken to cover their tracks, and the fact that Glenn Marks had kidnapped Hendrix's son and ex-wife, he must be ready to take the revenge he'd promised during the torture session in Arizona.

Or all their suppositions could be wrong, and Glenn Marks would bail on tomorrow only to show up at a moment whose importance was known to him alone. It could even be that he would kill David and Judy, dispose of the bodies so they would never be found, and then disappear into some hidden corner of the world, leaving Hendrix with the constant agony of knowing without ever knowing for sure that the last of his family was dead.

If that was the play, at least now they had a good shot at tracking Marks down. Bringing him to justice would be the hollowest of victories in that scenario, but Hendrix would know what happened and the President would be safe.

He mouthed a prayer that his son and ex were still alive, and that the killer would show up tomorrow as expected.

CHAPTER

18

HENDRIX REFILLED THE water glass and crossed the room to the couch. Nancy Marks was on her side, facing the cushions. By Perlutsky's estimate, the sedatives should have worn off an hour ago.

Nancy was awake, Hendrix figured, listening, plotting her next move, working out her story as the sun began its descent outside the window.

He dumped the water on her head, making sure most of it went straight into her exposed left ear.

She rolled backward onto the floor like she was spring-loaded. But with her hands bound behind her and her feet cinched up tight, there wasn't a lot she could do except try to roll up onto her shoulders and kick him.

He saw she was tensing to try it, but then she spotted the gun pointing at her dripping-wet face and the tension went out of her. She stared at him evenly, but she was struggling to keep her breathing under control.

"Good girl," he said. "We have plenty of time to talk before our big day."

"What the fuck, Hendrix?" she said. "I was set to meet you at the diner when a crazy Secret Service bitch kidnapped me and stuck a hypo in my neck."

Hendrix shook his head. The nine always made such a satisfying sound when you racked it.

"Seriously?" she said. "I'm on your side, Hendrix."

He shook his head again and jammed the barrel of the gun into her dry ear. He put his left hand on her throat and exerted pressure on her larynx until her eyes started to bug out.

After he let up, she coughed for several seconds before regaining the ability to speak.

"Okay," she said. "Your son and your ex are safe. We can work out a trade. My dad is as protective of me as you are of them."

Hendrix pulled the gun out of her ear and stood.

"You'd better fucking hope so, Nancy," he said.

*   *   *

Five hours until the trek to Camden Yards. The game was designated a National Security Event, which gave the Secret Service great latitude to close streets.

Perlutsky had set up a three-block-wide cordon, giving Hendrix a clear path up the middle street to the stadium. At twelve thirty, he would knock his hostage out again, cuff her to the wheelchair now folded in the closet, and push her the two clicks to Camden. Flat road, no sidewalk obstructions, rooftop watchers to spot stray civilians for interception, drone coverage, the works, all the way up to a no-fly zone over the central city.

There were bottles of water and deli sandwiches in the fridge. There was a Keurig with coffee and tea pods arrayed around it. Everything they needed for their brief stay. But no Mentos, he thought.

"Hey," Nancy Marks said from the couch. "I need to piss."

He turned to her, nodded, then made a sweep of the bathroom, emerging with the lid from the toilet tank, which he set on the breakfast bar. He hadn't seen any other loose fixtures she could turn into weapons.

"I'm not an idiot," she said. "I know I'd be dead the second I walked out of here alone."

Without acknowledging her statement, Hendrix yanked her to her feet and frog-marched her into the bathroom. As he stood behind her, he trained the gun in his left hand on her back.

"If you fall into me, you'll see in the mirror how big an exit wound these rounds make."

She held his gaze in the mirror before blinking in acknowledgment. He cut her wrist and ankle bonds loose with the tactical knife in his right hand.

"Keep your hands at your sides," he said. "Walk to the toilet, turn around, drop your pants, and do your business."

When she was seated, she hunched forward and rubbed the circulation back into her wrists.

"You going to run some water for me?" she asked.

He shook his head. "This is your chance to heed nature's call without ruining your wardrobe. Time to take it."

She did, relaxing into it even with the gun trained on her and Hendrix watching.

"You killed that woman in her bathtub. This would be fitting payback."

"That was Daddy's doing. I was with you when she was killed, remember? But go ahead, Hendrix," she said. "If you never want to find out where your son and his mama are."

"We can end this right now if you tell me," Hendrix countered. "We can secure them and skip the drama."

"I'd like to do that," she said. "But Daddy is a stickler for op sec. I have no idea where he took them. That way, we're both protected."

"For now."

"Hendrix, if you and I have learned anything in the past two years, it's that now is all we ever really have."

She stood facing him, pants around her ankles. Holding his gaze, she stuck three fingers of her right hand into her mouth and then ran them down her black silk blouse.

"You can stop right there," Hendrix said, feeling his face flush.

"Your loss," she said. She bent to pull her pants up and then turned toward the sink.

"Skip it," he said. "You won't be shaking anybody's hand."

She placed the middle finger back into her mouth and sucked on it as she walked to the doorway, then turned around and placed her hands behind her back, bending slightly forward as she did.

Hendrix zip-tied her wrists, walked her back to the couch, and retied her feet after she sat.

He pulled a chair over from the dining area and sat facing her in the space where the coffee table had been before he'd stowed it in the closet next to the wheelchair when she was still unconscious.

"You're the first man to see me nude in many years," Nancy Marks said.

"Attractive woman like you, that surprises me," he said.

A sad smile crossed her lips.

"I'm sorry about your daughter," she said. "She was a lovely girl and a good friend to my Dana. They loved each other."

"I'm sorry about Dana," Hendrix said. "I wish more than anything that I could have saved them."

They sat with that for a while.

"This is my father's operation," she said, finally. "Dana meant everything to him. My relationship with him is more . . . complicated. But he and Dana were best friends. If it wasn't for his need for revenge, I wouldn't be here now. I do blame you for my daughter's death. of course, but I'm not like him. In a way, it was a blessing."

"You didn't have a problem killing innocent people to cover for him," Hendrix said. "And leading Melody Sanchez into his crosshairs."

"Inviting her to that veterinary conference was Daddy's idea," she said. "The original plan was for me to lure your ex to Dallas and kill her at Dealey Plaza to get your attention. But then you went and charmed the pants off that animal doctor. She made a much more devastating target, even though the relationship was new."

Nancy Marks paused and made a pouting face. "You two were even going to get a dog together."

Hendrix mustered all his willpower to keep from strangling her to death.

"Oh, yeah, you were wired for sound," she continued. "Your house. Your truck. You found that transmitter in Dallas, but we didn't need it anymore. I was riding shotgun by then."

"You drugged me at the Book Depository."

Nancy Marks nodded. "Roofie in your water, Hendrix. Daddy and I needed to put the finishing touches on the Arizona plan, and I had some hotel videos to erase."

"The mailbox receipt in the librarian's car," Hendrix said.

"Came straight out of my pocket when I leaned over that seat," she said. "If it makes you feel better, I agree with you that Montoya's a shitty detective. Guess it takes one to know one."

"The warehouse in Phoenix," he said.

"I made the 911 call after I confirmed you made it out. I didn't think you could do it, but Daddy was sure you would. He said you'd crawled your way out of certain death at least once before."

"He mentioned my Special Forces training when he was torturing me," he said. "There was an incident that led to several deaths. The press accounts afterward played up something I did to save myself and some colleagues. It was minor, but it made for good copy."

Hendrix shook his head, thinking of the times he'd watched her step away to call in leads and resource requests to the FBI. She'd danced him across the country like a marionette.

"Hannah Sutton, all the other innocents," he said. "You're a monster, Nancy."

"I learned from the best, Hendrix. Daddy's persuasive, as you experienced. I took no pleasure in it. And the weirdo gun dealer, innocent? Whatever, fuck him, just like that Hitler-loving Proud Boy in Tucumcari."

"What about my son?"

"David is alive. If we play this right, he'll be okay."

Hendrix needed to believe her. "And his mom?"

Nancy shook her head. "Daddy saw her as extraneous. He said no man ever sacrificed himself to save his ex-wife."

Hendrix felt light-headed.

"She only left me to protect Davey," he said.

"I know," Nancy said. "We talked quite a bit over coffee when I was her friendly neighbor setting her up for a trip to Dallas. She had a decent relationship with her new husband, and she wasn't ready to forgive you, but you were still the one."

"Was it . . ."

"Absolutely painless, the way I heard it. In her sleep, the first night. Away from the boy. He thinks his mom is being held elsewhere. My father took David away the next morning."

Hendrix returned to the kitchen sink. He filled the water glass, drank it down in one long gulp, then gripped the counter with both hands. He tried to blink back the tears, but there was no stopping them.

"Where is she?" he asked.

"Daddy dissolved her in acid."

Hendrix pushed back from the counter and rubbed his forehead hard with his right palm. He wanted to scream. She was so matter of fact,

"You said he taught you how to be a monster. What kind of a monster is he?" Hendrix demanded, picking the gun up off the counter and pointing it at her.

"He's the worst kind," Nancy Marks said. "He's the highly trained kind who sees himself as the wronged hero out for vengeance."

Hendrix nodded and lowered the gun. He could barely focus on the words as he pictured the woman he'd loved melting inside a plastic barrel.

"Listen," Nancy said. "I'm going to help you get your son back. And not just because it may save my own skin. This needs to end with us."

Hendrix nodded, regaining his composure. "What was a blessing?" he said.

"What?" she asked.

"You said it was a blessing, Dana dying. Why? Was she sick?"

Nancy shook her head. "No, she wasn't the sick one. It was a blessing because it meant her adventures with grandpa were over."

"Jesus," Hendrix said, sitting back down on the chair.

She nodded as she saw the horror on his face. "That's also why no one gets to see this hot bod if they don't force me to strip at gunpoint. Daddy's that kind of monster, too."

"Complicated . . ."

"Doesn't even begin to cover my relationship with him, correct. When my mom caught him, she freaked out and threatened to call the police. He took her by the arm—I remember he grabbed it so hard his fingers indented the skin—and guided her into their bedroom. He closed the door, so I couldn't make out much of what they said, but I could hear the ebb and flow of the fight. She yelled at him for quite a while, but he just kept responding with his eerily calm voice until he wore her out. I fell asleep at some point. The next morning, she was gone, and Daddy made us French toast for breakfast."

"She left you there with him?"

"For years that's what I thought," Nancy Marks said. "But as I got older and no one ever found a trace of her, I realized he must have killed her that night. Your ex wasn't his first."

"Did you ever tell anybody about what he was doing to you?"

She looked at him in disbelief. "Hendrix, I was nine years old. My father was fucking me, and my mama had disappeared. He kept reminding me he was all I had now, and that his love for me was pure. He's a professional sociopath, trained by the government to bend people to his will. So no, I didn't tell anyone."

"But you ran away later and had a family?"

She laughed. "Wrong again, but keep trying. Daddy hand-picked a boyfriend for me in high school, a nice, neglected kid who was looking for a father figure. Daddy befriended him, bought him beer, took him to ball games, and encouraged a romance with his daughter. He would drive us to the movies and give us plenty of alone time at home. I was getting too old for him anyway, though he used to fuck me a couple times a week for tension relief."

"And your boyfriend . . ."

"Never knew. He enjoyed how experienced I was for a sixteen-year-old, but he never connected any dots. And then senior year, I got pregnant."

"Did you know whose it was?"

"You mean was Dana my *daughter* and my *sister*?" She shook her head. "Daddy was too careful for that. The baby was Billy's, and then pretty soon after we found out it was a girl, Billy was gone, too."

"Your dad killed him?"

"No, Daddy started making Billy's life uncomfortable until he split. I don't blame him. And then Daddy was right by my side in the hospital. He was very tender with me. I never saw him happier than when he held Dana for the first time. If I didn't think too hard about why he was beaming, it almost felt like a warm family moment."

Hendrix wiped away a tear that had escaped down his cheek.

"I haven't been able to cry about it for a long time, so thanks for that," she said. "We had a couple of pretty good years, if you can believe it. Daddy held off on Dana and didn't bother me too much. I was in the Naval Academy by then and ended up at the Bureau. I was a good agent, too. A true hard-ass pro. No emotion, just intelligence, drive, and a lot of anger. I rented an apartment in Silver Spring, but Daddy made himself a key and started on his many adventures with Dana."

"And no one ever knew?"

"Maybe Dana shared something with Becca. Who knows what kids tell each other. But no one in a position to help her ever found out. And then you took away Daddy's only happiness the day you saved the First Lady. He snapped. He kept saying that his princess died so the lesbian mongrel desecrating the White House could live. The icy self-control that helped him terrify his Al-Qaeda torture victims, that was all gone."

"Why didn't he come after me right away?" Hendrix asked. "I was easy to find. With my life falling apart, I would have been even easier to kill."

"It's like he said during your sessions with him: he needed you to suffer at his hand, to feel his torment. But that's only part of it. He needed a project to keep from eating his gun. And boy did he come up with a doozy. He'd get everyone's attention with his assassination spree, and then kill you, your son, and the President for his big finish."

"But that's not going to happen," Hendrix said.

She went quiet. He could see the calculation in her eyes as she worked out what to tell him. After nearly a full minute, perhaps triggered by Hendrix's emotional reaction to her molestation story, Nancy Marks began convulsing in choking sobs. With her hands bound behind her, the tears and snot flowed down her face. Her eyes grew puffy and her breathing came in ragged gasps.

If it was a performance, it was first-rate. Hendrix got a dish towel from the kitchen and cleaned her up. He kept the gun trained on her with his free hand.

"I need water," she whispered.

He got her a glass and tipped it up so she could drink. That calmed her breathing as the tears dried. She looked spent. After all the years of abuse, maybe her emotional dam had been breached. If so, Hendrix wished it had happened before she'd gotten Melody and Judy killed, and delivered David to her abuser.

"He was counting on your confidence to trip you up," Nancy Marks said. "As usual, he was right."

"What are you talking about?" Hendrix demanded.

"Before I killed the gun dealer, I was part of the stadium sweep team here. I checked in with Sutton's credentials and the Baltimore crew was none the wiser. The White House contingent assumed I was with the Maryland office."

Hendrix felt his scalp tingling. "What the fuck did you do?"

"Calm down, Hendrix, I'm about to tell you. We can show Daddy he's not always in control."

After Nancy Marks walked Hendrix through the setup, he called Perlutsky.

"Get the President on the line," he said.

"It's nearly midnight," she said.

"This can't wait. Get her on the phone now."

Hendrix stepped into the empty hallway, closed the door behind him, and briefed the President and Perlutsky on the latest intel about the assassination plot.

"I'm in process of having my deputy wake up the dumb shits from the Maryland office to make a photo ID of daddy's little helper," Perlutsky said. "Meanwhile, we have to call this trip off."

"But he's got the boy," the President said. "If I don't throw out that pitch, Marks will ghost us and . . ."

"I can't—I won't—ask you to risk your life for my son," Hendrix said.

"I agree, Madame President, it's too risky," Perlutsky said. "Even if Nancy Marks is telling the truth, who knows what she left out—or doesn't know. Glenn Marks is one compartmentalized motherfucker."

For once, the President took no for an answer. "We don't announce the cancellation until time of first pitch," she said. "And I take Marine One to Baltimore as scheduled. If he's on site, we'll still have a chance to grab him once he realizes the jig is up."

"I don't love that plan, but it keeps you out of direct danger," Perlutsky said.

"Thank you, Madame President," Hendrix said.

"Hang on," Perlutsky said. "We've confirmed Nancy Marks was on site as part of the sweep. Son of a bitch."

"Get the bomb squad out there now," the President said. "But do it quietly."

"Already in process," Perlutsky said. "We're bringing them in through a utility tunnel."

"I can't believe that fucker planted a bomb in the goddamn rosin bag," the President said. "I thought I'd seen my last IED when I left Afghanistan. Probably would have worked, too."

"What about my end of the operation?" Hendrix asked.

"You can still set up in your perch, but I'll grab Nancy before you head over," Perlutsky said. "No reason to bring her with you now. He won't be in the mood to do a hostage swap once he figures out his daughter was the one who disrupted his plot."

"Okay," Hendrix said. He realized he was unlikely to see David alive again. "How close are you?"

"I'm five minutes away," Perlutsky said. "I'm getting confirmation on the bomb disposal, and then I'll take Nancy Marks back into custody."

As Hendrix cut the connection, he heard a scuffling sound coming from the apartment, like something had fallen onto the tiled kitchen floor.

"Fuck," he said when he opened the door and saw Nancy Marks next to the sink. She'd worked her legs up the cabinet, kicked the burner phone off the counter and then rolled onto her side so she could make a call.

"Daddy!" Nancy Marks yelled. "They found the bomb! It's a setup!"

She raised her head to look Hendrix in the eyes and snarled, "You need to kill that boy now, Daddy."

Hendrix took three quick steps and kicked Nancy Marks full in the mouth, snapping her head back into a cabinet and knocking her cold. Blood flowed from her split lip, but it looked like she'd live. When he picked up the phone, the line was dead. When he redialed the number she'd called, no one answered.

CHAPTER

19

Perlutsky arrived a few minutes later with two other agents. They took Nancy Marks to get medical attention while Perlutsky and Hendrix figured out their next move.

"We'll work on her to give up his location, but she was probably telling the truth about not knowing," Perlutsky said.

Hendrix nodded. "Let me know if you get anything out of her."

"We will. Meanwhile, I'm taking this with me," she said, snapping the rifle case closed. As she picked it up, she added, "It was a low-percentage play. I'm sorry."

"I'll hang onto the burner in case he calls again," Hendrix said.

"Copy that. Let me know ASAP if he does. We'll put every resource into the search and rescue."

"If he calls, I'll need to start jumping through whatever hoops he sets up." Hendrix picked up the nine from the kitchen counter and tucked it into his waistband.

"I don't understand why Nancy changed her mind again and went back to daddy," Perlutsky said.

"She saved the President's life and finally asserted her independence from Glenn," Hendrix said. "But maybe saving David wasn't part of her plan. Maybe she wants the same revenge against me that her daddy does."

"Apples and trees," Perlutsky said.

As she started to leave, Hendrix said, "One more favor?"

She released the doorknob and turned back to him.

"I need a vehicle," he said.

*   *   *

Ten minutes later, an agent dropped off keys to a Secret Service SUV. It was a midnight blue Bronco, parked across the street from the building's front entrance.

Before he left, Hendrix made a sweep of the apartment. He slipped the knife into his back pocket, grabbed the open bag of zip cuffs and the pouch holding the second tranquilizer dose. Then he opened the closet door and saw the wheelchair.

"What the hell," he said, pulling it out. Might as well save Perlutsky's team a retrieval trip. And who knew what might come in handy if he found his son's kidnapper?

After stowing the chair in the back, Hendrix climbed into the SUV, adjusted the seat, buckled up, and pressed the start button. He made sure the burner was still on before sliding it into the cup holder to his right. His left foot was throbbing, but he couldn't take one of Linda Corboy's painkillers until this was over.

Where to now? Hendrix wondered. The monster might still be nearby. Perlutsky had checkpoints set up five blocks around the stadium in case he was in the neighborhood and tried to slip away.

Loosening his death grip on the steering wheel, Hendrix pulled his own cell phone out of his pocket and opened the browser. Where had Lincoln's train car been stopped relative to the stadium today?

While he was punching search terms into Google, the phone rang, and he almost jumped out of his skin.

"Nancy Marks was telling the truth," Perlutsky said. "The rosin bag was packed with C4."

"Are you heading back to the White House?" he asked.

"As soon as I finish kicking asses in the Baltimore office," she said and cut the connection.

Hendrix killed the motor and thought it through. Glenn and Nancy Marks had thrown up such a fog of diversions it seemed impossible to tell what was really happening. Had Hendrix and Perlutsky disrupted the plot, or were they still playing right into Glenn Marks's hands somehow?

Hendrix went over the events of the past two days. Discovering the murder of the National Gallery employee. The killing of the gun dealer. The kidnapping of Judy and David. The discovery that an FBI agent had been murdered and replaced by Nancy Marks, who had spent several months posing as Judy's neighbor to set up her murder and David's kidnapping. The discovery of the connection between Becca and Dana Marks. The subsequent apprehension of Nancy Marks and the dramatic events in the safe house.

Always one step behind.

Except for the lucky break of Perlutsky tracking down Nancy Marks so quickly in DC.

It reminded him of how lucky it was that Glenn Marks had left the woman Hendrix had known as Hannah Sutton alive in the bed of his truck. That, of course, had turned out to be bullshit.

It was after midnight. Hendrix was exhausted, grasping at straws. Shaking his head, he dialed the White House switchboard, identified himself, and got connected to the President immediately.

"Nobody's sleeping tonight, Hendrix," she said. "What have you got?"

"Madame President, I need you to wake up the DNI and get the entire CIA personnel file on Glenn Marks," he said. "I have to see it right away."

"I'll get Perlutsky on it," the President said. "Nancy Marks is at the Baltimore County jail infirmary under observation for possible head injury. We'll interrogate her in the morning."

"Don't involve Perlutsky or anyone else. This stays between me and you."

"What the fuck are you thinking now, Hendrix?" the President demanded.

"Crazy late-night thoughts," he said. "Humor me. Station the on-duty agent you trust most outside your bedroom door. Do not leave the personal residence until you get the all-clear from me. No one in or out. It may not even be safe for you to try to get to the bunker."

"Got it," she said.

"Do you still keep a nine in your bedside table?" he asked.

"I'm looking at it right now," she said.

*   *   *

While he waited for the personnel files to hit his in box, Hendrix resumed his Google search on the Baltimore Plot.

Camden Station, where Lincoln changed trains for the last time on his inaugural trip to Washington, had been integrated into the stadium itself. It had recently housed the Sports Legends Museum at Camden Yards, but the station, at 301 W. Camden Street, was now vacant while the state of Maryland sought a new tenant.

Hendrix started the SUV and headed there.

* * *

He found a spot around the corner from the station and reflected that Lincoln's body had lain in state here for a day on its postmortem trip back to Illinois in 1865. Hendrix wondered how many of the Baltimore plotters had stopped by to gloat.

If they don't get you coming, they'll get you going.

His phone screen lit up. Incoming call from the White House.

"The DNI had the files sent via secure link," the President said. "Follow the instructions in the email and you'll have temporary access. There are a lot of records, given the length of Marks's career and the number of missions he ran in Afghanistan and various black sites."

"Got it," Hendrix said.

"The DNI asked me to remind you not to copy anything you see. I had to grant you emergency top-secret clearance and the lawyers aren't happy about it."

It was slow work, first getting in with the clunky password protocol and then reading the files on his phone. He needed reading glasses but had to settle for pinching and zooming passages that looked promising.

Hendrix skipped the training and recruitment files. All roads seemed to lead back to Afghanistan with this guy. Hendrix followed along on Glenn Marks's torture tour from Kabul to black sites in Europe to Guantánamo and then to Yemen and the UAE in 2007 before the file ended abruptly.

As Hendrix read the brief report of the UAE interrogation, it became clear why the trail had stopped there. Glenn Marks was familiar with the head of the guard at the UAE military installation where the CIA conducted its interrogations of suspected Al-Qaeda operatives. They had worked together when the guard was part of a 250-troop contingent the UAE had sent to southern Afghanistan in 2003 to support U.S. efforts to root out terrorists and hold the Taliban in check.

That familiarity may have influenced Marks's decision to leave the guard solely in charge of a prisoner undergoing active interrogation while he went to the CIA's dedicated SCIF to brief the DC working group on their progress—which was sparse, as was so often the case with "enhanced" interrogations.

Protocol was to work in teams of two: two interrogators, two guards. In this case, it was two interrogators but just the one guard.

That had been a fatal mistake. When Marks returned to the interrogation room after forty-five minutes, he found the guard sitting in a folding chair, gun on the floor by his side, staring at the bloody corpses of the prisoner and the other interrogator.

The guard turned to Marks when he opened the door, raised his hands in surrender, and explained the prisoner had planted an IED that had killed his wife and three children on their way to school. It was part of Al-Qaeda's effort to terrorize the UAE in response to its interference in Afghanistan and Yemen.

When the guard had told the prisoner who he was and why he was taking his revenge, the other interrogator tried to stop him, so the guard shot them both to death in the soundproof room. It was finished now, he said, and he only hoped to see the scene once more on the security footage before he was executed.

The murdered interrogator's name was Anton Perlutsky.

Hendrix called the President and let her know what he'd discovered. She said she'd check the connection between Anton and Amanda Perlutsky and stay buttoned up in the meantime.

"How did you pick Amanda Perlutsky to lead the team?" Hendrix asked.

"After the bombing, we cleaned house," she said.

"I remember."

"We constructed the new detail from the next wave of agents coming up. I interviewed them all personally. Perlutsky stood out. Intelligent, competent, not part of the boys' club."

"It was a gut call?"

"Yeah," the President said. "And she's not out, but I could tell she was gay. That gave me the extra bit of comfort the First Lady and I needed at that time. Call it tribal trust." She snorted.

"It's understandable," he said. "Let me know what you find out about the family connection, if there is one."

"Hendrix, you know as well as I do, there has to be. The Bureau has a team waiting at her house in case she shows up there before coming back to the White House."

"She doesn't live with Nancy Marks?"

"No," the President said with a chuckle. "That was my first thought too. Her place is only two blocks from Nancy's, so that could still be the connection. But since Amanda's in the closet, the relationship wouldn't be in her file."

They shared a moment of grim silence. "One more thing," Hendrix said before hanging up. "When we closed up the safe house, Perlutsky took my sniper rifle. Stay away from the windows."

CHAPTER

20

HENDRIX FELT THE fog lifting. First Glenn and Nancy Marks, and now Amanda Perlutsky—they were good, but he and the President were finally a step ahead.

He recalled Nancy Marks saying it had been years since a man had seen her naked. Even if the molestation story was more gaslighting, that line rang true for another reason: She wouldn't want any man to see her if she had settled down with the right woman.

It was a working theory, but it matched the known facts. Anton Perlutsky had died because Glenn Marks fucked up. If Amanda Perlutsky was Anton's young daughter, Glenn would have felt obligated to help her.

Assuming Amanda had been living in DC with her mom while her dad questioned terrorists, Glenn Marks had likely played the godfather role, helping financially, showing up for graduations, maybe getting her started in law enforcement. Perhaps even inviting the Perlutsky family to spend time with him and his own daughter. A daughter with whom Amanda may have formed a deep and lasting connection.

There probably wouldn't have been a Billy in that scenario. That meant the pregnancy came a few years later, via sperm donor, after they'd started their parallel rise in the FBI and Secret Service. Staying in the closet would have meant Nancy Marks played the role of single mom burned by a no-good suitor or an ill-advised fling, while Perlutsky became her constant companion and Dana's Aunt Amanda.

With that one secret, one that was nobody's business, intact, their lives and careers had proceeded in a promising fashion. Maybe Glenn picked up Dana from school once every few weeks so his daughter and Amanda could have a date night.

The spring stayed coiled—until the bombers entered the school and blew their lives apart.

Glenn Marks would have been the mastermind, no question, but amid all that terrible grief, he may have been even more persuasive than usual when he laid it all out for Nancy and Amanda. Just like the guard in that UAE facility, they would have their revenge. But with the school bombers dead, any revenge would have to come at the expense of the Secret Service sniper and the First Family he had been protecting.

Hendrix dropped the clip out of the nine into his palm. Fully loaded.

"I'm coming for you, Davey," he said as he drove the clip back home and opened the door of the SUV.

*　*　*

The old train station was shrouded in shadow. Hendrix saw no light or movement inside as he scanned the front of the building. He stood in the gutter just behind the SUV, where it might be more challenging for a sniper to tag him from an upper floor.

Hendrix decided he'd learned everything he could about potential traps—jack shit. Considering his options, he decided on one he'd learned not in the Army or Secret Service, but way back in high school. It was during an outing to a wilderness paintball range where he and a motley assortment of classmates had assembled for several rounds of capture the flag for some kid's birthday one spring.

Hendrix was a good shot even then, but he was so cautious in the first two rounds that he never got a good target to shoot. He remained unscathed, but he was bored. In the third round, the flag flew atop an exposed ridge. Everyone who tried to sneak up on it was picked off by the defending team.

Sensing his moment to have fun, Hendrix sent two members of his patrol around the far side of the ridge to draw attention.

Once the defenders started popping off shots at the two runners, Hendrix began strolling up the ridge, fully exposed, shotgun at port arms.

The nearest defender was crouched behind a rock near the base of the ridge. Hendrix reached him quickly enough to take him by surprise. One shot, one opponent down.

The kid grinned and headed back to the staging area to fuel up on snacks before the next round.

This further emboldened Hendrix. "Any of you assholes want to come out and play?" he shouted as he briskly hiked to the midway point of the ridge.

This provocation drew out two sophomores who had been stationed behind a hillock covered with bushes.

As they stood and took aim, Hendrix sprinted toward them, firing six rounds in rapid succession before diving headlong into a shoulder roll as the defenders' paintballs pocked the dirt behind him.

One of his six rounds had taken out the taller of the duo. The remaining one shouted, "We hit you. I know we hit you."

As the kid was talking, Hendrix rolled sideways and drilled him with two rounds from a prone position.

The sore loser continued griping as he left the battle zone, but a referee confirmed Hendrix was unmarked.

That left just one defender between him and the flag. He reloaded, broke into another run, and launched himself past the stand of brush where the last kid was hiding. Firing blindly as he passed the bushes, Hendrix caught his opponent with two point-blank shots that would leave colorful welts. The paint-splattered defender shook his head as he walked away, rubbing his throbbing arm.

After Hendrix grabbed the flag, he surveyed the scene from the top of the ridge. Members of his team were coming up behind him, but the other slope remained heavily defended. He had to get the flag back to a spot down in the valley equidistant from both sides of the ridge. He could simply backtrack and take the now-easy victory, or . . .

"Fuck it," he said and began trotting down the other slope, popping defender after defender as they turned and tried to tag him with paint. He took out twelve opponents in total that round. His classmates talked about it for weeks. The local Army recruiter caught wind of it. The rest was history.

The stakes had been infinitely lower back then, of course. Hendrix couldn't barge into the old train station shouting and shooting. But he was done being manipulated at every turn. Like the day on the ridge, he needed to do something unexpected.

He and the President had one advantage: They were nearly certain Amanda Perlutsky was part of the plot.

They had already used that information defensively, making sure the President was buttoned up in the residence. But Hendrix realized they could use the intel offensively, too.

He climbed into the SUV and called up directions to the county jail.

Nᴀɴᴄʏ Mᴀʀᴋs ᴡᴀs sitting on an exam table in the jail infirmary, dangling her legs off the end and sipping from a bottle of water. They'd cleaned the blood off her face from the gushing nosebleed Hendrix had started with the tip of his shoe. Other than a blue bruise on one cheek, she seemed about as fresh as anyone could be at two in the morning.

Hendrix stayed far off to the side, out of easy view, as he talked to the on-duty doctor in the hallway.

"No sign of concussion," the doctor said. "Assuming we didn't miss a bleed, she'll be cleared for questioning by seven." He nodded at the Secret Service agent sitting in a chair on the other side of the doorway. Hendrix recognized him from the pickup.

"Where's your partner?" Hendrix asked.

"Catching some sleep," the young agent said. "Perlutsky said Marks is a low-risk detainee—especially after you kicked the shit out of her."

"You did that?" the doctor asked.

Hendrix nodded. The doc waited for an explanation. When one didn't come, he filled the silence. "As you can see, we've got the situation under control." He cleared his throat. "Your presence might do more harm than good."

The young agent looked like he was about to speak up in agreement but stopped when Hendrix held out his phone to him.

"You're going to want to take this one," Hendrix said.

The agent placed the phone to his ear. The conversation was short, but not at all sweet.

"Yes, Madame President," he said after she'd finished telling him the state of play. "Anything he needs. Got it. Thank you, Madame President."

"You understand who Junior was talking to?" Hendrix asked the doctor. He nodded.

"Great," Hendrix said. "Thank you for providing a clean bill of health for our prisoner. Unlock the door and we'll be on our way."

When Nancy Marks saw Hendrix walk into the exam room, she dropped the water bottle and played the scene for all it was worth.

"Doctor, this man assaulted me when I was cuffed and on the floor," she said. Hendrix couldn't tell if the terror in her eyes was real, but it was clear his appearance wasn't part of her plan. Good.

"Ma'am, I'm—"

"Showing us out, doctor," Hendrix said. "You're showing us out and then you're keeping your mouth shut. This is a national security emergency, and this woman is a terrorist. If you do or say anything that impedes my investigation, you'll get to know this place from the other side of the bars."

Again, the doctor nodded.

"He's going to kill me," Nancy Marks pleaded. "Agent Burroughs, you saw what he did to me in that apartment. You can't let him take me."

Burroughs shot Hendrix a nasty look, but then stared at the floor when he saw Hendrix's grim expression.

Hendrix spun Nancy Marks around with both hands on her shoulders and pushed her face down onto the exam table hard enough to make her bounce on the rubber cushion. He zip-tied her hands behind her back, giving the ties an extra tug so they'd dig into her wrists whenever she moved them.

He pulled her up by her hair and held a hank of it in his right fist. Any sudden movement and she'd be wig shopping.

Hendrix could tell Burroughs was ready to start punching, so he held up his other hand, palm out.

"She's part of an active plot to kill the President," Hendrix said.

Burroughs relaxed his muscles a bit, but Hendrix could see he still hated everything about this.

"What are you going to say when Perlutsky calls?" Hendrix asked.

"Exactly what the President told me to say," Burroughs replied. "That Marks has a likely brain bleed and she's been transferred to Walter Reed for testing and possible surgery. The doc says it's serious."

"Good," Hendrix said. He turned to the doctor. "And if she asks to talk to you for confirmation, you back Agent Burroughs completely. Tell her you hope they got her transferred in time to save her from stroking out."

"We don't say stroking out," the doctor said.

"I don't care if you call it a five-alarm cranial whoopsie-doodle, doc," Hendrix said as he dragged Nancy Marks into the hall. "Just make sure Perlutsky fucking believes it."

"GET IT OUT of your system, Hendrix," Nancy Marks said after he'd maneuvered her into the passenger seat of the SUV and bound her ankles together tightly. "Because none of this matters. You heard me tell my father to kill sweet little David. I burned Daddy's mission to kill the President because she doesn't deserve to die. But we will make you pay for what you did to Dana."

Hendrix ignored her, pulling another long plastic restraint out of the bag. He pushed her head against the headrest and zip-tied her neck to it.

"You'd better pray we don't get into an accident," Hendrix said. "If we do, that thing'll saw through your windpipe so fast your scream will come out as a whistle."

He walked around the front of the SUV, keeping an eye on her. When he got behind the wheel, he glanced at the clock. Nearly three AM.

"Back to the ballpark?" Nancy Marks taunted. "That train has left the station."

Hendrix decided to make his play.

"What the President and I told Burroughs and the doc about keeping Perlutsky in the dark about you? It was a show, right out of your playbook, Nancy. We have your girlfriend in custody," he said. "She told us everything."

Nancy Marks jerked her head toward him, cried out, then slammed her head against the headrest. Blood trickled down the left side of her neck where the zip tie had bitten into her.

"She didn't tell you everything."

"No?"

"She doesn't know where Davey is. Daddy kept both ends of the operation compartmentalized. You know what that means, don't you, Hendrix?"

"Enlighten me," he said.

She laughed, even as the tears streamed down her cheeks. "Once again, you've managed to protect the First Family and lose your child."

* * *

Hendrix pulled over a block from the entrance to I-95 south and walked behind the SUV, both so Nancy Marks wouldn't overhear him and so he could get a break from seeing her murderous face.

He swiped away the 3:30 showing on his phone screen and dialed the White House switchboard.

"I'm heading your way," Hendrix said when the President came on the line.

"At least there's no traffic at this ungodly hour," she said. "You should be back before five."

"This was the only time of day Afghanistan felt peaceful to me," Hendrix said.

"Starting to be like that around here too," the President replied.

"We were right about Perlutsky," he said.

"Which part?"

"All of it. She's playing on your team, like you thought, but she's not on your side. Nancy Marks confirmed they were gunning for you. Marks thinks you're safe because she told us about the rosin bag, and we took Perlutsky into custody. But we know Amanda's still on the loose, and she's got the right rifle to take you out at long range."

"Amanda hasn't checked in, but I couldn't call out the dogs until we got confirmation," the President said.

"Madame President, we don't know for sure there aren't more conspirators in your detail. If we tip our hand now and Perlutsky gets word, she's in the wind."

"And David . . ."

"Yes."

"What's your plan?"

"I'm going to track her down myself, quietly."

"I'll give you until six, and then I'm calling in the FBI."

"Copy that. Meanwhile, stay inside the residence, keep away from the windows, and don't open the door for anyone but me."

"You just love telling me what to do, Hendrix," she said. "But let's get back to the natural order of things: You are authorized to do whatever it takes to neutralize Amanda Perlutsky. There will be a full pardon waiting for you if you need it. Just take her the fuck out and get your son back."

*　　*　　*

"Where's Amanda?" Hendrix asked through the open passenger door.

Nancy Marks turned her head to look at him, taking care not to cut the other side of her neck.

"You have her," Marks said.

Hendrix shook his head.

"You son of a bitch," she spat.

Hendrix showed her the hypo. "It's loaded," he said.

"Fuck you, Hendrix."

"Okay then," he said as he jabbed the needle into the meat of her right arm.

"Damn it!"

"Stings, I know," he said. "But as soon as I push this plunger, all the pain goes away until you wake up in a maximum-security holding cell. Last chance, Nancy. You help me find Amanda and my son, I'll keep you off death row and do my best to take your girlfriend alive."

"Daddy hasn't told me a thing," she said. "I'm just the decoy."

He moved the syringe enough to make her wince.

"But Amanda, that's another story," Hendrix said. "You brought her in. She's doing this for love. No pillow talk?"

Nancy Marks shook her head.

"Before you make that your final answer, know this: I'm not bound by any government rules. I don't work for anyone. I'm just a tired, angry father out to rescue his son from a maniac, and I will do whatever it takes to get him back safely."

She was staring straight ahead. He grabbed her chin with his free hand and turned her head to face him.

"There's something else you need to know," Hendrix said. "The President has a full pardon waiting for me, and she has authorized extreme measures to take down Amanda. *Encouraged* would be a better word. You're looking at a trained killer with an absolute need for justice. I will destroy your world if you don't give me what I need."

He let go of her chin, but she didn't turn away.

"She isn't going to use the rifle to shoot the President," Nancy Marks said. "She's going to use it to detonate the bomb she planted outside the residence as her backup plan in case Camden Yards didn't work out."

"If you knew the President was still in danger, you weren't trying to save her life when you told us about the bomb at Camden. Why, then?" Hendrix demanded.

"To protect myself," she said. "I didn't want to be wheeled into that stadium unconscious while you and Daddy had your final showdown. Too risky. Besides, this way, the President and First Lady both die. No loose ends."

He jammed the hypo home and Nancy Marks went out.

Then he hit redial on his phone and got the President back on the line.

"There's a bomb outside the residence, Madame President," he said. "Get down to the bunker. Right fucking now."

The sound of an explosion came over the line and the connection died.

23

THE SECRET SERVICE SUV had the most powerful engine available, and Hendrix tested its limits as he barreled down I-95 toward the Beltway.

Ten miles outside the city, he popped the radar of a trooper waiting on an entrance ramp, but Hendrix answered his flashing lights with a set of his own and the patrol car dropped away.

Good choice, he thought as he took his hand off the nine.

Hendrix finally got through to the FBI director and briefed him on what he knew. There was already a large contingent of agents on scene at the White House, the director said, plus ATF and Homeland Security. Perlutsky was on the run. They had not yet secured the President and First Lady.

"There's a problem with the bunker," the director said. "The main access door is jammed shut and the air supply is cut off. We have a team working to saw through the door, but it's slow going."

"Has anyone been inside the residence?" Hendrix asked.

"Yes," the director said. "There's a lot of smoke and debris. They haven't found the President or First Lady yet. The residence withstood the blast better than expected. Steel-reinforced walls helped. The odds are decent they survived and made it to the bunker. Once we get comms back up, we'll be able to track them via security footage."

If they got out of the residence, Hendrix thought.

The National Guard was being deployed to set up a wide perimeter around the complex. Hendrix told the director he had Agent Nancy Marks in custody and would be at the White House within fifteen minutes.

As he entered the Beltway, he saw thick black smoke rising from the residence. Perlutsky had pulled it off. He prayed the President and First Lady were alive.

He had been connected with Johnson in the residence when the bomb went off. If she and the First Lady survived the explosion, the protocol was to head straight to the bunker, as the FBI director noted. And the bunker was now a tightly sealed death trap. How much air would be left when the rescue team got through a door designed to withstand nuclear attack?

*   *   *

The scene at the White House was as chaotic as he'd expected. The expanded perimeter had not yet been secured. Hendrix parked on a nearby side street, made sure Nancy Marks was still out, and hobbled to the front gate, where he found the FBI director coordinating the response.

When the director saw Hendrix, he sent an agent to let him in.

"Anything?" Hendrix asked. The director shook his head.

"With Perlutsky gone rogue, you'll need to re-vet the entire White House Secret Service detail, starting with anyone she personally hired."

"We're on it," the director said. "The Secret Service isn't happy about it, but given the circumstances, they agreed to let us lead the investigation."

"Not that your team is entirely clean," Hendrix said.

"I take full responsibility for Nancy Marks," the director said. "But we've seen no indication of a broader security issue in the Bureau."

"Anything I can do to help?"

"If you know a back way into the bunker, let us know. Otherwise, we're fully resourced at the moment."

Hendrix spotted one of the Secret Service agents from the Baltimore safe house walking across the East Lawn.

"Any word from inside?" Hendrix asked as he got closer.

The agent shook his head. Like Burroughs, he looked like a recent recruit.

"The FBI's freezing us out," the agent said. "They think Perlutsky was behind this."

"I'm afraid she was," Hendrix said.

He fell in beside the young agent. They soon found themselves near the White House perimeter fence, away from the investigative action.

"When I went to see Nancy Marks at the jail infirmary, Burroughs told me you'd gone home to get some sleep," Hendrix said.

"I did. I only live a couple blocks away. I rushed back when I heard the explosion."

Hendrix nodded. "What's your name?"

"Tomlin," the agent said, reaching for his ID.

"It's okay, Tomlin, I believe you," Hendrix said.

But Tomlin's hand came out of his jacket with a pistol, which he pointed at Hendrix's face.

"Amanda said you'd come back here," Tomlin said. "Nancy's in the hospital with a brain bleed because of you. Amanda is furious."

So the cover story had worked.

"Is that where Amanda's headed, Walter Reed?" Hendrix asked.

"She's not that dumb," Tomlin said.

"What was your role?" Hendrix asked. "If Amanda detonated the bomb, why did they need you here?"

"We knew the bomb wouldn't kill the President and her wife," Tomlin said. "That was to get them down to the bunker. Once I heard they were inside, I made sure they'll never get out alive. It's like a presidential roach motel."

"Jesus Christ," Hendrix said. "Was someone close to you killed in the school bombing, too?"

"No," Tomlin said. "I'm a Proud Boy. There's quite a few of us in law enforcement now, as you found out in Texas. We're done letting that mongrel desecrate the White House."

He needed to keep Tomlin talking until someone happened by their quiet little corner. Otherwise, the kid had him. The gun never wavered, and his finger never left the trigger. Hendrix was out of moves.

"We're done here," Tomlin said.

"Glenn Marks is going to be pissed if you kill me before he has a chance to get the revenge he has planned with my son," Hendrix said.

"I don't answer to Glenn Marks," Tomlin said. "I answer to Amanda Perlutsky, and she says you've done enough damage. It's time for you to die."

Hendrix flung himself to the right as the shot rang out.

After he hit the ground, Hendrix discovered he was unscathed. How? It was a point-blank shot.

He looked up and saw Tomlin on the ground next to him, leaking brains onto the neatly trimmed grass.

President Wyetta Johnson stood a few feet away, pointing her nine-millimeter at the dead agent.

"Charlie Mike, butterbar," she said.

A stampede of FBI agents came running, guns out. *Could have used you guys earlier*, Hendrix thought as he stood. He was finally getting the hang of the medical boot.

"Don't shoot," he shouted. "It's the President. She's alive."

Portable spotlights confirmed Hendrix's statement. The agents lowered their weapons.

"I had it handled, showboat," she said.

"You're welcome, Madame President," he replied. "I thought you were in the bunker."

"No way," she said. "The trusted agent you told me to post at my door—I sent her and the First Lady down there and hid out in the Map Room. Until I saw your sorry ass. It's lucky for you I don't do basements."

Hendrix nodded. "Thank you for saving my life."

"Now we're even," the President said. "Any word on David?"

"No, but I have Nancy Marks. The charming Mr. Tomlin indicated Amanda still thinks she's at Walter Reed with a brain bleed."

"Head over there. I'll send backup to meet you. Now, if you'll excuse me, I have to retrieve my wife from that hell hole before she runs out of air."

Hendrix saluted and watched the President jog back to the White House. Impressive woman.

CHAPTER

24

HENDRIX MADE HIS way through the phalanx of FBI agents and hobbled back to the SUV. Nancy Marks was still out, but she was stirring.

As he started the vehicle, the burner phone rang. He grabbed it from the cup holder and opened the line.

"Nice work, Mr. Hendrix," Glenn Marks said. "You saved the President from certain death in Baltimore and you're not even on the payroll anymore. Too bad we had a surprise waiting for her and the First Lady at the residence."

He didn't know the President was safe. Hendrix hoped they'd get to the First Lady in time. But he needed to focus on another rescue now.

"I want to speak with my son," Hendrix said in as even a voice as he could manage.

"And I want to speak with my daughter," Marks said.

"I've got her."

"Put her on the line and I'll do the same with David. He's such a nice little boy."

"Nancy's sedated," Hendrix said. "She'll be out for another hour."

"I wish I could believe you," Marks said. "But Amanda says she's undergoing emergency surgery at Walter Reed because you bashed her head in."

"That's not true," Hendrix said. "That was the cover story we gave the doctor in case Perlutsky called to check on her."

"Which she did on her way back to the White House."

"Your daughter is right next to me," Hendrix said.

"But how can you prove that? The phone I gave you has no camera, and there's no way I'm going to let you send a file from your regular phone to mine."

Hendrix tried to think.

"I'm afraid time's up," Marks said. "I don't believe you have my daughter, so there's no way we can make a trade. Once again, we both lose. I still have something very special planned for you and David, though."

"She told some disgusting stories about you, Glenn," Hendrix said, desperate. "Those are all going to come out now, unless . . ."

"Unless I hand over your son and then I get thrown into a black-site hole with my reputation unbesmirched? No, Mr. Hendrix, I'm well past the point of reputational damage control. Besides, I gave her that story to tell you, to make her more sympathetic. It worked, didn't it?"

"You're a master of the mind-fuck, Glenn, congratulations," Hendrix said. "But how's that working out for you? You got your partner killed in the UAE, you've murdered innocent people all across the country in a pointless quest to avenge your granddaughter's death, and now you're about to lose your daughter rather than trade her for a little boy who deserves a chance to live."

Hendrix was driving around the predawn streets, looking for something, anything that would lead him to the voice on the phone. His only other option was to try to intercept Perlutsky at Walter Reed. But like Tomlin had said, she probably wasn't that stupid, or blinded by love.

"You don't have my daughter, Mr. Hendrix. Drop the fiction. It's too late."

"Tell me where to go. I'll park and open the passenger door. If Amanda's with you, she can use the sniper scope to verify I've got Nancy. Or you can come check on her yourself. And then we can make the trade. Everyone lives to fight another day."

"Columbus Circle," Marks said after a pause. "Park in front of the fountain, open the door and await further instruction. I hope you're telling the truth, Mr. Hendrix. My daughter is all I have left. You know the feeling."

* * *

Five minutes later, Hendrix pulled into Columbus Circle and stopped in front of the fountain where there would be a clear line of sight for anyone with a scope on the street. He reached across Nancy Marks and pushed the passenger door open.

He rolled his window down and scanned the perimeter, but it was still too dark to see much. She could be anywhere. His position was too exposed for one person to defend. After an excruciating three minutes passed, the burner rang.

"Amanda confirms you have my daughter," Glenn Marks said.

"Are you ready to make the trade?" Hendrix asked.

"Not exactly," Marks said as Amanda Perlutsky smashed Hendrix in the temple with the butt of the sniper rifle.

CHAPTER

25

WHEN HENDRIX CAME TO, he swatted at the trickle of blood running from his scalp into his ear and immediately regretted it. The dent in his left temple wasn't quite as painful as what looked in the rearview mirror like a broken eye socket. His vision in that eye was blurry, but his right eye was working fine.

Nancy Marks was gone. Perlutsky had left his phone and the burner. He opened the center console where he'd stashed the nine. Empty. There were no messages on the phone, no new calls to the burner, and there had not been enough of a disturbance to draw official notice, especially with all the commotion at the White House. It was 5:35. He'd been out for about ten minutes.

Hendrix shook his head to clear it, triggering a shooting pain that almost blacked him out. He settled for some deep breathing as he looked around for any sign of Perlutsky. A dull dawn was breaking, and traffic was picking up.

Then he glanced at the rearview mirror and saw it: a blue Post-it curling up from the glass. He reached up and unfurled the note. There was an arrow drawn on it, pointing out the passenger side of the SUV, and a notation: 6 AM.

Hendrix followed the direction of the arrow, scanning across the street. Nothing but a park. Which one? He called up his location on Google Maps. Lower Senate Park. He searched for its history. Nothing useful. He tried Upper Senate Park. It had been the site of the Washington Depot train station from 1851 to 1907.

The article he'd read in the safe house about the Baltimore Plot was still open on his browser. Hendrix pulled it up. So many trains, so many stations. But there was one he hadn't paid attention to: the station in DC where Lincoln arrived after thwarting the assassination attempt.

Abe had finished his grueling inaugural trip on February 23rd at six AM when the train he had secretly taken from Baltimore arrived at the Washington Depot. It was also called the New Jersey Avenue Station, because it had been located at New Jersey Avenue and C Street Northwest.

That was now the location of Upper Senate Park, with its tree-lined view of the Capitol dome and large central fountain. It was less than a mile away down Louisiana Boulevard, which lay in front of him.

A jolt of adrenaline surged through Hendrix as he started the SUV. When Glenn Marks set up the hostage swap, he'd had to pick someplace Amanda Perlutsky could get to easily from wherever they were holding Davey. She could have gotten to Columbus Circle and back to the park with Nancy Marks in less than ten minutes.

Whether this endgame was part of Glenn Marks's original setup or an improvisation after the Camden plan was disrupted, it would be just as deadly to David.

Hendrix glanced at the phone. It was 5:46. He ran a red and shot down Louisiana Boulevard to the park.

* * *

When Hendrix saw Perlutsky's SUV parked on C Street just off New Jersey Avenue, he didn't hesitate. Jamming the accelerator to the floor, he slammed into the side of her vehicle at full speed, tipping it on its side.

After he pushed away his airbag, Hendrix opened the door and dropped onto the pavement in a crouch. He crept around the door and surveyed the wreckage of Perlutsky's SUV. It was totaled, but there was no one inside.

They'd probably transferred Nancy to Glenn's vehicle, Hendrix thought. And since she was still unconscious, it must be nearby.

He looked around and saw a white panel van parked half a block further up C. He popped the trunk of his SUV and pulled out the wheelchair and a tire iron.

It was 5:51.

He rolled the chair up the street to the van. The windows were tinted, and he saw no sign of movement inside. He went around the back and checked the doors. Locked. He used the tire iron to break one of the windows and saw Nancy Marks on a blanket inside with his nine tucked in beside her. She was starting to rouse.

He reached in through the window and opened the back door. After retrieving his gun and dragging Nancy out by her feet, Hendrix zip-tied her to the wheelchair and started pushing it up the path toward the fountain, which lay about a hundred yards ahead through a stand of trees.

5:56.

Glenn Marks and Amanda Perlutsky must have heard the crash. Meanwhile, his left eye was shot, and the damn medical boot was slowing him down. They had every advantage.

"Come on out, you assholes!" he yelled as he neared the clearing where the fountain lay.

A small chunk of concrete popped out of the sidewalk next to Hendrix as a bullet dug into it.

He remembered how they used to tell each other to "get small" when the action heated up in Afghanistan.

Hendrix crouched behind Nancy Marks and pressed the nine to her right temple.

"One more shot and you can say goodbye to dear Nancy," he called out.

"Help!" came a small, muffled voice from the other side of the fountain.

"Davey!" Hendrix shouted. "It's your dad. I'm coming to get you."

He stayed in a crouch and pushed the chair ahead of him.

"You're too late," Glenn Marks said, stepping out from behind a column on the far side of the fountain.

"David is wired to a bomb set to go off at precisely six AM, the same time Lincoln arrived here way back when," he continued. "It's not quite as elegant as what I had planned for you at Camden Station, but it'll have to do. You'll never rescue David in 120 seconds. Or more like 119, 118 . . ."

Glenn Marks was at his eleven. Amanda Perlutsky stepped out from a stand of bushes fifty yards away at his three. She had the rifle trained on him, but without bracing herself, she'd have to be a damn good shot to hit him without tagging Nancy, too.

Hendrix had a clear shot at both of them, but they were beyond easy pistol range. And even if he shot one of them, the other would still be in play.

"Dad!" David called out. "Dad, I'm in the water. Come get me! Please!"

"We knew you'd take Nancy's word that she was handling Michigan," Glenn Marks taunted. "Just like with the bombing, you always choose the President over protecting your own family. You've got less than a minute to come to terms with that fatal character flaw."

Hendrix watched a nasty smile play across Amanda Perlutsky's face. Which shot should he take? He thought back to the day of the school bombing, the shouts for him to stand down, the terrible carnage he'd unleashed. The choice he'd made that had sentenced his daughter to death, just as Glenn Marks said.

For five precious seconds, he froze.

And then it all became clear.

"You know what?" Hendrix called out. "Fuck all three of you. Davey, I'm coming."

He pushed the wheelchair as hard as he could.

The motion was enough to wake Nancy Marks up. "Amanda!" she screamed as she spotted Perlutsky.

Hendrix shot Nancy Marks three times as she rolled down the path between her father and her lover.

Perlutsky dropped the rifle and ran to Nancy. Glenn Marks ducked out of view.

Hendrix hobbled around the fountain and saw his son. David was duct-taped to a pillar, a bomb with red numbers on a timer next to his head. The seconds were counting down from 20 now, 19, 18. He sluiced into the shallow water and propelled himself forward with two strong kicks of the medical boot.

Then he stood and pulled the utility knife from his pocket.

"Dad!" David shouted. "Look out!"

Hendrix felt the searing fire of the bullet tearing through his left shoulder. He used the momentum of the shot to spin to his right. Falling backward into the water, he shot Glenn Marks, who was lining up his own handgun but died before he could pull the trigger again.

Out of his good eye, Hendrix saw Amanda Perlutsky cradling Nancy Marks's head in her arms. The timer on the bomb was ticking down past 10.

He stood and yanked it free. With five seconds left, Hendrix hopped three steps away from Davey and hurled the duct-taped device as far as he could manage.

The bomb landed at Amanda Perlutsky's feet.

Hendrix turned and shielded David with his body. At that moment, Glenn Marks claimed his last victim.

After Hendrix felt the heat behind him subside, he cut his boy free.

"Close your eyes," he said as he picked David up with his right arm and began limping out of the fountain toward the squad cars converging on the street below the plaza.

He felt his son's face burrow into his shoulder, hot tears soaking into his shirt.

"I've got you," Hendrix whispered into David's ear. "Daddy's here."

CHAPTER

26

I T WAS A near thing, but the rescuers managed to extract the First Lady and the Secret Service agent from the bunker before it ran out of air. In the end, Glenn Marks's plot had amounted to nothing. But just as Lincoln had discovered after Baltimore, this President would never be able to rest easy.

They found no trace of Hendrix's ex-wife. Glenn Marks had made Judy disappear just like his daughter had done to the real Hannah Sutton in Dallas. With no sign of his mother, Davey's nightmares grew worse. It was an experience Hendrix had never wanted to share with his son.

David was terrified of being left alone, but Hendrix had to go in for round after round of official questioning as the entire alphabet soup of agencies under the DNI fought for investigative scraps. There was talk of congressional subpoenas. And he was once again a cable-news fixture worldwide.

Ellen Reynolds, Becca's counselor from the after-school program, proved to be as kind as she had seemed the morning she identified Nancy Marks from the photo on Hendrix's phone. Reynolds reached out to him as soon as she saw the coverage and volunteered to babysit David while he untangled the legal mess. Hendrix gratefully accepted, and David took to her right away.

Judy's parents were too old to take David into their home in Michigan. They also blamed Hendrix for their daughter's disappearance and probable death, perhaps rightly so, he reflected. They FaceTimed their grandson every Saturday morning and told David they couldn't wait for him to visit, but that was the extent of it.

Judy's new husband, the rekindled high school flame David had learned to call Dad in the two years Hendrix was away, wanted nothing to do with the situation.

"Fox News has been camped out on my front lawn for a week," he told Hendrix during their only call. "I could lose my job over this. I can't be involved. I'm sending David's toys and clothes to his grandparents. Please tell him I love him."

Hendrix hung up without a word. Meanwhile, it seemed that his best friend the President was once again following a strict no-contact protocol with Hendrix. It was necessary because of the multiple ongoing investigations, but it was also the smart play of a woman months away from ramping up her campaign for a second term. She was a politician. Why should Hendrix be surprised she'd made a promise she couldn't keep?

If it hadn't been for Ellen Reynolds, the counselor he'd never met when Becca was alive because he'd always been too busy to pick her up from school, he and David would have been utterly alone.

"Where are you two staying?" she asked when Hendrix came to pick up David on the third day after he was hauled aboard the official questioning merry-go-round.

"One of those extended-stay places," Hendrix said. "Someone tipped off the reporters, though, so between the TV trucks and the nightmares, we aren't getting much sleep. I'm looking for temporary quarters until the FBI, Secret Service, and the intelligence agencies are done with me."

"I have a better idea," Ellen Reynolds said. "You'll stay right here."

"I couldn't," Hendrix said.

"Listen to me," she said. "I've got a spare bedroom. David is comfortable here. It would mean not having to shuttle him back and forth. Plus, we're high up in an apartment building well shielded from TV trucks. I've thought this through. Everything about it makes sense."

Hendrix nodded. "I can't believe your generosity," he said. "You're an angel."

"No, Rafael, you're the only angel around here. I just help where I can. Like I told you at Starbucks, you did the right thing at the school that day and you shouldn't have to keep paying such a terrible price for it."

They moved into her spare room, and Ellen set up a daybed for David so he could sleep next to his dad.

The media figured out where they were within two days. Though the TV trucks were indeed kept at bay, speculation mounted about Hendrix's relationship with Ellen Reynolds. The hard-core conspiracists insisted they'd had an affair two years ago and planned the school bombing together. The regular gossips thought they were taking advantage of the current tragedy to shack up. Meanwhile, Larry Farnham, the Fort Stockton cop, was out of the hospital and awaiting trial in Texas, which didn't stop him from stirring up all manner of shit on right-wing conspiracy sites.

"We should leave," Hendrix told Ellen at the end of the second week. "It's not fair that you're being dragged through the mud for a good deed."

They were sitting at her cheery orange kitchen table nursing the last two glasses from a bottle of cheap red wine. She put her hand over his and said, "They can say whatever they want, Rafael. I know who I am and why I'm doing this, and I have a pretty good idea of who you are, too. I'm not worried. You're not going anywhere until you're clear of this mess."

When Hendrix went to bed that night, he kept thinking about her hand on his, calm and warm and reassuring. He slept better that night than at any time since before Melody Sanchez had been murdered.

As the weeks dragged on, David's anxiety level remained high. Hendrix reached out to a doctor who'd been mentored by the therapist who'd treated him after Afghanistan. She said she'd be happy to help David if she could—and Hendrix, too, given the fresh trauma he'd endured over the past two years.

Soon after David started his sessions with the doctor, he was getting better sleep. He had even pointed to his eye, then his heart, then at Hendrix one night at bedtime. The haunted, feral look that had so often flashed across his son's face was mostly gone, thank God. Hendrix had gone in for a couple of sessions, too, but he knew he had a lot more work to do to become the emotionally healthy parent his son needed.

It's a process, Hendrix reminded himself. Don't force it. It was a mantra he'd picked up from his physical therapist. His left shoulder was healed from the gunshot and had decent range of motion, though he still woke up most mornings stiff and sore until he massaged and stretched it. The tooth implants felt like the real thing, as the Arizona doctor had promised. Better yet, his toes felt like a permanent part of his body again. He was even thinking about starting to run. He remembered several good trails in DC that he wanted to revisit.

As for his left eye, surgery had repaired the socket
and his vision was saved. Hendrix would have to wear
an eye patch for a couple more months while the orbital
bone mended. When he lifted the patch to check the
healing progress after the swelling had died down, Hendrix noticed a small scar forming next to the corner
of the eye. It looked like the tip of his own personal
constellation.

It was spring and cherry blossoms ringed the Tidal
Basin like cake frosting. The investigations were ongoing,
but the questioning of Hendrix had ended for now. There
was nothing left to ask. For the first time in many years,
he felt unburdened. It was a feeling he wanted to keep
experiencing.

Chuck Corboy reached out from Amarillo one fine
Sunday morning in early April and told Hendrix he was
glad he'd survived Nancy Marks and her father.

"I knew she was trouble after Tucumcari," the trooper
said.

"People tend to reveal their true nature in moments of
crisis," Hendrix said. "Thank you for having my back even
when I made it difficult."

"If it wasn't for my wife, you'd have gotten the bum's
rush."

"We both know I deserved it."

"Nancy Marks deserved it," Corboy said. "But you're a
good man. You're not quite as easygoing as I am, but your
personality comes in handy when the chips are down."

"Your approach seems pretty effective, too," Hendrix
said.

"When you get sick of the DC humidity this summer,
Linda and I would like you to bring your boy down for a
visit. I've got something of yours I want to return."

"What is it?"

"Your telescope, Hendrix. Nancy Marks left it in the Camaro. It must mean something to you if you lugged it from Fort Stockton to Dallas and Los Angeles and then all the way back here. I saw the plaque on the bottom with the inscription from your parents."

"Thanks for saving it," Hendrix said. "I thought it was gone for good."

"It'll be waiting here for you and David."

"I've been looking forward to teaching him about constellations like my dad did with me," Hendrix said. "This summer seems like the perfect time for it. Maybe I can teach him how to ride a bike while we're down there."

"Big Bend National Park is a great place for stargazing," Corboy said. "My wife hates camping, but I could take you guys down there for a couple days. Heck, I spend half my life driving around under the Texas stars. I might as well learn something about them myself."

"Sounds like a plan," Hendrix said. He was sitting on Ellen Reynolds's small balcony, watching the shadow of the Washington Monument creep across the Mall.

"What sounds like a plan?" Ellen asked as she slid the door open and joined him.

"Stargazing under the Texas sky," he said. "Elevating ourselves above the cruel cares of the world."

Ellen placed her left hand atop Hendrix's right, as she had done so often lately.

But this time, unlike any of the times before, she laced her fingers into his.

"Listen," she said. "I'll be here when you come back. I'd be happy to have you two stay here longer."

Hendrix leaned toward Ellen and kissed her cheek. "I can't ask you to do that," he said. "But I've decided to stay in DC. Once we get set up, we can see each other like normal people instead of fugitives."

Ellen smiled. "I'd like that," she said.

Before he could say more, Hendrix's phone rang. It was the White House switchboard.

"Hello?" he said.

"It's Cleo Johnson, Rafe."

"Madame First Lady, I'm honored," Hendrix replied.

"I wanted to thank you for saving our lives," she said. "It seems to be something of a habit with you."

"Your wife saved my life that night at the White House too."

The First Lady chuckled. "You'll not be surprised to know she mentions that fact whenever I bring up your bravery on our behalf."

"That's Wyetta," Hendrix agreed.

"Yes. But while she may have a few foibles, she is a woman of her word, and she is your friend. She asked me to see if you are available for an unofficial meeting tonight at Off the Record."

"Of course," Hendrix said. "But how is she going to pull that off?"

"She'll take one of the old tunnels out to see you. She said if they were good enough for JFK, they're good enough for her. I told her she'd better not be out visiting her own version of Marilyn Monroe."

"I'll keep an eye on her," Hendrix promised.

"I know you will, Rafe," the First Lady said. "I'm counting on it."

"NICE RIDE," HENDRIX said when he found President Johnson incognito in a borrowed wheelchair and a U.S. Navy ballcap at a back table in the Hay-Adams Hotel bar.

"I vowed never to sit in one of these again after all the months of rehab and prosthetics hell I went through," she said. "But if Off the Record is the place to be seen and not heard in DC, I had to make sure no one would know who they were seeing." She lifted her head long enough to flash him that cocky smile.

"The Navy cap is a nice touch," Hendrix said.

"It's a better disguise than the chair in some ways," she agreed. "I confiscated it a few months back from the desk of some junior West Wing staffer who'd clearly never heard of the Army. Luckily, I hadn't gotten around to incinerating it."

Hendrix took a seat in front of the two fingers of very fine bourbon she'd ordered for him. She raised her glass, the twin of his, and they quietly sipped. And then she chuckled.

"What?" he asked.

"With that eye patch, you've finally made the transition from rough-trade dreamboat to strip-club pirate," the President said.

Hendrix couldn't help smiling even as he shook his head. "Still offensive," he said.

"So all's forgiven?" she asked as they both leaned forward to maximize their privacy.

"For your radio silence after the school bombing?" Hendrix asked. "Of course. So long as you never pull any shit like that again."

She nodded. "But that's not the only reason I called you here."

The President waited for Hendrix to respond, but he just worked on his bourbon. It wasn't a chore.

"You ready to saddle up again?" she asked, finally.

"Back on your detail?"

"Hell no," the President said. "Even after you're clear of this shit, you'll still be the dictionary definition of political liability."

"What, then?" he asked. "Alphabet agency?"

She shook her head. "Hendrix, you know the part of the defense budget that looks like a zebra?"

He smiled. "Black and white but not read all over."

"Exactly," she said. "Underneath one of those black redaction bars, there's funding for a small, top secret intelligence agency that reports directly to the commander in chief. No bureaucrats, no generals, no commemorative hats."

"No oversight?" he asked.

"Hendrix, there's always oversight if you fuck up badly enough."

"So I won't fuck up."

"Now you're getting it," she said, raising her glass. "You'll have a no-show cover job in the Commerce Department, something that makes it easy to explain international travel. You'll be briefed on the rest as soon as I get your clearance restored. After the smoke clears."

Hendrix nodded. "So I've got a few more weeks."

"At least," she said.

"Time enough for some stargazing with my son."

She looked up again and smiled, softly this time. "It worked for me, Hendrix. It'll work for Davey, too. Just follow the North Star back here when you're done. We've got a lot to do."

"Hooah, L.T.," Hendrix said to himself as the President rolled away. "Hooah."

AFTERWORD

ALTHOUGH I LOVE U.S. history, I was only vaguely aware of the Baltimore Plot, an 1861 conspiracy to assassinate President-elect Lincoln, until I began researching political assassinations for this book. The Baltimore Plot has many disturbing parallels to the January 6, 2021, insurrection at the U.S. Capitol, which makes it particularly relevant now. I reviewed many sources, but found Daniel Stashower's 2013 book, *The Hour of Peril: The Secret Plot to Murder Lincoln Before the Civil War* (Minotaur Books), especially illuminating.

Hendrix's experience during the deadly swamp phase of Army Ranger School has its roots in a February 1995 disaster. As the *Washington Post* reported that March, "Four U.S. Rangers died of hypothermia while training in a Florida swamp last month because their superiors led them into unknown waters that were too deep and too cold during a routine exercise that disintegrated into a nightmare of mistakes."

The young men who gave their lives that tragic day were Second Lieutenant Spencer Dodge, Captain Milton Palmer, Second Lieutenant Curt Sansoucie, and Sergeant. Norman Tillman.

For Hendrix's description of the Kafkaesque highway-defending mission in Afghanistan, I am indebted to Erik Edstrom, a U.S. Army combat veteran who served in Afghanistan and in 2020 published *Un-American: A Soldier's Reckoning of Our Longest War* (Bloomsbury). Edstrom shared the highway story in a provocative, insightful 2021 *Politico Magazine* essay.

And to prove I'm not some highfalutin scholar, I'll let you know the gas-station fight was inspired by a gripping YouTube video of a motorist fending off three hapless carjackers with nothing but fast thinking and a steady stream of unleaded fuel.

Speaking of pop culture, one of my favorite moviegoing moments has always been the promise made at the end of James Bond films. In that spirit, I will leave you with this:

Rafe Hendrix will return.

—*Frank Sennett, June 4, 2022*
Copyright Frank Sennett 2022

ACKNOWLEDGMENTS

I F YOU ENJOYED meeting Rafe Hendrix, please join me in thanking the folks who helped make *Shadow State* the best novel it could be.

On the personal front, I am indebted to Keir Graff for his close reading, excellent advice and constant friendship. I am also grateful to my familial readers, chief among them my mother, Leslie McClintock, and stepfather, Michael McClintock. Hard to do better than getting great insights from a fellow University of Montana creative writing MFA and her English professor husband. Thanks also to my wife, Denise, my oldest son, Nick, and my daughter, Emma, for their feedback and support. To my pre-reader toddler, Frankie, thanks for not destroying Daddy's laptop on the occasions when you picked it up and ran around the house with it while laughing maniacally.

On the professional front, I am beyond thrilled to be working again with Matt Martz and am in awe of what he has accomplished with Crooked Lane. Let's not wait another ten years to work together again. Thanks also to Terri Bischoff, an editor I now trust as much as Matt thanks to her spot-on suggestions and deep genre knowledge. The rest of the Crooked Lane team has been wonderful to work with as well, including David Heath, Dulce Botello, Molly McLaughlin, Kate McManus, Rebecca Nelson, Madeline Rathle, and Melissa Rechter. And I can't imagine a better cover than the one designed by Nebojsa Zoric. I look forward to many adventures with them to come.